TRAP
GOD

PUBLISHING

THE LIBRARY OF CONGRESS HAS CATALOGED THIS EDITION AS FOLLOWED:
TRAP GOD 2018911808
FIRST EDITION: SEPTEMBER 2018

ISBN 978-1-7327993-0-1

Cover design by: Helen Nneka "Ifedi"
Edited by: Donald "The Preacher Man" and
Moiz Mangaloorie

DIXIE DOG POUND PUBLICATIONS
7025 CR 46A Ste.1071 #312
Lake Mary, FL. 32746
Visit our website at:
www.DixieDogPoundEnt.com
DixieDogPoundEnt@gmail.com

PUBLISHING

Dedicated To my Brother Leroy

I love you and miss you forever.

ACKNOWLEDGMENT

First and foremost, I would like to thank and praise Jehovah. The one and only true God. Creator of all things!!! With you guiding a person, anything is possible. Without you, nothing will prosper. I am forever your humble servant, and all praise goes to you. I would like to give thanks to my beautiful wife inside and out, Bree. You are truly amazing, and heaven sent. I will go to war and slay the devil himself for you. Thank you for the push. Thank you for believing in me. Thank you for standing by my side under the worst conditions. You've demonstrated our vows. For better or worse and for that I give you a Kings heart on a platter!!! I am forever indebted; I love you to the moon and back. Next, I want to thank my mother. I love you Irene Posley. You are truly the definition of a strong black woman. I admire your qualities, and my father was truly blessed to have someone as remarkable as you did in his life. For you, I will move mountains just to see a smile on your face. I also shot out to my children. There's nothing daddy won't do for you. I'm grinding hard to give you the best life possible. Y'all bring me

PUBLISHING

the best joy ever. And to my brother's four children and one granddaughter, I love you, and I'll always be there for you. To my siblings, Gracey, thank you for all the Bible wisdom you shared with me. You are the most humble and gracious woman I know. You've always been wonderful to be around. Quinney our birthdays are the same I love you, and I do need to say that more, LOL. San Paid Lady, I love you and thank you for holding me down on a ten-year sentence. Mary, you are the most innocent person I know, I will always protect you from any harm. I love you, Dr. Viola Posley. Thank you so much, Blackfoot even though you criticize this book. I know it was your way of motivating me. I understand your thought process better than you think, I love you. Thelma "Ella Mae"! Thank U, Thank U, Thank U!! You gave me the game up close and personal. A real front row seat. Coming up you were the illest chick I knew, and you turned me into the boss nigga I am today. I love you, and will always be there for you. Vickie you are my heart, you the realist out of all, I understand you and thank you for always listening to me. I'll always take care of you, I love you. And Buck; LOL Man, words can't describe where we at. Thank you for everything, you gave me swag or should I say sauce, and your wisdom is unreachable. Myself a certified GANGSTA, RETIRED BRICK BOY, Would come to you in the middle of the night, carrying a duffel bag filled with bricks and money, to ask you questions about people and life. And you would always have the right answers, and break it down in terms I could understand, and digest it. I love you forever, my brother's keeper. And to Curtis Junior, Ben, and Shorty Boy, Thank you Niggas for everything you taught me, and for making the Posley brand and legacy, certified GANGSTAS! And to Sugar Momma, Barbran, Genie, y'all are the definition of Boss women, before the definition came out. And can't forget Metal Mouth, Boss of all Boss women. And to my father-in-law Phil Snyder, thank you for the wisdom you gave me, you are truly wise and a wonderful man. I look forward to getting as much guidance and wisdom from you as I can. You inspire me. And here's the BABY, LOL. And to my Niggas that are no longer with me. I've lost too many to name, so I won't name any names, in fear I might leave someone out. Y'all rest in peace I do this for y'all. And to my niggas locked up. Too many to name so I won't name any names, in fear I might leave someone out. Free all of you; all of you are in my prayers. And to any and everyone who has ever motivated me, helped me in any kind of way. Thank you, and we HERE!!!! DDP ENT... in the building. I'm going to push this shit like I use to push them bricks, just in case you were wondering LOL, and to my haters, I'm teleporting, multitasking for you lames. And planet hopping if you fast. But I don't waste time or energy on haters. Just know its Bugatti taillights. I hope everyone that reads this; enjoy this book and the rest that comes from DDP publishing. Peace out!!!!

Migo Bugatti

SUBMISSION GUIDELINES

Submit the first three chapters of your completed manuscript to Dixiedogpoundent@gmail.com

Subject line: Your books title

The manuscript must be on a file and sent as an attachment.

Also provide your synopsis and full contact information.

If sending multiple submissions, they must each be sent in a separate email.

If you have a story but don't have a way to send electronically? You can still submit to:

Send in the first three chapters, written or typed or your completed manuscript to:

DIXIE DOG POUND PUBLICATIONS
7025 CR 46A Ste.1071 #312
Lake Mary, FL. 32746

Do not send original manuscript. Must be a duplicate. Provide your synopsis and a cover letter containing your full contact info.

Thanks for considering DDP

TRAP GOD

BY

TALTON A POSLEY

PROLOGUE

"Now you listen here young blood, take your time out there, and don't rush nothing. Just let the game come to you like an alligator lying low in the swamp waiting as still as a rock for his food to come."

Bo Diddley paused to take a hit of his Newport as he let his words sink deeper into the young nigga's mental. He took another hit from the Newport releasing the smoke from his nose into the prison cell, as he locked eyes with this young nigga he came to view as a son. Breaking contact with him when he closed his eyes, he spoke some more words of wisdom, but the truth was he was speaking to himself. "I want you to cleanse your soul of all the bitterness and hate that's in there from all the people that ever wronged you by forgiving them and never forgetting them. You got a second chance out there, and a nigga would give their right arm to be in your position. Go out there and represent for all the real OG's that's never getting free.

I believe in you. You got what it takes to change the world. I've been in 20 years, and I haven't met one youngster who has a mind as sharp as yours."

Bo Diddley was from Miami where he reigned as king. He been down for 20 years and was in the federal penitentiary for moving truckloads of cocaine. When it came to the street politics, Bo Diddley wasn't just the president he was the dictator.

In the last five years, Bo Diddley had spent a lot of time and energy into the molding, shaping and building a young nigga that was an up-and-coming street politician with the likes of Frank Lucas's potential. The streets called him "Grill," but old-school gangsters called him "Sponge" because all he did was slide around soaking up all the game. Bo Diddley called him "Tony Montana" the black cuban.

After observing for five years, the old-school cats agreed upon conscience without questions and doubts that this young nigga Alton had gifts and talents beyond his years. The youngin had the IQ of two hundred and mastermind qualities. And for more proof just look at the T-Rex size footprints he made in the concrete all around the U.S.P. Coleman penitentiary.

Being that he was from a small town that wasn't even on the map called Sanford, Florida, he had to play the game harder and smarter than everyone else. Before a quarter of his sentence was done, everyone there knew where Sanford, Florida was. And they also became familiarized with the small town inside of it called Midway. Alton had managed to flawlessly manipulate and monopolize the prison system.

He had made $100,000 smuggling weed inside the prison. He controlled the majority of the weed that circulated from cellblock to cell block within the prison. What he had done was manage to defy the odds by making money and providing for his family with his hands tied behind his back and without catching a new charge.

Many people before tried to bring the street hustle game to the penitentiary. A high percentage of them failed and added more time to their sentences. Alton was one of the small percentages who escaped that fate.

Lockdown! Lockdown! The officers spoke over the intercoms. After hugging, giving daps and shaking hands with everyone he fucked with, the lights were out in his two-man cell. He was sitting on his bunk smoking his last joint. When the last glow of his joint was gone, he closed his eyes, and begins to fall into deep meditation, reaching down into the core of his inner being. He had reached a motivated state focusing and projecting himself towards his future goals and destination on the outside. He begins visualizing the possible paths that would lead him to his goal and destinations and away from them as well.

He mentally calculated all the possible effects and side effects of his future actions and reactions of every point, line, and intersection. He considered all the people, places, and things that are found in the equations of solutions and circumstances that he might encounter doing his path to greatness.

Hours later, the words from his inner being broke the silence of his trance state. The low inaudible sound that preceded from him in the conscience of a mantra were the words, sentences, and paragraphs of the seven pages of a modern blueprint plan he had written, fine-tuned and

4

memorized for the past 5 years. It read like Hitler's "Mein Kampf" (my struggle) that he had written in prison. Alton had visualized the many paths that his future might take him as he closed his eyes, laying back on his bunk to reflect on his past life of victories, failures, and missed opportunities. The clearest reflections he had were of the last five years of all the scheming and hustling he had done only to lose most of what he worked for and to lose his son's mother. She ran off with damn near all the money and to add insult to injury she was fucking his little cousin that he had raised like their son. All thoughts that related to his reflection on life with her was of all the risk that he took bringing shit in and grinding it down to the smallest gram. After taking all these risks just to build a future for them, his only thanks was to be disrespected and slapped in the face by her like he was the bitch.

He was honest with himself that he still loved her, but could never be with her again because she had to pay one way or another for what she did to him. He wanted her to see first-hand, up and close whom she crossed and what type of nigga he really was and would still be once he got back on the streets. He understood that the best weapon of revenge to get back at anyone was without a shadow of a doubt was "Success." He knew he would be successful, the God of Abraham had told him that on numerous occasions. Being incarcerated had taught him so much like the ancient Magi, the power of the mind. Anything you visualize you can bring into reality. The only thing that ever stopped him in the past was the broken focus of visualization. One example of this power happened when he was fourteen. He visualized that he would take over his block and city while having the most expensive cars, the finest hoes, and the most money and he did just that and much more. Once he got into the FED's custody, he pictured himself making fifty grand while being behind the wall. As soon as he learned the game, not only did he make fifty, but he made a hundred grand. Drifting a little further in thought, he set his mind on all his moves, from the smallest to the insignificant, to the childish, and all the major moves he planned to make. One small familiar step he knew would be easy was conquering Midway, Sanford. He had great confidence he would do this. After hustling behind the prison walls where your every word and action was monitored then recorded by the most advanced state of the art audio and visual equipment, then analyzed, scrutinized, and held up under close examinations by one of the nation's top federal experts, he knew on the outside world he would be able to move more freely and camouflage himself more easily. Most of all he learned that the dope game was not the game, just a pawn on the chessboard of the game. It wasn't the road, just a stepping stone to the road of greater things. With those last thoughts, Alton fell into a deeper place in his sleep state. "Patience is my shield, surprise is my weapon, patience is my shield, and surprise is my weapon."

Alton's trance was broken as he heard the actions of the C.O. sticking his keys into the cell door twisting it open and walking away. Alton cracked open his eyes glad that he would only see these walls a couple of more hours. It was time to go.

Grabbing the last bar of soap out of his locker, he hit the shower cleaning and scrubbing his body unmercifully while smiling, picturing how he would be in some pussy by nine o' clock.

The memory of the pussy was of this Italian girl named Brittany that was coming to pick him up. He had already given her the script, and she had been practicing her lines for the last five years, preparing herself to play any role he told her to play. Brittany already had in her mind that Alton's first couple of hours was going to be a porno movie. Brittany's resume was that of a fine ass valley white girl with the body of a video vixen who was more loyal than that bitch Tasha. So far she proved her loyalty by riding with him for five years and then dancing to whatever music he played her.

She wasn't even his girl! She was really just a fan of his, who was begging him in every freaky letter she sent him to have a scene in one of his movies once he hit the streets. So far she had made the cut and a few hours from now she would be playing her first leading role. The thought of it was crazy sometimes, the truth was he only fucked her three times but couldn't really remember the episodes because she was just another face in the endless sea of pussy when he was balling out of control on the streets. That made him smile again knowing that Brittany really had no idea what she was getting into. She recently dumped some lame ass dude who was her boyfriend at the time. She didn't even know the difference between a lame as a black dude and a gangster. All her freaky white ass was in love with was some black dick. With all the shit that she'd done for him, there was still no way he would fall weak for her or any female again in his life. He was through loving a bitch. He would rather be loved than to love. Love only turned into hate for him.

"Come on lil nigga get out that shower thinking about that baby. You're going to be all in that ass in about two more hours," laughed, Convertible Burke. Smiling, Alton turned the water off, dried himself, got dressed, and then walked back to his room for the last time.

The rules of the game were they catch you and beat your ass before you leave. He knew they wouldn't try that shit with him. He was tried and a proven "G" through and through. He had come to the penitentiary and represented in ways nobody had done before.

As he was placing on his prison uniform, everyone that he had looked out for and effected in some kind of way came to pay their respect saying goodbye to him. A few had tears in their eyes wanting to go with him and others of joy for him knowing he had graduated from "Harvard" (Coleman Penitentiary). Coleman was considered that in the FED's. His cellmate for the last five years (Dexter Brown) a Sufi Muslim was the last to come. He truly loved Alton like a little brother. He was the one to take Alton's mind to another level. The power was already there as Dexter went to tell Alton all he had to do was just activate key brain cells that were lying dormant.

Damn near everybody thought he was crazy: They called him a bug. Dexter name came because he spent most of the time in his cell. He spent the majority of his time in the meditative forms of prayer or studying anything that belongs to the esoteric aspects of the macro and micro universe. All he ever did was read educational things on the mind, body, spirit, and soul. So he improved, Alton's vision and taught him how to read people, how to understand the human mind, how to send and receive telepathic messages about the inner self. He learned about the inner self, the little voice that most people ignore. He taught Alton to trust it. He gave Alton books to read daily. The knowledge he received showed him that we as African Americans had that gift since the beginning of time. Cultural people meaning Africans, Indians, and Hispanics were in tune with it more than any other race. He showed him how to use it to his advantage, and Alton loved him for it.

"You know I love you right? Please be careful and don't lose focus. Keep your eyes on the prize, not the money because it will come. Always be true to yourself and don't forget your mission. Listen to the voice, and it shall never lead you wrong. The moment you stop talking and listening to it, you will be brought back here. I'll pray for you day and night." "Mosley, report to R&D." A voice blared from the loudspeaker.

"Now let's make salot."

Alton wasn't a Muslim, but he always prayed the Muslim way with Dexter. After making prayer, he gathered his phonebook and the few things he was taking with him and headed towards R&D.

The compound was open, and nigga's said their goodbyes to Alton. Some were really happy to see him go, others had the expression of hate on their faces and Alton could read them. Dexter walked him to the gates and looked away with one tear running down his face. Alton stepped through the gates of R&D, and an officer placed him in a cell and handed him a box with his things in it. He looked at the black Air Force one's in amazement, visualizing the first steps on the path of greatness he was going to take them. Shedding his prison clothes felt as if he was taking off a thousand pound weight made of hellfire. Feeling as light as a feather, this was the lightest he felt in five years. Putting on his new socks, boxers, red Monkey shorts, and a black Polo shirt felt like a blanket of cool water on his skin. Once completely dressed he looked at his reflection in the mirror. He was 5'11 and 150 pounds slim when he came in, but now he put on 25 pounds, weighing 175 all muscle and ripped up like he'd been cut with a razor blade. Not an inch of body fat. His father was Indian, so his hair hung to the middle of his back in long braids. He wasn't handsome nor pretty. He had the isocratic noble look and bearings of a Nubian Prince or King.

"Mosley are you ready? While you're in there smiling you'll be back. I saw your kind a million times before. Once we let you scum bags out, you come right back within six months!" A fat redneck officer yelled.

Alton looked at the cracker and said, "I'm going to your house and put all 10 inches of this big black dick down your wife's throat and up her ass. Then I'm going to fuck your daughter. Pussy ass cracker, you will never see me again unless it's on T.V. Now do your fucking job and give me my check! Can't you see that bad bitch up front waiting on me? I got shit to do."

The officer's face turned as red as a coca cola can.

Alton just grilled him, knowing the officer couldn't do shit to him do to the fact he was going home. The officer handed Alton the one thousand dollar check and whispered nigger as he walked off.

The walk through the three sets of doors brought Alton to where Brittany was waiting for him. She jumped out of her chair, hugging and kissing him. Walking out together towards the parking lot, Alton had his hands all up under her skirt, making sure she stuck to the script and didn't have on any panties.

Brittany handed him a pair of Gucci shades out of her Gucci purse. They walked hand and hand towards the sun on May 27, 2005, at nine o'clock a.m. Alton got in the passenger seat and closed his eyes telling Brittany to hurry up and back the car up. He didn't want to look back at the place. As the saying goes, you never look back. Brittany put the car in motion and spun out of the complex. Handing Alton the blunt of purple, she hit the play button on the radio, and Young Jeezy immediately came out of the speakers, *"If you're looking for me I'll be on the block with my thang cocked, cause I'm a rida."* The song played as Akon sang the hook. Alton laughed out loud allowing the sunlight to hit his gold grill. He didn't want to hear any of those other dudes because he had fallen in love with Young Jeezy's music. He knew Jeezy was a certified trapper. So far Brittany had been playing everything by the script. He told her to pull over while he ran around the car and got in the driver seat. Puffing on the blunt, he told her to put her back up against the door and show him her pussy and play with it. After watching long enough, he pulled his dick out smiling. She attacked his dick like an animal sucking and licking on it. He busted a nut in her mouth, and she swallowed every drop of it. He looked at his reflection in the rear-view mirror and said, "Hello, welcome back it's your time now."

CHAPTER 1

SHORTY WANNA BE A THUG

"One, one, two, one, four!"

"Again, Again."

"One, one, two, one, four. One, one, two, one, four!"

"Alton, you're not moving with it!" The boxing instructor growled at him through his gritted teeth.

"Break! Put your gloves down, Alton. Until you get yourself together, you're just going to go through the numbers."

Alton's arms hung by his side after taking the gloves off. It felt as though he was holding a ton of bricks. His adolescent frame gave off steam, as he was trying to suck fresh oxygen into his lungs. Panting frantically, Alton's intense breathing caused it to feel like fire was traveling through his body.

"Why are you so out of breath?" the instructor questioned.

Alton just looked at him still breathing hard, knowing the reason for his breathing was caused by the one drug he loved the most, weed. Alton knew that it was affecting what his boxing instructor taught him were the qualities of a True Champion. The "Triple A" (Alertness + Ability = Advantage).

This motto was supposed to be exercised in any situation. Deep down he knew something was wrong with his performance. He wasn't performing up to the level he usually did in his past training sessions.

Alton was thirteen going on forty, wise beyond the youthfulness of his age. A lot of the older generation that watched him grow up always referred to him as having an old spirit. An old man baby, the baby boy, and the rut of thirty-six children. Many people labeled him. The "Last Don" was how he thought of himself. Alton's father, Curtis Mosley, was sixty years old when he fathered him. His mother, Irene, ironically was thirty-six when she gave birth to him. She was the mother of eight children, all who were born from Alton's father. Irene first met Curtis when she was fifteen years old babysitting Curtis's other children. Although he was married at the time, sly Curtis had his eyes on her.

Curtis credentials read like a collective treasure of Donald Goines novels. He was a king player, a pimp, a full-time gangster, and the definition of a bonafide hustler. Although Curtis only had a second-grade education, he was a genius at whatever he set his mind to. Who knows, if he was born in a different place at a different time, he always believed he could have been a CEO at a fortune five hundred company.

Curtis humble beginnings were in the heart of the State of Alabama, better known as the Dixie Camellia State, where the motto was "We Dare Defend Our Rights." At that time in the 1920's and 30's, African Americans, especially women, were taught to be submissive. Curtis accepted the first part of that with a solid disposition by staying out of the way of the "Law." What he couldn't accept was the second part of Alabama State rights, whereas, a man had the right to beat his wife to a bloody pulp. In this case, it was his mother being beaten by some nigga claiming to be his stepfather. Nobody cared nor was anything being done about it. In the prevailing consciousness of the time, his mother was a leper times three. One-being born an Indian, two-a female, and three- a whore. All and all, she was still his mother, and he was willing to die and kill for her. One day in a calculated act of murderous rage, Curtis killed the fuck nigga. The act sentenced him to three years in a reform school. After doing his time, he moved to Florida, where he ran through three different wives and countless other women.

Curtis was a full-blooded Black Cherokee Indian, with looks that could kill. His long, black, curly hair made every woman that looked his way want to have his baby. He had a tribal mentality to the 1st degree with a belief system that was based on the ways of his ancestors when it came to having children. He believed that the more children a man had and was able to support and raise defined how powerful a man's medicine was. He single-handedly took care of all 36 children including all his wives. That's why his squaw's (wives and daughters) and (braves) sons called him Big Chief.

Big Chief worshipped the Great Spirit whom he referred to as "The Hustle God." He lived his life as if he was the most zealous, disciplined missionary of the Hustle God that ever lived. Many times he came close to sacrificing his life to the Hustle God on the streets. As a missionary, in his younger years, he took his religion from state to state and from city to city, bringing his wives and children along to spread the hustle. As he got older, his ways in the Great Spirit of the hustle got wiser and sharper. He began concentrating the network of his hustle to four connecting counties: Orange, Brevard, Seminole, and Volusia.

The sermon he lived, recited, and preached was "Hustle Hard." He studied books on nature, memorizing ancient text that was considered as holy as the Bible or the Koran to the Indian culture. He taught his tribe how to read those holy words, teaching them that hustle is like a seed growing into a tree, which is the same as a penny being flipped into a thousand dollars. He also taught to never throw good seeds on the bad ground because that's the same as putting good money on top of bad money, a worthless hustle. He constantly stressed, "If what you got in your hand is a harvest, plant it in some good ground as a seed."

He taught his tribe to be aware and not to limit themselves to one form of seed. Meaning, to not get trapped into one kind of hustle as so many blacks do in the drug game because drought season will come and no fruit will grow. By you knowing only one hustle during a drought, you start doing desperate shit just to make it. A true hustla, Big Chief could make something out of nothing! He could barter, trade, or sell anything to make a profit. He would always emphasize that *a true hustler could sell water to a fish and air to a bird!* What set Big Chief apart from other hustlers was his innate ability to weigh the hearts and souls of a man at a glance. In Big Chief's world, there was only two type of people; customer or competition.

Surviving those savage years during the route reconstruction period of slavery imprinted a suppleness and craftiness that intertwined like snakes around prey. He passed all of his knowledge in nature down to his children. Some received more than others. He recognized that Alton embraced what he was taught more than anyone else. Because of this, Curtis was harder on his tribe, especially on Alton. He lived by the principle, *"If I give you a fish I'll feed you today, but if I teach you how to fish you'll eat for a lifetime."* Even though he had a lot of money invested in many places, he didn't give his children anything except the bare essentials needed to survive. He provided them food to eat and a place to stay. Anything else they wanted they'd better hustle hard for.

Alton didn't really understand nor did he care for all those riddles and sayings. In fact, he felt that his father treated him like shit. He knew the nigga had the money to get him brand new clothes, shoes, and the latest video games but in Alton's eyes, his family was poor. Dirt poor. His attire consisted of either clothes from goodwill or hand me downs from his older siblings. His diet was even worst, from eating road kill, picking up cans off the road, or picking fruit and vegetables from someone's field during harvest time period. Not to mention being picked up from school by his father in an old beat up, crusty white station wagon. He was sick of this shit. Sick of getting into fights at school because other kids always laughed at him.

Alton was losing his edge and his Triple-A with the boxing, and he no longer had the urge to want to fight. His father was a golden glove, and so was two of his older brothers, but what had any of that boxing shit done for them? *Nothing.* They didn't have anything to show for it. The real reason that his father had placed him in boxing was to teach him discipline because he was always getting into fights at school. It had actually done him some good because he hadn't been in a fight at school in a while. He had even become good at boxing, placing 1st in his last four tournaments. His record was 5-1, and the only loss he had was for hitting his opponent after the bell rang.

"Listen here Alton, I know What chu doing! I've known for a while because I watch you come into the gym high, and now you're moving all sluggish. I've been training you since you were seven years old. I know what to expect out of you. Your timing is way off, and your reaction speed is slow motion." The trainer reached out and placed his hand on Alton's shoulder.

"Listen to me Alton, if you don't straighten up and I mean fast, you're gonna get knocked out when you go to Tampa to fight little Tyreek Sims."

For a second chill went through Alton when he heard that he would get knocked out. He shook it off, knowing what his trainer was saying had some truth to it. Tyreek Sims was no walk in the park. His records were 6-0 at thirteen years old, and he was rated as the best in the state in his weight class of 90 to a 100 pounds.

"You gotta stop smokin that stuff, it ain't good for you. I've been down that road you goin and it will get you nowhere. You got a lot of talent. But if you don't perfect your craft and stay training in the gym, it will all be for nothing."

Alton just stared at his trainer thinking, if he only knew the thoughts that were going through his mind. He no longer cared about boxing. His mind was on getting some new shoes, clothes, and gold jewelry ASAP! The last thing on his mind was the tournament he had coming up next month.

"Do your dad know you're smoking weed?" The trainer asked.

"Who said I was smoking weed?" Alton responded back, moving his shoulder so that his trainer's hand would fall off it.

"I say your smoking weed! I've watched your performance, and I smelled it in your clothes before you changed into your boxing gear. Boy I was once your age, and I know when a kid is going down the wrong path, so don't get smart with me!" The trainer shot back.

The trainer turned his back to Alton and took a couple of steps. "I've been thinking about what to do for the last month. Should I tell your father about this one or no? What are you trying to do end up like your older brother? Let me guess which one Shorty Boy or Leroy?"

At the sound of his brother's names, Alton looked at the instructor with murder in his eyes thinking, where the fuck did he come off talking about his brothers? He didn't know shit about his brothers or their lives. The trainer saw the look of rage in Alton's eyes, shaking his head in despair, thinking to himself that if Alton only knew where he had come from and the hardship it took to get where he was at now. He had boxed and was raised right alongside Alton's older brothers, but unlike them, he was able to escape the madness that had trapped them. Even the thought of going to prison when he was 18 ran across his mind. He then gloated on his accomplishments by coming home, getting his life right and starting this gym after realizing he didn't have what it took to go pro. But both Shorty Boy, Leroy and his friends had what it took. Shaking his head again he thought about all the wasted talent that continuously got lost in the fast world of the streets. And now Alton, the youngest out of 36, was drifting down the same road. The shocking and sad thing about the whole situation was that he had more talent and was better than both his brothers at the age of 13. The trainer took a deep breath, telling himself that he was going to give it one more try.

"Alton, what do you think I should do?"

Alton shrugged his shoulders saying, "Do whatever you do!" He walked away heading to the locker room where he stripped off his boxing gear and put on his clothes. Coming back out, he took one last look at the gym where he had anointed the floor with his boxing gloves and shoes in the middle of the ring.

From his office window, Meneeffe watched Alton leave walking across the parking lot. Usually, Mr. Mosley would be waiting, but Alton had left one hour early. The trainer checked his watch that read 6:00 PM knowing that Mr. Mosley would be there by 7.

At exactly 7 o'clock Mr. Mosley pulled in the parking lot. Meneeffe walked to meet him at the car to tell him what was going on with Alton. Mr. Mosley just listened, knowing the trainer was right. When he finished, he shook his hand telling the trainer, "Thank you." He proceeded to drive back to the house the same way he came, hoping to spot Alton walking. He brooded to himself thinking dark thoughts as he drove like he had seen this in another place another time before. *Déjà vu.*

The mean streak that showed up in Alton reminded Curtis so much of the blood he brought to the city decades ago. The blood he hadn't seen up close in a long time. His first two wives were not what you would call ideal women. They weren't raised right, and he considered them all ignorant.

It was different from his last wife Irene and the eight children he had from her. They had good blood, especially when comparing them to his other twenty-eight children. They were considered menaces to society. They were either killers, pimps, players, hustlers, hoes, prostitutes, or just plain out nobodies as far as the standards of society go. He didn't want that for this set of children with Irene. He knew this would be his last go-round, and he wanted the best for this bunch. So far he was doing okay because all of them were on the right track. Everyone over eighteen had their high school diploma, a good job, and a few were even in college, but this last one scared Curtis more than all the other children he had. He saw that same old blood that started showing up in him at a very early age every time he looked at the boy.

The boy had more charm than a leprechaun, and he was a master manipulator. He was the exact replica of Curtis in more ways than any kid he had. He had his good looks, his old ancestor warrior spirit, and could stand on his own two feet. He didn't want to lose this one like he had lost the other two sons, Leroy and Shorty Boy. But the truth was he started losing Alton little-by-little when he lost his 2 brothers. Shorty Boy was at the prison called, "The Rock," serving 2 life sentences for two murders. And on top of that, the boy had killed someone else while he was in that place. Curtis had to accept the fact that he would never see him come home again. It made him sad because he was the one that put the "go hard and zero tolerance" in all his children.

He didn't consider that the laws of the land were changing and America wouldn't stand for that kind of savage behavior. Out of all his children, Curtis only had one to be killed. His favorite son Leroy was shot in the head at the little club down the road from the house called Jimmy Hamp. Leroy was deadly with his hands. After catching a dude cheating in a card game, Leroy beat the man unconscious while Shorty Boy watched him. The man's cousin got up from the bar and calmly walked over to where Leroy mounted his cousin, put his gun to the back of his head and squeezed the trigger. He then picked his cousin up and calmly walked out the juke joint. Shorty Boy had a pistol and fired at the man, but the gun jammed. The nigga laughed at him and continued to walk out of the place. Shorty Boy had to watch his brother get slaughtered like a sheep watching another sheep.

In the end, he placed Leroy's lifeless body in the car and brought him home. When they got there, the image that still hurts Big Chief Mosley to this day, was seeing his sons soaked in the lifeblood of his beloved son Leroy with fragments of his brain matter all over them.

Big Chief went crazy! All the little children stood around watching as he cursed God one minute and begged him the next for Leroy to wake up. Eight-year-old Alton stood still clenching and unclenching his fist. He stared at his brother's dead body lying on the floor with his eyes wide open, looking at the ceiling as if he was trying to find his soul. All Alton felt was a cold rage that went through his body like electricity.

He loved his brother! He remembered his brother coming to the house slap boxing and wrestling with him then gave him five dollars after they were finished. He had grown accustomed to the routine every weekend like clockwork. Now a fuck nigga had taken that away! It was then at a young age that he vowed to never let a nigga kill him. Big Chief contemplated all this as he drove, admitting to himself *"this boy was gonna be a real problem"* and he didn't have the legs to chase him.

Twenty minutes after Alton had left the gym, his sister's boyfriend Teke spotted him walking. He was a pitch black gangsta looking motherfucka with pointy ears like a cat and a gold grill with six to the top and bottom. The nigga always stayed smiling at God only knew what. He pulled over in a black Camaro with tinted windows and rolled down the window on the passenger side.

"What's up nigga? Get in da car fool." Teke said in a crisp voice.

"Where are you coming from?"

"The gym," Alton responded.

"The gym, huh?" Teke repeated Alton's words as if he was trying to size him up.

"You think you ready for me?"

Alton just looked at him. Teke smiled showing his grill. Teke was BAD BUSINESS! Alton's mom didn't like that her daughter was fucking with him.

Teke had just come home from the pin on a murder charge, and the word on the street was that he was a certified head bussa and jack boy. He was always robbing people and getting into shootouts. Alton didn't know if any of that was true. Even at thirteen, Alton knew that the streets talked like hoes and bitches.

Teke fired up a blunt. "Fool let me hit that blunt," said Alton. Teke just smiled knowing that this little nigga was going to be ruthless when he hit the streets. It was only a matter of time. Mr. Mosley was getting too old to watch this one, plus jit was always around him at his sister's house, trying to steal his weed. "Curtis's baby boy," Teke would say all the time laughing. He passed the joint and watched him smoke it like a champ while leaning back and listening to Scarface. *I never seen a man cry. Till I seen that man die.*

Teke reached in his pocket pulling out a $20 bill from a fat knot of cash wrapped in a rubber band. He knew Alton was watching his every move. Teke gave a single $20 bill to Alton then reached in his consul where Alton spotted an all-black pistol, 2 bags of weed, and a pill bottle full of the stuff they called crack or rocks. Teke gave him a bag of weed then pulled in the park around the corner from his house.

"You know I can't drop you off at the house because Mr. Mosley will kill both of us," he said as he gave his brother-in-law some dap and watched Alton get out the car walking towards all the other little wannabes. Out of all ten of them, Teke thought Alton was that *one.*

He replayed every minute and detail of his recent encounters with Alton. Replaying back the scene when he asked Alton was he ready for him, and all the boy did was just look at him with those eyes.

"Those eyes had a familiar glow," Teke thought. He saw them every time he looked at himself in the mirror. He had the eyes of a *Predator.* He began laughing out to himself thinking the streets were in for a surprise. Teke knew jit's bloodline was ruthless and bout that action on the male and female side. It wouldn't be long now before Alton married the game. He was around his sister all the time. His sister was a real thoroughbred ass bitch, and Teke had made her his main a long time ago.

The weed had passed through and took hold of Alton's system. Very soon he would have to go full time just to support his habit. Right now, Teke and his other relatives gave it to him, and that's the only way he stayed high. Occasionally, he would steal out of Thelma's stash that Teke gave her.

Walking towards his crew at the park, Alton was happy he had something to smoke. His nephew, Sean, walked towards him dribbling the ball. They were only 6 months apart. They were the same height, same weight, practically the same everything. They were terrible when they got together! Sean was Alton's sister Gracy's son. He lived in Oviedo, another part of Seminole County, but he was in Midway on Dixie Ave every day because of school. Gracy would drop Sean off in the morning and go to work in Sanford as a police officer. After school, he would walk home with Alton and the rest of the kids to his grandmother's house.

"What's up Unc? You out of boxing class already?" Sean asked.

"Hell yeah, I'm tired of that shit," Alton replied.

"Unc, you see I been quit that shit. I ain't got time to be goin' down there every day. Man lets go get some weed."

"Shit I already got some, Teke just looked out for me. We just gotta go get a blunt from Miss Moses." Miss Moses was the neighborhood bootlegger. She sold anything from liquor and tobacco to chewing gum and hot sausages.

On the walk to Miss Moses, they argued about who got the most pussy and who had the best pussy. Alton had all the girls, but Sean wasn't too far behind him. They just ran the train on a girl last week in the next neighborhood over. They got their blunts and headed back to the park. After they fired up, they played a little two on two.

Once the lights came on at the park, they headed home. Sean's mama was usually there waiting on him. Alton really didn't want to go home right away because he knew he was about to get it from walking out of the gym. He headed home hoping his father was either gone or passed out from all of the Seagram's Gin he had drunk throughout the day. As they approached the house, Alton could hear his mama Irene's loud voice cursing like a sailor.

"I done told you motherfucka's about running in-and-out my house while the air is on! I got a trick for ya'll motherfuckas. I'm gonna cut the whole damn air conditioner off and let you sons of bitches burn up. Shit, ain't nobody got no god damn money to throw away! How da fuck you expect the house to ever stay cool?"

That was Alton's mother. She talked so loud and cussed so much you could never misinterpret what she was saying. You could hear her voice in another county! All the neighbors knew all the Mosley's business because of Irene. She was a very obnoxious woman. Sweet as the sweetest pie but when she got started or was going to throw one of the fits she went at it all day and all night for hours. People say a person couldn't argue by themselves but Mrs. Irene could. When she started everybody just left the house. Sean looked at Alton then smiled and said, "That's your mama." Alton's sister Gracy was walking out the house as they were coming up.

"Sean, you got your things?" Gracy asked while grinning and smiling from ear to ear. Irene's ranting and raving didn't bother her. This was her comedy hour. After dealing with absurd crimes and rude co-workers, Gracy needed this laugh.

Sean quickly grabbed his things then ran to the white cougar his mother was driving. "I'll holla at you Unc!"

Alton just looked at Sean and his mother as they left the madness of the house. He wanted to go over Sean's house where it was peaceful. He had the newest gadgets and video games. Alton walked up the steps thinking, *let the madness begin!*

It was always something going on at the house. It was the family meeting place, a friendly gathering place, and most importantly it was the family refuge house. That's why Alton always thought there was drama going on there. Everybody in the family brought their issues and problems to the house. It was always overcrowded, and people were always coming and going.

The thunderstorm started soon as Alton stepped in the house. His mother forgot all about the cold air when she laid eyes on her son.

"Motherfucker! Oh, why yo ass walked out on Mr. Meneffee? You think me and your daddy got money to spend on yo ass and you don't appreciate it! And he told your daddy you smokin dope. Boy, if I catch you smoking somebody gonna have to holla in my ear to get me off you! You think you grown? I don't know where you picked that shit up from. You just like them motherfucker's from Titusville! You ain't gonna be shit! All me and your daddy do for your ass, and all you wanna do is smoke some dope? That's why yo ass be eating up all the damn cereal! If I catch you, I'm gonna beat the black off yo ass! Little manish motherfucker! When your daddy get home, he got something for you! We gonna take your ass down to the clinic and get a drug test.

Out of all things she could have said to him, the mention of his dad spooked him. His mind started racing, imagining all the things his dad could do to him. He knew firsthand how Big Chief could torture him without laying one hand on him. Big chief always said, "It's more than one way to skin a cat!"

Big Chief had a thousand ways to break a person, while Irene had only two ways. Talking shit or whooping your ass. But oh well, he'd rather face his daddy than to deal with his momma. With that last thought, Alton headed in his room that he shared with his brother Billie and his nephew Mark.

Mark was his nephew from his sister Barbaran who was strung out on crack. She had another son, Raymond, who was her pride and joy. He had recently been killed by his best friend in Titusville. She didn't handle it too well and had a mental breakdown. Mark eventually got taken away from her and put in a foster home. He was taken out of the foster home by his grandmother and grandfather and was brought to Sanford to live with them.

Mark was in the room snickering.

"What the fuck are you laughing at?" Alton sneered at his nephew.

"Man she been arguing to herself for the last two hours." They both laughed knowing that the woman was crazy. "Grandpa said he gonna put you on the wall when he gets back."

They both knew what the wall was. Big Chief would make them stand up with their backs against the wall and their arms straight out. He would have them stay like that until they got tired. Alton was hoping Big Chief would make him clean the yard or something, but knowing his daddy, he would stay on that damn wall for at least two hours.

"Alton and Mark!"

Irene's voice stopped their conversation like the crack of lightning. Get y'all ass outside and get them damn clothes off that line! Don't y'all see its dark outside? Them clothes been on that line since yesterday. Y'all the laziest bitches I don ever seen!"

Alton and Mark thought different. Work was all they did. Nobody else had to do anything but the two little ones. Billy, his other brother, who was two years older than him was at his job. Buck, who was four years older than him, was at his girlfriend's house. Nobody was left but him, Mark, and the other grandchildren that were too small to do anything. They were taking the clothes off the line when they heard the horn blowing from the front of the house. Their eyes locked with each other. Both boys knew what the blowing of the horn meant. Big Chief Curtis was home, and he was drunk. The boys rushed grabbing the basket of clothes and hurried to take them in the house. Both boys took a look out the window. True enough, Big Chief was staggering drunk barely holding himself up as he stumbled into the house.

"Irene, come tell Mark to go outside and bring them two turtles on the porch from the car. Tell him I said take them bags of cans out of the car and put them with the rest." Irene did as she was told. At times, she felt like she was one of his kids because he had raised her right along with his other children. In fact, a few of his children were older than her.

"Mark, you heard what he said!" Irene yelled.

Mark hurried up and did as he was told because he knew from first-hand experience, shit could get real ugly, real fast when Big Chief was drunk.

"Where that fish mouth motherfucker at?" Big Chief asked in a slurred voice. Fish mouth motherfucka was the name he gave Alton because his mouth was so small like a sheep head fish. When he was a baby, they couldn't even put a spoon in his mouth.

Nowhere to run, Alton thought. He stepped out of his room facing Big Chief.

"Sir?"

"Now all that money I spent on those classes and yo ass want to walk out on that man and leave your clothes and shoes on the floor!" He spoke in a slurred low voice, stressing each word while measuring Alton behind slanted cat-like eyes. Alton wasn't fooled by Big Chief. He knew that he was famous for dulling a person's senses to sleep, then exploding, catching you off guard and by surprise. "All that money??"... He said in a low, slow voice. "Right!" He slurred. Licking his lips constantly was a sure indication that he was drunk. Even though he knew the explosion was coming it still caught him off guard making his heart skip a beat. Alton willed himself to remain calm and still, looking at Big Chief wondering what this old motherfucker had in store for him. He knew his daddy had a thousand ways to torture someone. Alton felt that he had to answer a question Big Chief already knew the answer to was just one form of his many tortures. "You can't talk boy?" "Yes, sir." Alton shrieked. "Well then talk boy."

Alton could tell his daddy was fucked up because he was slurring heavily and licking his lips constantly. Alton didn't say anything but just looked at his daddy as he laid back on the couch like he was king of the world. "Get yo ass on that wall and you better not move until I fall asleep and wake back up, you got that?" Alton still didn't reply, he just did as he was told. It wasn't a question, it was a command. Nobody contested Big Chief, not his children, friends, or wife. Nobody! He would get really aggressive if someone even raised their voice at him.

Honestly, the wall was a place Alton did most of his thinking. It was a place where his body was forced to remain still, but his mind veered off. The one thing that was on his mind at that moment was why his dad hadn't brought up him smoking weed. He wanted everything ran concurrent not consecutive.

He stayed on the wall for the Cosby Show, A Different World, and Sanford & Son. He studied his dad, watching him closely timing his breathing trying to decide if his dad was sleep or playing possum. He decided that he was asleep and started to move a little, lowering his arms down some and resting his back against the wall a little. One of Big Chief's eyes opened as soon as Alton tried to relax a little. *Fuck! This nigga ain't human,* Alton thought.

When the first segment of the news came on his mom came in and rescued him. That was one of the privileges of being the baby boy.

"Go take a bath and get ready for school in the morning."

He left the wall thanking God for his mama. His whole body was hurting, and he felt stiff as a mummy all over! An hour later Curtis puffed on his cigarette. He didn't want

Alton smoking weed, but all his brothers smoked it. He knew that trying to keep the boy from smoking after he started was like trying to stop a kid from having sex. We gonna have big trouble out of that one.

"Irene, he got that blood running through him. I'm getting too damn old to be chasing him. Nothing doesn't faze him, and he is just like I was, so damn fearless. He's gonna be a damn thug just like the rest of them. Just be glad you only got one. I'll play the part as long as I have to, but he ain't gonna listen to me much longer. You didn't say nothing about what that coach said about him smoking weed did you?"

"Yeah, I said I was going to take him to get a drug test," Irene confessed.

Curtis didn't want her to mention it to him. He didn't want to reveal his whole hand.

"Bring me my food," Curtis demanded.

Irene scurried to the kitchen to grab his plate. For a minute, she thought that Curtis was over exaggerating and maybe Alton was just going through something. But on second thought, Curtis was always right. *Always.*

CHAPTER 2

WELCOME TO THE GAME

The year was 1995, and everyone was listening to Tupac, T.H.U.G L.I.F.E (The hate U give lil infant fucks everybody) music pierced the minds of everyone. Young Alton was standing on the corner of 21st and Dixie Ave. in Midway. The 21 D is what the boys called it. It was okay for him to hang on this corner because nothing was going on in this part of Midway. It was considered downtown, the quiet part of Midway and all the old people lived in this part.

As long as he wasn't hanging uptown where all the drug dealers, killers, and prostitutes were, he was on good ground. He was standing there waiting for his crew so they could go steal something from Walmart. Usually, on their way from Walmart, they would cross over highway 17-92 and go into the white neighborhood's to steal BMX bicycles.

They would bring them back to da hood and sell them for $10 or $20 to buy some weed to smoke.

As the leader, Alton handled the business part of things once they completed their weekly missions. He would go buy twelve nickel bags for $40 dollars and get his team-high as fuck. He would always save four bags to sell to the white boys at school for $10 dollars each. He and his crew basically got high for nothing. Making something out of nothing just came naturally to him.

He heard the music *Shed So Many Tears* before he laid eyes on the car that turned the corner where he was waiting on his crew. The car was a 1973 green Chevy Caprice. He immediately recognized it belonged to Fatso. He had a reputation for being "The Man" in Midway. Alton put on his cool face as he nonchalantly watched Fatso ride by him real slow with the music blasted. He was leaning against the driver door sitting real low, holding his steering wheel with his left hand. The car was the baddest thing Alton ever saw. It was a type of two-tone green and dark money green with airbrushed pictures on the side. The inside was leather, trimmed in the same green as the outside. It was hot as hell today, but you couldn't tell the way Fatso was leaning in the car with the windows up. As he got further down the road, he opened up the doors and revved the gas.

Alton was in love with that car. He wanted one just like it. He sat down on the corner daydreaming about that car and vowed that he was going to do whatever it took to get him one. He imagined all the pussy he would get by driving that car. He knew he could pick and choose whatever girl he wanted. From that day on, Alton made up in his mind that he was getting in the game and he didn't give a fuck who didn't like it.

He was a straight A student in school, but that didn't mean shit because all the girls seemed like they were attracted to dumb guys with money. As he sat there, his mind continued to look ahead.

Summertime was coming up, and the school would be out. He'd be damned if he didn't have the freshest and flyest gear when school started back at Seminole High School. Ain't no way in hell was he gonna be caught alive with some clothes from the Goodwill. *"FUCK!!"* he thought to himself, "I ain't wearing no hand me downs neither. I don't care if it's one of the neighbors or a family member, I'm just tired of them trying to give a nigga a handout." He paused for a minute and had to check himself on his last thoughts about everyone trying to give him a handout. Trab, his dawg that stayed a couple houses down from him, was two years older. He was his Brother Billie's best friend, and he did everything out of real nigga love.

Trab was his mother's only son and was spoiled to death. He acted like he was Alton's older brother and the truth is he wished he was. Anytime Trab had something, he made sure Alton had it. He would even give him shoes and clothes way before they got old.

Alton was still in a daze when his partner Apeman rolled up. "What's up, you didn't hear me calling your name?"

Alton thought to himself, and chuckled, *this nigga look just like an ape in real life.*

"Hell nah, I ain't hear you. Man, you seen Fatso car?" Alton asked.

"Yeah, I seen it a couple of times at the party last Sunday. Him and Stack was arguing about who paint was the wettest."

Stack was another big-time drug dealer from Midway, who also had a badass whip, a throwback 1969 Impala. Apeman's parents were young, and of the new school era, so he was able to do whatever and hang with whoever he wanted. The party he was talking about was held at the Center, a building in a park around the corner from his house. Alton parents would kill him if they thought that he was over there. Alton and Apeman talked back-and-forth about cars and who had what until all the members of his squad showed up.

The city bus arrived 10 minutes later, and they hopped on the one that was in transit to Walmart. They were planning on stealing some hats and watches. Alton set there listening to his team talk on the back of the bus. They were arguing about who was the best fighter on Mortal Kombat out of Sub Zero and Scorpio.

As he sat back contemplating about what they were doing and observing his atmosphere and the conversation, he suddenly had an epiphany. All of a sudden his situation seemed stupid, the conversation seemed stupid, and what he was planning to do seemed stupid. Seeing that car earlier put everything in perspective for him. It put his mind on some grown man shit.

They got off at Walmart and went inside to go on their usual stealing spree, which they had mastered down to a science. After another safe getaway, they headed for the white neighborhoods that were across Highway 17-92 where they would steal bikes.

It was always sweet in the white neighborhoods because they would just leave their bikes laying in the yards or in open garages unchained. One person looked out with rocks or something to throw in his hand, while the other person went into the garage and stole the bikes. It worked every time like clockwork.

Everyone had a new bike but Alton. He wanted a BMX with pegs in the front and the back. He passed up a lot of them waiting on the right one until he finally seen the one he wanted.

It was something about this particular bike that interested Alton. As they were leaving the neighborhood, he noticed that the same bike he had been looking for was the same bike in the garage they passed by. Without hesitation, Alton walked to the garage where he noticed the bike was not chained. "Sweet sack," Alton thought to himself. He grabbed the BMX bike and was halfway out the driveway when he heard, "You little muthafucking nigger, you wanna steal my kid's bike?"

Looking back, he saw the biggest cracker he'd ever seen standing at the garage door of his house with his shirt off and bare chest showing! He reminded him of those men in the old slave movies that his mom would watch from time to time. Alton picked the bike up and took off like a bat out of hell! Once he got a couple of yards down the road, he jumped on the bike and pedaled like he was racing for his life. Alton glanced back wondering, *where the fuck was Apeman?*

Two shots rang out like a cannon. The man was shooting at him! Putting his head down he pedaled even harder, praying he didn't get shot. Alton noticed a cut on a side street and was able to get out of dodge of the cracker that was shooting at him. Thanking God for his getaway, Alton's mind started to wonder *where everyone else was.*

The squad knew the script;

One got the bike, and the other person was supposed to play lookout by yelling or throwing rocks at whoever came out.

At the realization of possibly getting killed, he began pedaling with anger and thought about how Apeman had left him for dead. He hated a scary nigga. I'm gonna beat that nigga ass when I catch him, he thought to himself. Alton road his stolen bicycle to his girlfriend, Ayeshia's house in Georgetown. Ayeshia's mother worked at Checkers and didn't get off until 9 PM. He figured he would stop by and get some pussy before he headed to Midway.

Ayeshia was fine as hell. She resembled the actress Stacy Dash, from the pecan tan complexion to the beautiful hazel eyes. All the niggas from the hood wanted her but she belonged to one nigga, and that was Alton. They had been dating for a minute, and he was responsible for taking her virginity.

Reaching 7th St. in Georgetown, he rode his bicycle up to the store. All the hood niggas from Georgetown hung out there. Ayeshia was on the pay phone.

"What chu doing up here?" Alton asked.

Ayeshia walked towards him, smiling with her hands on her hips.

"I was just calling yo mama house looking for you."

Reaching him, she threw her arms around his neck and started kissing him. You could tell she was excited to see him. Pulling away she said, "Let's go to the house."

They took off across the street. Alton hid his new bike in the backyard just in case her mother came home early, and he needed to make a quick escape.

"Go in the room while I take a bath."

Even though she was young, Ayeshia was grown as fuck. She did things that you wouldn't expect a girl her age would do. Before she ran the bath water, she put on an R. Kelly CD.

Fifteen minutes later she came into the room wearing see-through thongs and a lingerie top, smelling like Victoria's Secret. She walked up to him smiling seductively. Alton was sitting on the edge of the bed in nothing but his boxers. Ayeshia bent down and kissed Alton gently on his forehead. Alton smiled as he grabbed her close to him. With no hesitation, she climbed on top of Alton and pushed him back on the bed whispering in a lustful voice, "Lay back." Ayeshia was so damn aggressive. She grabbed Alton's hard dick out of his boxers. Alton already knew what he was in for. She reached down with her hand guiding his dick inside her, then rode him like she was a grown ass woman.

"Do you want me to go faster or slower?" She whispered in his ear.

Alton told her to go faster, and she did as she was told. He then flipped her over holding her legs in the air as he pounded the pussy. She dug her nails into his back asking him to slow down because he was hurting her. Alton just ignored her and pounded harder until he was finished.

Ayeshia slapped him on the back, snapping on him about being so rough. He thought sex was all about beating the pussy until it made her scream. If you weren't doing that, then you weren't doing nothing. She made him take a shower with her, and after they were done, they took turns drying each other off. Alton had to leave real soon because her mom would be there.

Putting on his clothes, he reached into his pants pocket and felt a twenty dollar bill. *Damn,* he thought. He wanted to give it to her, but that was all he had at the time. He knew all the dope boys across the street were throwing money at her.

Fuck it, he said to himself and gave it to her. She kissed him and asked, "Do you want me to keep my hair like it is now or get micro's?" He told her it didn't matter. Alton kissed her goodbye, got back on his bike and headed back to Midway.

The whole ride back he was thinking about how he was going to fuck Apeman up for not letting him know someone was coming. *Damn, I could of got shot! Fuck this, ain't no money in the shit no way,* Alton thought.

Alton finally made it to his sister Thelma's house. She lived on the other end of 21st St. in a 3 bedroom house. When he got there, he hid his bike in the shed in the backyard. He began to walk down the 21st St. in the opposite direction where Dixie Ave. crossed over.

Everybody that went with him on the mission was at the corner except Apeman.

"Where Apeman?" Alton asked.

Everybody said they hadn't seen him. Little Ron, the biggest member in the crew, said he heard the shots and thought Alton got hit. Alton didn't respond, he just told them to go sell two of the bikes to Miss Josephine on Crawford Dr.

"Try to get $30 for both of them", he directed. The boys rode off on the bikes to go and handle business. Alton on the other hand, went to the park to wait for them to get back with the money but was really hoping Apeman showed up.

An hour later, the boys came back to the park with the money. Alton stuck the money in his pocket without counting it, then got on the handlebars of one of the boys in the crew named Jolly. He towed him to the weed lady's house who went by the name, Mary J. Alton's sister Thelma and Mary J were best friends.

Mary J looked just like Mary J Blige. She was fine as fuck and always had something short on when she came to the front door. She answered the door wearing a mini skirt and a halter top. Mary J stood there with her right hand on her hip looking Alton up and down like he was a fresh piece of meat.

"What's up Alton?"

"Nothing." He said nonchalantly.

"Let me get some weed for thirty dollars."

Mary J liked this lil nigga. He was fine as fuck. She was just waiting for him to get in the game so she could fuck him. If it wasn't for Thelma and how crazy she was, she would have already fucked the young nigga. His young ass had it going on. She was twenty-six, but that didn't mean shit. She was going to take that young dick.

Mary J. walked up the stairs to get the weed. She knew he was watching so she let her skirt rise up, showing him she didn't have no panties on. She looked back at him smiling. "Boy stop looking up my skirt before I tell Thelma on you." She paused at the top of the stairs standing bow-legged with her hands on her hips, poking her ass out.

"Plus little nigga you know you can't do nothing with no grown woman."

Alton just smiled at her, saying nothing while thinking how he would fuck the shit out of her old ass! He knew Mary J was just talking shit about how she was going to tell his sister. Shit, she was the one who had been selling him weed for the longest.

She came back with the half ounce of weed for him for the $30. She must have been feeling really generous or something because he had never got the weed loose before. People always gave it to him in bags.

"When you shake all your little friends come holla at me in a couple days. I need you to do something for me."

"All right," Alton said.

He left Mary J's house, got back on the handlebars and headed back to the park. The whole time he was smiling and wondering what she wanted him to do.

As they pulled up to Miss Moses house to get some blunts, he saw Little Ron pulling up. Little Ron informed Alton that Apeman had sent him to Miss Moses to get some blunts so they could smoke. Alton told Jolly to go back to the park and not to tell Apeman that he saw him.

Ten minutes later Alton arrived at the park and saw Apeman sitting on the bench with some other jit's. Alton jumped off the bike and ran up to him.

"You pussy ass nigga! Why you ain't let me know dude was coming!?"

Apeman stood up. "Nigga fuck you! I wasn't about to get shot for you!"

That's all Alton wanted to hear. He knew Apeman thought size meant something but he was going to show him.

"Fuck nigga you know what time it is! Shoot me a fair one!" Alton said, cracking his knuckles.

"Nigga you ain't said shit!" Apeman growled back at him.

All of the other kids moved out the way. Alton knew this was more than just a fight for cool points. This fight was for control of the crew. The funny thing about the whole situation was that he didn't want the crew no more anyways. He wasn't a thief, he was a hustler. But he was still going to beat this fuck nigga's ass for pulling that shit!

They squared off. Alton took one glance at the way Apeman had his hands up and how he was standing flat-footed. He knew without a doubt that Apeman didn't have a chance against him. Alton crouched low, staying on the balls of his feet. With a sudden spring like a lion, he slipped in and hit Apeman with a mean left jab, followed by an uppercut. He then finished it off by coming over the top with an overhand right. Apeman went down like a sack of potatoes.

"Get your bitch ass up!" Alton taunted.

Apeman rose up off his hands and knees and charged Alton, throwing a few wild punches. Alton easily weaved and ducked like he had been taught so many times before.

"You ready to go back down fuck nigga?!"

Alton could see the fear all over Apeman's features, and he fed off it with primal hunger. It was like he could taste his fear. Apeman no longer was Apeman in Alton's eyes. He had become a prey, and Alton was a predator. This was power in its most addictive form. The ability to conquer and subdue another human being mentally and physically no matter how much or how hard they resisted. Alton had grown to love the power of having knowledge that his combative skills were greater than his opponents. Apeman was fighting with his emotions, and he could not stand a chance against Alton's cold, calculated technique and skill.

Apeman threw a wild hook and Alton weaved it. Alton then threw a left punch to the body connecting with Apeman's ribs. He knew he could've finished it, but he wanted to toy with his prey some more. Backstepping out of Apeman's lazy uncoordinated reach, he circled him. Alton told Apeman to come on. Apeman threw another wild punch and Alton ducked it, positioning himself on Apeman's inside. Instantly, Apeman tried to grab Alton and overpower him with his weight, but that's just what Alton wanted him to do. Apeman made the mistake of stretching his upper body out by trying to grab him. Alton hit him with a right hook to the body so hard that it knocked the air out of Apeman. Alton threw one last right uppercut that knocked Apeman off his feet.

Apeman was on the ground balled up like a baby, crying holding his face and stomach. Alton stood over him glaring with a coldness in his eyes.

"Where the weed at?" Alton barked at him. Apeman fumbled in his pocket and gave Alton the weed.

"Getcho bitch ass up and get from 'round here!" Apeman stumbled to his feet and began to make his way down the pathway to go home. Everybody stood around appalled at what had just happened.

Alton casually took out a blunt and began to roll his weed as if nothing had happened. Everyone knew he had boxed, but they never saw him fight outside the ring. They only saw possible encounters with different niggas at school and other parts of Sanford, but the dudes always backed down at the last second.

Alton fired up four blunts putting them in rotation with the crew. When the smoke session was over, he gave everyone a dap and a little weed for themselves to smoke. He took one last look at the faces of his crew and thought about how young and stupid they looked. Right then and there he decided that he was done with his crew. Alton told them he would holler at them later and left the park heading for his sister Thelma's house.

Once he got to Thelma's spot, a man's voice answered to his knocking on the door.

"Who is it?" The man yelled.

"Alton!" He said, responding in the same tone the man had used.

The door opened, and it was Thelma's new boyfriend, Joe, smiling from ear to ear showing off his gold grill. Everyone called him Trucker.

"What's up lil nigga? I saw that bike you got back there. Who you stole it from?"

"Man, I ain't stole shit! Somebody let me hold it." Alton said defensively, walking past Trucker into the house. His sister was sitting in the living room reading a Jet magazine when she overheard the conversation between Trucker and Alton.

"Boy, what I tell you about cursing witcho little-grown ass!"

"Thelma leave that man alone!" Trucker said.

"Man. Where at?" She said in a mocking voice rolling her eyes.

Thelma was his mother's fourth child. She was one of the finest bitches in Sanford but don't get it twisted. She was a straight *gutta* bitch. She set niggas up to get robbed, trafficked bricks of cocaine, shot niggas, cut bitches, just about anything you could think of, Thelma was on all of that! She had much respect in the hood. All the dope boys and hustlers loved her. She loved gangsters, and if you were a pussy, you couldn't fuck with Thelma. She would take your sac, set you up to be robbed, and spend your money in the mall!

Alton liked hanging at her crib because he could hear real street gossip all day long. This was the closest he could get to the streets without getting in.

"Let me get some money sis?" He said in front of Trucker to test him and see what he was really about.

"Boy, I ain't got no money!" Thelma responded, looking at the gold diamond ring she had on her finger.

Trucker quickly reached in his pocket and asked Alton what he needed. Alton shrugged his shoulders and said, "Whatever you want to bless me with."

Trucker started smiling as he handed Alton a fifty dollar bill. He told him not to spend it all on weed.

"He better not be smokin no weed, he ain't grown," Thelma said looking at both Alton and Trucker with daggers in her eyes.

"Come on brother-in-law, let's roll. Thelma give me your keys!"

She reached into her purse that was sitting on the table and handed Trucker the car keys. When he turned to walk out, she looked at her brother and winked at him. Alton shook his head thinking to himself *what a devilish actor his sister was.*

Trucker drove to another part of Midway called The Camp. He pulled in front of a ran down building that had a whole bunch of street bums loitering around. Alton sat in the car staring at the scene all around him.

"What you waitin on bruh? Come on, get out the car." Alton snapped out of his daze and got out the car, following Trucker into the ran down building. They walked down a hallway where Trucker stopped at the 7th door. Bending down, he reached into his sock and pulled out a single key. Trucker stuck the key in the lock and opened the door glancing at Alton, with his gold teeth grilling at him.

"Walk light in here and don't drag no mud in here with you," he spoke in a sing-song voice that echoed in Grill's mind as he disappeared walking through the door. Alton was left in the hallway by himself, confused not understanding what Trucker meant by *"walk light."*

Stepping in the front door, he spotted a black mat with white block letters stitched into it with the words "DOPE

MAN." He hesitated to go in wondering about the words on the mat. *Fuck it,* deal with it later were the words that formed in his head as he took a deep breath and crossed the threshold. Alton made sure he didn't step on the mat. He saw that he was in the foyer of a small, two bedroom apartment. To his left was the kitchen and to his right was a closed door. In front of him was the living room where Trucker was in the middle of it. He watched as Trucker removed wads of money out of his pockets and a brown bag and throw it all on a table. Trucker stopped and looked up at Alton.

"Bring that safe out from under that bed in that room on yo right."

The safe was gray with black trim and about two feet long and two feet wide.

Alton brought the safe in the living room and placed it on the table. Trucker opened the safe and put black rubber bands around the money he was counting. Alton looked on in awe. He'd never seen so much money in his life! It was stacked on top of stacks in the safe!

After placing the money from the table into the safe and closing it, Trucker stood up, motioning Alton to follow him as he put the safe back in the room. He opened the closet in the room and turned on the light switch. Alton's eyes got big as fifty cent pieces! There was enough arsenal of guns to supply an army! Alton's eye locked in on four assault rifles that were hanging in rows. He was no stranger to guns, but these were the kind he had only seen in movies. There were lots of handguns stacked on top of a crate. Trucker reached for the black Glock 40 that was on top. He popped the clip out inspecting it, making sure it was loaded. Putting the clip back in, he cocked it back letting a round slide back in the chamber.

Trucker tucked the gun inside the waist of his belt on his left side. Turning around, he locked eyes with Alton and said "Listen here little nigga, I've been wantin' yo sister for a long time. Ever since I was yo age, I had a thang for her, and now I got her. I don' heard 'bout you too jit. That nigga Teke be comin' on the block all the time bragging about how nice his little brother-in-law is with his hands. Well now, you my little brother-in-law! We family."

Trucker was from Midway too, but he moved back to Miami when he was 12. Most of his family was from Miami. He was back in Midway at 18 years old.

"All these niggas scared of Teke. I'll kill a nigga real quick, and he knows not to come at me any kind of way! I want a reason to kill him!" Trucker's facial expression went from hate to murder instantly.

"Bruh, I got those four wheelers in the other room, so whenever you want some rec just come down here and tell my Uncle Tony to let you get them. Come on let's go."

It was just getting dark after they left the apartment. Alton started walking towards his sister's car when Trucker stopped him in motion and pointed to a car with a black cover tarp over it. Trucker went over and snatched the cover off and said, "Dis' what we riding in."

Alton's eyes lit up like a kid on Christmas when he saw the 1972 sparkling wine colored dunk with a brown convertible top sitting on chrome thirties and lows. Alton just started smiling at how the surprises kept coming and coming.

"I haven't let these pussy niggas see this yet. I just got it up here from Miami," Trucker bragged. Alton saw that the inside was the same peanut butter color as the convertible top. Trucker cranked the car, and it sounded like a race car engine was under the hood.

Leaving The Camp, they turned on the road called Sipes Ave. Trucker sat the Glock 40 in his lap as they rode in silence a couple of minutes while he tried to find the right CD to vibe to. Trucker dropped the top, and *It's Like Candy by Eight Ball and MJG* came on. The lyrics to the song jammed loud through the 6-12 inch speakers Trucker had in the back. Alton couldn't believe he was riding in one of these cars. As they pulled up to Midway and Sipes Ave., he thought to himself, *if his father could see him now, he would kill him.*

Trucker reached into the car console pulling out a lighter and a blunt he had rolled earlier. He fired it up and took a couple of pulls then passed it to Alton while coughing. Alton took one puff of the blunt and started coughing uncontrollably. After he got his coughing under control, he hit the blunt again and passed it back.

Alton was so high he leaned back in the seat just so that he could get himself together. He couldn't hear his own thoughts because the music was so loud. He caught himself beginning to be submerged into the beat and lyrics. It only motivated his will to obtain.

Sipes Ave was crowded as usual. There was always something going on every Sunday. You'd think it was a block party or a parade the way everybody from the hood gathered together. Everybody that was somebody or trying to be somebody was out, either on some business shit or some pleasure shit.

Trucker pulled up to the hole in a wall juke joint called Jimmy Hamp and backed the car in with the music still cranked up. All of the gangsters were out because it was Get Fresh Sunday. This day had become a ritual where black people came together to get their shine on. The gathering had been going on ever since Alton could remember. At one time black folks use to gather here after church to trade goods, gossip and mingle. Now black folks came here to trade drugs, show off their whips and flex their money and jewelry. Everything was a competition.

Alton spotted that nigga Fatso, flexing hard in his red BMW. He was wearing a baby blue jogging suit with a matching Kangol hat. Fatso made sure not to leave any jewelry at home. Every part of his body was glistening with gold and diamonds.

A nigga named Stack was stunting in a candy apple red 69' Chevy Caprice with peanut butter interior. And then there was another '73 Caprice, candy light green with cocaine white interior sitting on gold daytons. It belonged to another dope boy named Spark whose father, Jimmy Hamp, owned the juke joint. Jimmy Hamp had become a millionaire off of street money, and he spoiled Spark.

Alton continued to observe the scenery as a 2 door red Cadillac sitting on the thirties and lows pulled up. It was a youngster named Lil Gee. Everyone started smiling. He was the youngest kid there with a car and was just two years older than Alton. Everybody was laughing because of how raggedy his car was, but it didn't look raggedy to Alton.

Alton was standing outside the car reminiscing on how this was the place his big brother Leroy got killed. He wanted to go inside, but the sign on the door said eighteen and older, so he stood by the car and watched everything. All of a sudden,he felt a set of eyes on him from the back. He turned around, and Teke was standing by the dice game looking right at him. The expression on Teke's face was one of utter disgust.

Alton felt a little nervous looking at him because he knew Teke thought of him as a traitor. Alton looked away but little did he know, Trucker had watched the whole exchange of looks between him and Teke. Trucker walked over to Alton and passed him the blunt.

Two other dudes walked over and gave Trucker and Alton some dap. One of them started vibing with Alton like he knew him. As he chopped it up with the dude, Trucker walked off. Alton followed his movements, watching him holla at this person and that person.

Trucker called Alton over and passed him another blunt. A dude name Kenny King said to Trucker "So you got your little brother-in-law with you huh Truck?" Trucker just smiled.

"You know damn well Teke don't like this," spoke another dude name Big Man.

"Yeah, well he better keep it to himself or get what's on his mind put on his ass." Trucker tapped his waistline as he spoke.

A pineapple Cadillac with gold diamond cut thirty's, and lows pulled up. "There goes Pretty," Kenny King said while spitting on the ground.

"That's a bitch ass nigga right there." Trucker stated. His face had a look of scorn as he looked at Pretty's car.

Pretty was a light-skinned dude who didn't belong in the game. He always got robbed or debowed and then would run and get Meat, his brother. Meat was about that gangster shit.

A nigga named Lil Alex robbed Pretty, and he did his usual, went and got his brother Meat. Meat shot Lil Alex in the head in broad daylight in front of everybody on the corner of Sipes and Midway Ave. Now he was in the county facing a first-degree murder charge. Meat was fucked for life behind Pretty's bitch ass, who shouldn't have been playing a gangster in the first place! Every man should be able to handle his own beef.

A car with two girls pulled up on the side of the road. It was Mary J and Debra. Debra was another one of Thelma's friends. Mary J rolled down the front window, releasing a thick cloud of weed smoke into the air.

"What's up?" She said to Big while staring at Alton like he was a piece of meat.

Alton broke away from the eye contact Mary J had him locked under when he caught Trucker motioning to him to come on. He followed Trucker's lead giving Kenny King and Big Man dap like Trucker did. Alton didn't want to leave, but he knew the real reason Trucker wanted to leave was because of Mary J. He had a feeling that she would go back and tell Thelma everything she'd seen.

They jumped in Trucker's whip and took off making a left on Sipes Ave. then a right on Highway 46. Trucker was hitting the gas like he was driving in the Daytona 500. Alton just sat back and enjoyed the ride. They rode across town through all the neighborhoods that he heard the kids from crosstown always talking about at school. Trucker pulled up on 13th St. and hopped out of the car. He went into another juke joint called Dread. Five minutes later, he came back to the car with two swisher sweet blunts and two sodas handing them to Alton. Trucker grabbed some weed he had in his pocket.

"I know you know how to roll the weed nigga," he questioned.

Alton didn't say nothing because he was high as a kite already. His mouth was dry as fuck. What he needed the most at the moment was something to drink. Alton placed the blunt and weed on his lap and popped open the soda. He guzzled it down like it was the last soda on the planet!

They were riding through Georgetown on Pine St. when Alton saw his girlfriend sitting on the porch with a lot of other girls. He tapped Trucker on the shoulder to get his attention. Trucker turned towards him and hit pause on the music.

"What's up?"

"Stop right here. That's my girlfriend up there," Alton said pointing towards the house. Trucker smiled at him and said, "Yeah, let me see what you working with."

He pulled the car in front of the house Alton pointed to. Alton motioned for Ayeshia to come to the car and she got up and begin to make her way to him. Trucker expected to see a young Barbie doll looking girl, but what he saw made him do a double take. Little mama had a stripper body, and she was bad as fuck. He knew right then and there that his brother-in-law better start getting some money quickly because if not he wasn't going to keep her long. Especially in this neighborhood. He knew how the niggas at the store got down on some real predator, no holds bar shit when it came to a bad female. She walked to the car, swaying her hips like a model walking on a Paris runway.

Alton opened his side door and stuck one leg out as she jumped in his lap asking him "Who you with?" He didn't hesitate to say his brother-in-law. After talking to her for a few minutes, he told her he would call her later. She kissed him and walked off. Trucker was amazed at hearing his brother-in-law spit game. He knew the little nigga was going to be big problems and it was only a matter of time.

As they were coming out of Georgetown, they made a left on Celery Ave, and the police got right behind them. Trucker turned the music down.

"Bruh, troll right behind us." He pulled the Glock out his waistline. "Hold this!"

Alton took the Glock and put it in his waistline, no questions asked. Trucker told him to cuff the weed, and he put all of it in his hand. By this time the police had turned their lights on. Alton's heart was beating so loud he thought Trucker could hear it. But it wasn't from fear, it was from excitement. Trucker pulled over putting the car in neutral, holding his hand on the gear shift. As soon as the police car pulled over and the officer got out, Trucker turned the music back up on full blast and put the car in drive smashing the gas pedal. He went straight through the light on Melonville and Celery Ave. doing the dashboard heading to Midway. Alton was smiling, having the time of his life while running from the police. They made a quick right on Sipes Ave. Alton looked back to see how far the police was behind them, but they were nowhere in sight. Trucker hit it down Sipes and bust a right on 20th St., pulling back up at The Camp. He cut the music off and parked the car back where it was. They jumped out and told some crackhead to cover it up. Trucker grabbed the gun from Alton, and they got back in Thelma's car. As he cranked up the car, he looked down at his pager and smiled.

"Thelma has been blowing my shit up. I know Mary J fuck ass done told her you was with me."

As they were riding back on 21st St. Trucker reached his hand across to Alton and gave him some dap.

"I like what you did when I handed you that strap. Don't ever panic."

He gave Alton another dap. He reached in his pocket and gave Alton $100 then looked down at his shoes and said, "I'm going to take you to the Magic Mall Thursday and make sure you buy your girlfriend a bracelet or ring, something to keep her entertained. You can keep that weed too."

They pulled up, and Thelma came out on the porch looking mad as hell! Trucker just started smiling giving her a sly grin.

"Why the hell you had my brother on Sipes with you? He ain't grown!"

"You and me used to come through there when we wasn't grown!" Trucker responded, rubbing his head with his right hand. Thelma walked up to him and looked at him in his eyes. Folding her arms right over left she said, "You act stupid or play stupid if you want to, but you know damn well as I do that my daddy will kill him, me, and you if he thought for a second I let him go with you up there."

Trucker thought to himself, *he might as well start killing because this little nigga was on the verge of coming up on his own.* Standing there with her hands on her hip Thelma continued, "And besides that nigga, why haven't I seen your car yet?"

Trucker knew all that other shit Thelma was talking about was a smokescreen for what she really was after. He walked towards her and grabbed her hand, "You know you will," he said smirking. She looked away from him pouting and biting down on her lower lip.

"Everybody been blowing me up talking about how they saw him with you." Trucker cursed under his breath, letting go of Thelma's hand while turning towards Alton.

"Hey little bruh, go home before it get dark. I'll see you on Thursday," he said while cutting his eyes back at Thelma. He knew Mary J wasn't the only one to call her. He was willing to bet his nuts that Teke bitch ass called her too. Both Thelma and Alton caught the look. Alton knew at this point it was time to leave. He gave Trucker some dap, told his sister goodbye and walked out the back door to grab his B.M.X out of the shed. Everything felt surreal to him as he rode his bike home. He still couldn't believe he had $150 to his name! To put the icing on the cake, he still had all the weed he got from Trucker and Mary J. The weed he broke off the crew was the weed he took from Apeman after he kicked his ass.

With all of the events of today, he felt the decision he had made earlier of not fucking with the jits from his crew no more was a great choice. He was on to bigger and better things now. He would start hanging Uptown where the grown man action was going down at. He broke off his train of thoughts remembering he had to go to school tomorrow and pedaled faster towards Uptown. He had one more stop he had to make before he went home.

He pulled up at the New Store, and a dude named Showtime was hanging out in the front. Showtime was the definition of a St. gorilla to the first degree. He stood 6'5 and weighed two hundred and fifty pounds. His skin was dirty black, laced with over a dozen battle scars and bullet wounds. If the devil smoked crack, Showtime would be him. When he was feining for a hit of crack he would transfer into a kamikaze nightmare, knocking out niggas and taking their sac. If that wasn't enough, he kept a big Glock nine on his waist side for those who wanted to take it to another level. Most of the niggas who were out there respected the game and gave him something to smoke or else their sac was at risk of being taken. Showtime was Teke's, right-hand man.

"Lil bruh what chu' doing out here by yourself at night?" Showtime stood there towering over him like a silverback gorilla towering over a little monkey.

"Man I need you to go in there and get me a blunt and some of those nickel bags they sale." An amusing sinister grin formed on Showtime's face as he considered this little nigga who he looked on as a little brother. Alton's father, Mr. Mosley was the father of Showtime's sister, Phebe, and had basically stood in and raised Showtime as a son when his biological father was nowhere to be found.

Still, the first law of the street was *only the strong shall eat. It cost to be the boss.*

"You got some money?"

Alton wasn't about to let Showtime know he had $150. That was asking for trouble.

"I ain't got no money," He said leaning on the handlebars. Showtime started scratching his chin like a dog scratching for fleas.

"Don't worry about it, I got you."

A couple of minutes later, Showtime came out the store with what he needed and handed the stuff over to Alton with a serious expression on his face.

"You know you owe me money right?"

Alton wiped the smile off his face as soon as he spotted the look in Showtime's eyes. Hearing what Showtime said made Alton grip the handlebars with a dead man's grip.

"How much?" He responded in a low whisper.

Showtime just stared at the little nigga in front of him thinking to himself that this jit was going to be *the truth*.

"I'll tell you how much and when to pay me one day. Now get your ass from up here before I take what's in your pockets!" Alton was scared, but he wasn't going to show it. He looked Showtime dead in his eyes and spoke in a tone of voice as cold as death.

"And you won't take nuthin from nobody else!"

Locking eyes with Alton, Showtime took a step closer with a grimace on his face. Alton tightened down on the handlebars and held his ground, glaring back at Showtime with fire in his eyes. Showtime broke eye contact first, laughing and scratching his chin.

"Lil bruh go home."

Alton looked at him for a couple more seconds, then turned his B.M.X around, letting out the breath he had been holding. Leaving the parking lot on his bike, he turned around locking eyes with Showtime one last time to mimic him by grinning. Showtime continued scratching his chin while following Alton on his bike with his eyes until he disappeared down the dark streets. Showtime was surprised when he recognized that he was breathing hard and that his heart was racing.

"Shit, I'll be damned, that lil nigga spooked me some," Showtime admitted out loud.

He lit up a Newport to calm his nerves so that he could get a good read on his feelings. The truth was, he couldn't remember a time that no nigga had ever spooked him, except Big Chief, Mr. Mosley. The man who helped raise him. Not even that nigga Teke spooked him. He respected and tolerated him because they had a long history together, but Teke didn't put fear in his heart.

"Shit!" Showtime said out loud. There was a feeling that came over him like a cold arctic wave of cold ice air that was able to freeze anything it touched in an instant. In this case, the cold arctic air was the force behind the little nigga Alton's words. *And you won't take nuthin from nobody else!*

"Damn, that lil nigga gon' be hell!" Showtime said to himself. His thoughts were interrupted by the voice of a female.

"Hey daddy, I know you got a hit of some good on you. Let me put this head on you for a hit." Showtime turned around looked in the direction of where the voice came from. It was a crackhead named Cathy who had been strung out on dope for years. Her beauty had disappeared years ago, and she was as thin as the wind. Her clothes hung loosely on her like a clown outfit, and she looked like the walking dead. Lust took over Showtime's mind as he took Cathy and disappeared around to the back of the store.

Meanwhile, Alton had arrived home and placed his bike in the backyard. He had already decided that he was going to keep the BMX bike and not sell it. In his head, he was calculating the money he had in his pocket and the money he would make in school selling weed to the white boys. Once he got into the house, he tried to sneak past his mama.

"Boy its dark outside, and you know you got school tomorrow. Where you been?" He looked her in the eyes stretching his arms out faking a yawn.

"I was at Thelma's house cleaning up for her. She paid me." She didn't say anything else, and he just went into his room and closed the door.

After everybody was sleep, Alton crept out of his room into the kitchen. He grabbed a single plate out of the cabinet and went back to his room. Mark slept on the bottom bunk with his legs hanging over the edge and his hands in his pants. Billie was asleep in the front room next to Big Chief, and Buck had his door shut.

Alton pulled out both bags of weed and poured them on a plate. He went to work stuffing the bags. He bagged 13 nickel bags out of the sack he got from Mary J and 12 from the one he got from Trucker. He counted two hundred and fifty dollars that he could make if he sold the bags of weed in school to the white boys. He couldn't believe all this money he would make! He was honest with himself and knew he would smoke some, so he rounded it off to two hundred plus the one fifty he had in his pocket. When it was all said and done, he planned to have three hundred and fifty dollars. Alton quickly pulled the dresser back off the wall and pulled up the new carpet that was laid over the old carpet. He tucked the money between them and placed the dresser back against the wall. As he was about to get the weed off the plate, Mark woke up. For a minute they just stared at each other.

"Where you get all that weed from?" Mark asked.

"Man shut up and go to sleep!" Alton said, grabbing the bags of weed off the plate and putting them in his pocket.

"Granddad gonna beat your ass if he finds it."

"What you gon' tell on me?" Alton shot back. Mark raised both his hands up. "Na'll, but you know his old ass is slick!"

He let his hands drop back in the bed, pulled the covers over his head and rolled over on his side to go back to sleep. Alton just looked at him. He stayed up all night thinking about money and what type of shoes he would buy. He was then distracted by the voice of his mother yelling and cussing, telling them to get up for school as usual but this time he was already up. He left the house thirty minutes earlier than normal.

Alton was the first kid at the bus stop. He rolled up a blunt and started smoking it, thinking about the weed he had in the waistband of his boxers. Halfway through the blunt his sister, Gracy pulled up to drop Sean off and waved at him.

"What's up nephew?" Alton greeted. "You know I had to put it on that fuck nigga Apeman yesterday."

"Oh yeah? We should whoop that nigga again when he comes to the bus stop." I can't let you have all the fun." Sean said with a smile.

"Na'll he a straight fuck nigga. He was crying like a bitch."

Alton passed the blunt to Sean then started giving him a detail by detail description of yesterday. He boasted about how it was the best day of his life.

As he was talking, Little Timmy walked up to the bus stop and gave dap to Alton and Sean. Alton rolled another blunt, fired it up and passed it to Little Timmy.

All the children arrived at the bus stop before the blunt was finished and the school bus arrived a couple of minutes later. Alton and Sean got on the bus last and walked straight to the back where their seats were always empty and reserved.

Ten minutes later, they arrived at Lakeview Middle School. Soon as Alton's feet touched the school property, he was on a hunt to find Whiteboy Billy before his homeboy Maurice aka Mann caught up with him. Mann was one of them young niggas from Washington Oats who had a little hustle in him as well. Billy was the school's weed head. His family was rich, and they spoiled him.

Alton spotted Billy by the snack machines.

"Hey, Billy what's up? I got some weed," he said giving Billy some dap.

"Hey bro let me get 4 of those dime bags. I got forty dollars."

Alton eyed him grinning from ear to ear. He led him into the bathroom and gave him 4 dime bags. Billy pocketed them and reached in his book bag to pull out a fat knot of $20 bills.

Alton eyed it like it was nothing. He reached into his boxers and gave Billy another dime bag on the house.

"Holla at'cha friends to see if they need some weed and tell them to holla at me!"

Alton left the bathroom giving Billy some dap and headed for his first-period class. In the class, he was daydreaming all period about money. He kept replaying the scene from yesterday over and over in his head. As they went to the second period, he hollered at a few more of the white boys he knew, selling a bag here and there. He saw his homeboy Mann making a serve to some Latinos. Mann spotted Alton as he was leaving the Latino's and headed over to him.

"What's up bruh?" He said, giving Alton some dap.

"Just coolin'?" Alton responded. They talked for a minute and came to an agreement to skip the 3rd period and go match blunt for blunt.

The third period came, and they went behind the school and smoked 2 blunts talking about the different clientele at Lakeview Middle. The fourth-period bell rang, and Alton told Mann that he'd holler at him later. He took off and finished the rest of the day of school.

Finally, his school day had come to an end as Alton heard the last bell rang. He ran into 3 more sells before he could get on the bus. He couldn't believe all the money he had made. On the bus ride home, he counted all the money he'd made. $90 was an honest day's work. *Shit, I could get used to this, Alton thought.*

When they got off at the bus stop, Sean walked with him to Miss Moses spot and bought some blunts. They went to the park and smoked one before Sean's mother came to pick him up.

Gracy was already there by the time they got home, so they gave each other dap, and he told Sean he'd see him tomorrow. Alton got on his bike and rode to his sister Vicky's house.

Vicky was the youngest out of all the girls his mom had birthed. She was hot in the ass and already had a baby before she turned 20 years old. She stayed in a 1 bedroom house that his mom didn't like him hanging around. Vicky's house was the hang out spot in the neighborhood, and she kept some wild ass jits around there all the time. Vicky talked to a younger jit from Midway that was only 17. He kept his friends over there like Vicky's house was the trap.

As Alton pulled up his sister was standing in the doorway of the house.

"What's up lil bruh? What brings you this way?"

"Just coolin'. I came to check on you and my little niece."

"Where you get that brand new bike from?" Vicki asked with a smile.

"Now why you gone ask me a dumb question like dat?" He leaned the bike against the side of the house and walked past her and into the living room. His little niece Titi was sitting there, and he picked her up and walked towards the kitchen. He knew Vicky had a refrigerator full of food and cabinets full of snacks.

"Where yo' car at?" Alton asked.

"Gipp black ass was supposed to go and get some weed. Shit, that was over an hour ago, and that nigga still ain't came back yet," Vicky said aggravated.

"Where the blunts at?" Alton questioned.

She grabbed a Swisher Sweet off the top of the refrigerator and gave it to him. He rolled a fat blunt and got her high as fuck before telling her he had to leave. The block was calling him. Alton got back on his bike and took off down Sipes Ave. As he was riding, he noticed his sister's car. He crept up a little more and seen Gipp shooting dice at a familiar gambling house. Alton walked his bike up to the dice game and stopped to get Gipp's attention.

"What up Gipp? Vicky still waiting for you to bring her the weed," Alton said with a smirk.

"I know. I'm just trying to get my money back from all of these niggas," Gipp said with a frustrated look.

Alton figured he would sit there and watch the dice game for a minute. They were shooting 3 dice at a time, playing a game called C-Low. Gipp's facial expression said a million words. You could tell he was losing because every time he rolled the dice, he would be cursing and giving money to another nigga they called Daddy-Low.

After sitting there getting tired of seeing Gipp get his ass handed to him, Alton decided to take off. As he bust a right on King St., he saw Showtime, Teke, a nigga name Kenny King and a bunch of other niggas that he didn't know. Teke caught a glimpse of him and gave him a mean mug that made Alton feel uncomfortable. Teke's facial expression was one of steel and immediately changed to a cheesy ass grin, showing a mouth full of gold teeth.

Maybe he ain't mad at me, and I was overthinking it, Alton pondered. *Fuck that! I'ma keep it moving.* He knew he would see Showtime later and eventually he would bump into Teke but now was not the time. Alton threw up his hand acknowledging them but kept pedaling like he was on a mission.

He came to Crawford Drive and seen a couple of his homeboys that went to his school. After sitting there and hollering at them for a while, he decided it was time to go.

Suddenly he felt tired and concluded that home was his next destination. Once he got home, he did an inventory and seen he only had 2 bags of weed left to smoke for himself if he wanted to make the two hundred dollars. He told himself he would slow down on the smoking.

Lost in his thoughts, he laid down, and that was all it took for him to fall into a deep sleep.

When Alton got to school the next morning, Billy was waiting on him beside the bus ramp with 2 more friends.

"Man, that was the best weed that I ever smoked! How much do you have with you? We want all of it."

He was about to say 11 bags because of the 2 bags he intended to smoke himself but quickly dismissed that idea because he could easily get more.

"Man, I got 13 more. Wassup?"

Billy and his 2 friends quickly calculated who would pay what and gave Alton $130. This was the most money he ever made on one deal. He said fuck school for today and walked straight off campus to the nearest bus station and got on the bus that would take him to the mall.

As he was on the bus on the route, he realized that he had never been to the mall to buy anything. He had only had the chance to window shop or buy food. As Alton walked through the mall, he grew more excited about being able to buy something. He got to Foot Locker and seen the new Jordans in the window on the shelf that said *New Arrival.* They were the white ones with the shiny black leather on the front. It was love at first sight! He knew at that moment that's what he had come to the mall for. Alton went into the store, grabbed the shoes and asked the sells clerk to let him try them on. The white man kept walking as if he didn't hear him. Alton was about to get frustrated until a young pretty black female walked up to him and asked: "May I help you?"

"Let me check these out in size 9," he said with authority.

She smiled at him and said "OK," and went and got the shoes and came back.

He was kind of embarrassed to take his shoes off in front of her because his socks were too long and folded at the bottom. When he took the old shoes off he tried to hide his socks. If she saw them, she was a good actor because she paid it no mind.

"If you don't mind me asking how old are you?"

Lying with a straight face, Alton said "16."

"Why aren't you at school?" She asked.

"Damn, you being nosey! But if you must know, I didn't feel good today," he barked back defensively. The girl just looked at him knowing he was lying about his age and why he was not in school.

Alton stood up and looked in the mirror at the shoes. He loved them and couldn't wait to show them off. After walking back-and-forth in front of the mirror, he caught the female clerk watching him. Being satisfied and feeling himself, he sat back down and took them off.

He's cute, the store clerk thought to herself. If he had been 16 for real, she might have given him some play. She was only eighteen herself and just graduated. She knew he was 14 or 15 at the most and she couldn't stoop that low.

"So do you want them?" She asked flirtatiously.

"Of course," Alton spoke like he wasn't new to this and bought shoes all the time. She was stunned because she saw kids like him come in here all the time trying on shoes they could never purchase.

She went to the cash register, and Alton followed her as she rung the shoes up.

"$110. Do you want some socks to go with it?" She asked with laughter in her eyes. He quickly remembered taking his shoes off. She must have seen his socks and thought she was funny. But he said yeah anyway, and she put a pair of black Nike socks on the counter. She then told him to wait for a second as she went to the back and grabbed a pair of black Jordan shorts that hung low.

"You need these too," she said smiling.

Alton was kind of nervous because he never bought clothes out the mall before and he didn't know how much it would cost. She must have sensed his nervousness because she told him he'll get a 10% off discount since he bought them from her.

She directed him to the dressing room where Alton tried on the shorts. He loved them. Once he came back, she told him his total was $130. She must have read his pockets because that was about all the money he had left except for the $20 bill he came to school with. Alton went in his pockets and paid her, then he smiled and told her thank you and walked out of the store. She watched him walk out of the store with his bow legs and couldn't help but think of how much a heartbreaker he was going to be.

She looked around and seen the white store clerk watching her. He had just told her not to long ago to watch him and his kind because he looked like he was going to steal something. Now she had made her 1st sale of the day. *Cracker,* she said to herself.

Alton walked to the food court and stopped to order him some Chic-Fil-A to kill some time. The school wasn't out for the next 2 hours, so he ate his food until the next bus came.

After he got on the bus, he had to look at his shoes and shorts again. He then noticed something red in the bag. It was a red Jordan shirt. The pretty ass sales clerk had given it to him without him knowing. He wondered how and why she did it. Then he figured that's why she sent him to try on the shorts and he smiled. He was so happy he had the whole fit that he couldn't wait to go back to school. The thought of hollering at the girl at footlocker came across his mind, but she was too old. But shit, if he had his money right, she wouldn't be.

Once he got off at Midway, he went home and put his things away and checked his stash. He had $200 plus the change he had left over from the mall. He decided to go see what Mary J wanted him to do, so he got on his bike and headed down 21st. He saw his old crew on the corner of 21st and Dixie Ave. Everyone was there except Apeman.

"What y'all doing?" Alton asked.

All of them in unison said, "Nothing. Chillin'."

"Wea you been hidin' at?" Little Ron asked.

"Man, I just been coolin' it."

He didn't feel the need to tell them none of his business because he felt like they were jit's and he was on to something new.

"I'll be back later and burn one with y'all," Alton said like he was in a rush to go.

"Alright." Little Ron shot back quickly.

He took off to Mary J's house and knocked on the door.

"Who the fuck is it?" She questioned with a lot of attitude. She swung the door open with her hands on her hip. Once she saw it was Alton, her attitude changed and she invited him in.

She passed him the blunt and told him he could sit down. She sat across from him with her legs wide open knowing he was watching her like an eagle watching his prey. She looked down between her legs, looked back at him and then crossed her legs smiling.

"First of all, I didn't tell Thelma you was with Trucker, Debra did," she said staring into his eyes to see if he believed her.

Alton was easily convinced that she was telling the truth. Mary J decided to move forward with her plan. Her main goal was to seduce him and not make him run off like a little boy. She began her plot by baiting him with the lust for money.

"But anyways do you want to make some money lil nigga?"

"Yea, doing what?" Alton questioned.

She rolled her eyes because she expected him to know what she was talking about.

"I want you to slang some weed," Mary J said bluntly.

Alton just smiled to himself. This was bingo because now he had 2 connects in a week.

"You smoking this shit so you might as well get you some money," she said with an attitude.

"That's wassup, how much do I got to pay for it?" Alton knew nothing in this world was free and everything had a price on it.

"Well I'll start you off with a quarter pound, and we'll see how you do.

"I'll just charge you two hundred dollars. You do good and bring me my money in a timely manner, the price will get better. But first, you gotta do something for me and can't tell Thelma or no one!" Mary J's voice suddenly became seductive, and she pierced Alton with lust in her eyes.

"Man what I look like telling Thelma you giving me weed." He was unable to read the lust in her eyes being that he was so young. Mary J wasn't talking about weed. Right now she was ready to fuck him. Her desired plot was that she was going to fuck him and raise him up, but Thelma or the streets couldn't find out! She knew Thelma would kill her if she found out, but the curiosity in her couldn't help itself. Dredd was convenient for her, but she wanted some young dick because she knew the younger they were, the more likely they would listen, not to mention the stamina.

Mary J decided to come up with a straightforward approach as she watched the expression on his face.

"Take them shorts off so I can suck your dick," she said in a very commanding voice.

Alton was thrown off guard for a second, but he refused to show shock or show her she intimidated him. "Come take them off," he commanded as he looked her straight in her eyes.

Alton didn't like being controlled, but on the contrary, he liked to be in control. Old bitch or not she wasn't going to tell him what to do.

Mary J quickly got up off the sofa, walked over to Alton and unzipped his shorts reaching inside his boxers for his dick. Alton was still smoking the blunt like he had done this a thousand times already. He reached down to help her retrieve his dick from his boxer's.

"Nigga take all that shit off, but yo' shoes, this grown-up fucking," Mary J said kneeling between his legs.

Once he got everything off but his shoes, Mary J grabbed his dick stroking it up and down, shocked at the size of it. She knew it was big because she heard his sister Thelma always bragging about it, talking about how big it was when he was a baby. But she didn't know it was this big! The boy had a grown man dick, and she knew she was going to love every inch of it.

She licked him slow at first from the base of his dick all the way to the tip of his head.

"Look at me," she commanded.

Then she spat on it and got it real wet while making sure she didn't break eye contact with him. She deep throated him and tried to put the whole thing in her mouth but thought to herself *she may have underestimated him.* Slob was running out of her mouth to the shaft of his penis as she began to use her hand to follow the motion with her mouth, stroking and sucking simultaneously.

"You think you can handle all this?" She said, more of a statement than a question.

"You think you can handle all that?" Alton replied back with a sly tone.

She stood up towering over him and lifted her skirt up over her head to expose she had nothing underneath it. Her body was like a stripper. Waist very small, with a lot of ass, thighs, and hips.

"I asked you, nigga. Do you think you can handle it?" She said slapping on her own ass hard making it sound like a gun went off.

Alton had never been with a woman with a body like this, and he damn sure couldn't wait. He began stroking his dick and told her there's only one way to find out. She smiled because she knew this little nigga knew he had a big dick. She wanted him to get it any kind of way he wanted it so he could always remember. Dredd didn't have the strength and stamina like a young nigga. She wanted Alton to stand up in that pussy! She wanted to do all the positions like she did when she was a teenager.

"How you wanna fuck me, nigga?" Mary J asked while bending over in front of him making her ass clap.

"From the back like a dog. Can I fuck you like a dog?" He asked smacking her on the ass.

"That's right nigga smack that ass! And that's how I want you to fuck me. Just like a dog." She said naughtily.

Mary J got on the couch, looking back at Alton and repeatedly slapping her ass hard. "Face down, ass up nigga! That's how I want you to fuck me. Now come and get it!"

Alton walked up behind Mary J while she had her ass hiked up in the air. He slid his dick inside of her pussy and began fucking her hard and fast right away. Her pussy was dripping wet like Niagara Falls.

"That's right little nigga! Pound that pussy hard, beat it up!" She urged Alton on.

He spread her ass cheeks and push them forward so he could get as deep as possible.

"Oh shit, that's what I'm talking about." Mary J groaned.

"You like it in deep like that?" Alton said aggressively.

"Just like that, you got it in me so deep."

Alton pushed his dick in as far as he could and thrust his hips as fast as he could. He was pounding the pussy with as much strength as his little frame could muster. The more she moaned, the more excited he got.

Mary J was about to cum all over Alton's dick. He was so deep inside of her, and she wanted to make sure he stayed there. She reached back and spread her ass for him so he could go deeper.

"That's right daddy fuck this pussy!" She screamed.

"Deeper daddy. Go deeper! I'm about to cum all over your dick! Make me cum daddy and pull my hair." Mary J moaned out in ecstasy.

Alton pulled her hair and fucked her faster than he ever imagined he could go. He was enjoying watching the waves in her ass every time he hit it. She was talking nasty to him, making him go faster, plus he had never pulled a girl's hair before. It was arousing him in ways he never dreamed about.

"Talk to me daddy, tell me to cum on that dick, and call me a bitch."

"Come on my dick, bitch." Alton barked.

"Oh yes daddy, make me cum."

"You like the way I'm fucking you bitch?"

"Yes harder daddy, I'm about to cum." Mary J screamed.

Alton pounded away while pulling her hair and Mary J began to grind back on his dick.

"I'm cumming all over that big dick, yes!" She moaned lazily.

"I'm not through with you bitch!" Alton said still pumping.

"Stop, let me clean your dick up baby." Mary J said panting out of breath.

Alton backed up out of her with an erection the size of the statue of liberty. He never saw his dick like that before. Mary J sucked and licked all over his dick while moaning.

"Oh, yes gotta keep your dick clean baby I made a mess." She said giggling.

Alton just looked at her like she was an animal. She was doing the things to him he had only seen in the XXX movies his dad tried to hide.

"Now let me get on the floor and hike this ass up while you beat it. Dogs fuck on the floor!" Mary J got on the floor and put a pillow down there for her face and her head.

"Now fuck me hard and as long as you want!" She said moaning seductively. Alton got behind Mary J then inserted his dick inside her. He continued to fuck her hard and fast. When Mary J heard his breathing change, she yelled: "Take it out and cum on my ass." Alton took it out and squirted his cum all over her ass, breathing hard and out of breath.

"Baby that dick so good! Now I'm gonna stay right here and play with this pussy while you go in there and get you some water," she said smiling.

Alton just looked at her and smiled. He never fucked any girl who just let him fuck as hard, deep, and as fast as he wanted. He was starting to get hard again already just thinking about it. After drinking some water, he went back into the living room to fuck Mary J again.

After they finished, Mary J went upstairs and got the weed and came back down. She handed him a quarter pound. Looking Alton in his eyes, she said, "Bring me the two hundred dollars as soon as you make it. Rule number one when you're getting fronted anything, always pay your connect first whether you make your profit or not."

Alton had the money to pay her now, but he wanted to see how tomorrow turned out because he wanted to get

Ayeshia a gift from the Magic mall. So he said to himself he'll come to pay her tomorrow. Alton told her bye, tucked the weed in his boxers and walked out the door.

It was almost dark when he got home. After everyone went to sleep, Alton bagged up 20 nickel bags and hid the rest out back in the laundry room behind the washing machine. He went back into the house and laid his new outfit out on the bed. He couldn't wait for school tomorrow.

Walking to the bus stop that morning, he smoked a blunt and felt like the coolest nigga in the world. He stood by himself while the bus came because Sean had stayed home for the day. Once he got to school, he saw Billy and two more white boys standing like they were waiting on him.

"What's up y'all straight?" "We got one hundred bucks we need ten dime bags," Billy stated, not giving any time for small talk.

Alton quickly told them to follow him to the restroom. He gave them twelve bags and told them every time they came with a hundred he would give them twelve. They were very happy when they left out the restroom. He made his rounds, talking and flirting with girls all day. He loved the attention he got because of his new clothes and shoes. Not to mention his new found income. Alton was becoming a trendsetter because everybody kept telling him how they were going to cop the new Jordans he had on.

As soon as school was over Alton got on the bus and couldn't wait to get to Midway. When he got home he took one hundred and fifty dollars from behind the rug and added it with the hundred he had made earlier at school then jumped on his bike and rode down 21st St. to head to Thelma's house.

As he pulled up, he spotted Trucker outside already waiting for him.

"What's up lil nigga? You ready to go?" Trucker asked smiling.

"Hell yea!" Alton said excitedly.

He motioned for Alton to come on as they got in the car and headed out of Midway. Trucker stopped at a few places and met a few white dudes who all gave him two or three hundred dollars. Then they got back on I-4 and headed to Orlando to go to the Magic Mall.

Once they got there, they went to a jewelry store that was owned by an oriental couple.

"How may I help you?" The wife said smiling.

"He wants to get a bracelet for his girlfriend," Trucker said looking at Alton with a sly smirk.

The old lady looked at Alton and walked toward him. Alton was busy looking in the glass at the gold chains he saw with crosses on them. He always wanted one and was visualizing himself with one of those gold chains on.

"The bracelets are over here, sir," the oriental sales clerk said pointing at a different part of the glass. Alton came out of his trance and walked to where she stood. He quickly looked at all the bracelets and decided on an XO bracelet he seen with the price tag of fifty dollars. He pointed to it and told her what he wanted. She cleaned it, and put it in a box and gave it to him.

Trucker had walked off, so Alton went back to looking at the gold chains. He saw the one he wanted with a broken cross that dangled. The price tag on it said five hundred. He asked could he try it on. The sales clerk looked nervous and hesitated at first, but when she saw Trucker, she handed him the necklace and let him look at it in the mirror. Alton instantly felt like a big man. He puffed his chest out and thought the necklace made him look older. Trucker knew he wanted the chain, so he decided to tell him something to motivate him.

"Get half the money for it, and I'll give you the rest."

"Alright," Alton said thinking to himself he only needed fifty more dollars.

"You got your girl the bracelet?" Trucker asked.

"Yeah. I only need fifty more dollars, and I'll have my half for this."

Alton didn't hesitate to let him know because things were always subject to change.

Trucker looked at his little brother-in-law from head to toe. He was going to buy the bracelet for his girlfriend for him, but this little nigga paid for it! And he knew that outfit plus them J's cost at least two hundred dollars. That's two hundred and fifty dollars he spent and was now talking about he had two more hundred! Trucker thought, *Fuck, I gotta help the little nigga out.*

"Mommy he already spent fifty dollars with you. Let him get the necklace and charm for four hundred." She quickly said OK with a smile.

Alton pulled out the two hundred dollars he had and watched as Trucker put the other two hundred on the counter. He couldn't believe he just bought this necklace for four hundred dollars! She told him to take off the necklace so she could clean it. Although he didn't want to, he did anyway. After she cleaned the necklace, she gave it back to him. It looked even better now as he put it back on. Alton couldn't stop looking at his chest. He felt big! Trucker watched him and smiled to himself.

Trucker and Alton walked around a little longer and came to a decision that it was time to go. When they got in the car, Alton told him to take him to Georgetown. As they drove off, Trucker was thinking to himself, *where did jit get all that money from?* He knew he only gave him one hundred and fifty dollars the other day. He kept driving pondering to himself.

"How you gonna get back?" Trucker broke his train of thought.

"I was gonna walk back," Alton said boldly.

"Man you trippin. I'll come back and get you in two hours, but next time you can drive over here. But just here and back though." Alton looked at Trucker shocked, "You for real man?"

Trucker looked at him and smiled. "I'm for real lil bruh, I got chu."

They pulled up to the house, and Alton got out and walked to the door. Trucker waited until his brother-in-law was in the house before he pulled off. Ayeshia opened the door and looked him up-and-down. She didn't see what he had on today in school because she went to a different middle school.

"Damn baby you look good. When did you go to the mall? I would have went with you," she said admiring what was in front of her.

"Yesterday," Alton said.

Ayeshia looked at the necklace on his neck. She grabbed it and started to play with it. She couldn't believe she had such a cute boyfriend. Something was different about him. Alton looked like he was older now. She kissed him like she hadn't seen him in forever.

Alton sat down on the couch and told her that he had something for her too. He reached inside of his pocket and pulled out the box which contained the bracelet and told her to open it. Ayeshia opened the box and took out the bracelet. She loved it and was ecstatic because no one had ever bought her anything but her mother. She kissed him all over his face and told him thank you. She now had the bracelet to match her necklace.

He watched her as she examined it and he felt powerful. Alton knew no kid his age was buying their girlfriend fifty dollar gifts. They sat down and talked for a while then he went across the street and got a blunt. He came back and sat down on the porch and began to roll his weed. When he finished, he fired up his blunt.

As the blunt was coming to an end, Ayeshia friends started to come over. They immediately noticed her bracelet and all were in awe. They talked, and he listened not saying a word. He paid no attention to them even though he knew he was being watched.

After a while, Trucker pulled up in the car. Alton told Ayeshia that he would call her later then kissed her goodbye.

He got in the car with Trucker, and they rode back to Midway and pulled up to Thelma's house. It was time for Alton to go home, so Trucker told him to come holla at him later.

Alton got on his bike and rode home, all the while feeling himself. He knew nothing about the game, but he wanted in. He no longer wanted to sneak and hide like a little boy. He wanted to be a part of the streets. When he finally got home, he went straight to his room and shut the door. Fuck all that hollering shit! He said to himself. He locked his door and begin to bag up more weed for tomorrow in school.

When he got to school the next morning, he saw Billy in the hallways chilling. Billy told him he had a little left over and didn't need any today. Alton went on about his day and still caught a few sales from other white boys. He and Mann hooked up, skipped a few classes and did their usual, matching blunt for blunt. Mann couldn't do nothing but notice Alton's new necklace, and he was fucked up about it. He knew he had to get him one.

They were the only ones making money and even though Alton had just started, it felt good to know he had something to show for it. A couple of blunts had passed, and the conversation had died down, so they decided to head back to school. They had got back right before the last period, and Alton couldn't wait for the end of the day.

After catching the bus home, he decided to go chill and hang out with his old crew so he could show off his new things. As he pulled up to the park, he noticed all the boys were out there, including Apeman. They all looked at him strangely as he pulled up to them.

"What's up y'all?" Alton said, breaking all silence.

"Nothing." They all said at the same time.

Alton pulled out a blunt and fired it up. Everybody awkwardly stared at him and Apeman like they were going to fight. He could see the fear in Apeman, so Alton decides to ease some of the tension. He passed the blunt to him, and Apeman accepted it and started smoking.

"Where you get this from?" He said while coughing.

"That's what I got," stated Alton, looking him in the eyes.

Just like that Alton went from being a friend of theirs to their connection. Apeman and everyone looked at their friend hard and realized that he was in the game. They looked at him and observed the clothes he had on and his necklace. They knew he had to get it on his own because his parents wouldn't buy it for him.

"You got some now?" Apeman asked, hitting the blunt a few more times then passed it to another kid.

"What chu talking about?" Countered Alton.

"Let me spend twenty with you." Alton reached into his draws and gave Apeman five nickel bags for twenty dollars. Then all the other kids at the park put together twenty and got the same.

"I gotta go handle some things, but I'll be back to smoke something else with y'all later."

What Alton rode off on his bike thinking Apeman wasn't looking too bad after only a couple of days of getting his ass beat. He was glad he didn't hurt his friend too bad. He was on his way to Mary J's house to pay her the money he owed her.

Alton pulled up on his bike, and Mary J was outside talking to Debra. Both of them looked at him and started giggling. He could tell they just were talking about him. Alton couldn't help but blush as he thought about how he fucked Mary J, his older sister's best friend.

"Heyyyyyyy Alton," Debra said smiling real hard.

Alton felt really strange after she said his name like that like she knew he did something.

"What's up?" Alton replied looking back at Mary J.

He looked away for a second at the passing car that was riding by because he thought he recognized it. As he turned around to face Mary J and Debra, he caught Mary J elbowing her, but he pretended like he did not see them.

"You can go in the house Alton, and I'll be inside in a second." Mary J said.

Alton put his bike down then went inside. He sat down and started rolling a blunt. After a few minutes, he heard Debra's car crank up and then Mary J came into the house. She just looked at him, analyzing his outfit. He was sporting his new Jordans and all black Dickies with the shirt to match. Her eyes then went to his neck, and she noticed his gold chain. In her mind, she had quickly added up $750.

She stood in the doorway, leaning against the front door with her hand on her hips as he watched her. She thought to herself, *he couldn't be done with the weed, and if he was, he fucked up the money.* But she didn't care because she felt that it was well spent. With his performance, she should have given him the weed anyway!

"Well I see you done got all fresh on a bitch?" She said in a joking manner. Alton looked at her and continued to smoke.

"I've been thinking about you ever since you left. You make my pussy wet every time I think about you and what you did to me. My pussy starts jumping and throbbing every time I think about your young ass. Hurry up and give me some of that dick before my kids come home." Mary J said in a sensual tone.

She had 2 kids that were in elementary school, so they were coming home in the next hour.

"Come get it, bitch!" These were the first words he said to her since pulling up outside. She began to come to him submissively.

"Damn nigga! I love when you talk to me like that." Alton interrupted her, "I got your two hundred dollars." He went into his pocket and gave the money to her. She looked at the money, then his feet, then his neck, then his face. She started staring into his eyes and knew this young nigga was the one! She took the money and put it on the table, and began taken off her clothes.

Mary J sucked his dick good and fucked him even better. After she was satisfied, she asked him how he made money so fast and who had bought him all that stuff. Alton didn't say anything, he told her he was straight on the weed, and he'll need some more in a few days.

As he got ready to leave, there was a knock at the door. Mary J got up and opened it. It was a guy name Looney from Midway. He told her he wanted to spend twenty dollars. She told Alton to serve him, and he did. Alton gave him four bags for twenty.

After the exchange, Mary J told Alton to start coming over to her house after school and serve the people that came. She gave him a key to the house just in case she wasn't there. He said alright then told her he was going home. He got on his bike and took off.

CHAPTER 3

POCKET FULL OF ROCKS

Summer was in, and school was out, and all Alton could think about was getting money! He no longer hung with his old friends but had developed a new set of friends, all except Little Timmy. But that friendship was cut short because Little Timmy got locked up for shooting his dad in the head for beating on him. Miraculously, his father pulled through. Also before school got out for the summer the FEDs had come through Midway and got all the big time drug dealers. Fatso, Trucker, Bumble, Dray, Pretty, and a couple of other cats all fell victim. Shit had got crazy, but Alton didn't see the after effects of the game, he just saw the glamorous life.

Alton had started driving a lot since he was fucking with Mary J. She let him drive her little hoopty to go check on his girlfriend and take her something to eat. There was a party tonight in Midway, and he was going, so he drove Mary J's car to the mall. He hadn't been in Foot Locker for a while, so he decided to go there first. Once he walked in, he saw the girl that sold him his first pair of Jordans. She was waiting on a customer, so he decided to wait until she was done and approached.

"What's up?" He said nonchalantly.

She looked startled at first trying to recognize where she knew the face from, then she smiled. "Hey you, how have you been? And why haven't you come back to check to see if we got any new arrivals?"

After speaking, she glanced at him from head to toe quickly taking in his new Hurackes, black Dickies, black T-shirt and nice gold chain. She thought to herself his young ass got it going on. He looked much older and better than the last time she saw him.

"I just been coolin' and I've been too busy to get down here," Alton replied to her question.

"So what can I do for you today?" She asked admiring everything about Alton's new look.

"I need a fresh pair of kicks for this event I'm going to tonight."

"What are you wearing?" Alton was still relatively new to this shopping shit and didn't think to get the outfit first.

"Nothing, I'm going down to Dillard's to find something," he said innocently.

"Silly, you always buy the clothes first if you looking for an outfit. Unless you just gotta have the shoes," she said smirking at him.

"Okay, is it for school, a wedding, a funeral, a party or what?" She just wanted to keep him talking.

"Party."

"What party?" She asked with her eyebrows raised.

"A party in Midway. Damn you nosey!" Alton said smiling back at her.

She looked at him before saying anything, thinking he's too young to get into a party.

"Aren't you too young to be going to a party out there in Midway?"

"That's where I'm from. Born and raised." He stated matter of factly.

"Well go to Dillard's, get your outfit then come back and I'll hook you up." She said popping her gum.

"Okay," Alton said and walked off. She just watched him thinking to herself, she was going to bust a move on him one day, but she had to wait until he got a little bit older.

Alton went to Dillard's and brought him some Tommy Hilfiger navy blue khaki shorts and a yellow and white Tommy Hilfiger shirt to match. Along with the outfit he snatched a navy blue Tommy Hilfiger hat. He was going to be fresh as fuck! Once he tried the clothes on, he purchased them and proceeded to walk back to Foot Locker.

When he got back, the store clerk was waiting on him smiling. She asked him to see his things, and he handed her the bag. She opened the bag and examined the clothes he bought and was immediately impressed with his taste.

She went and got him a size nine and a half of all white Air Force Ones to go with his new fit. As they were walking towards the register, he saw the new arrival sign advertising the new Jordans. He told her to let him get those too, and she was shocked. Not only did he go spend the money at Dillard's but he was buying two pairs of shoes. And he already had on a fresh pair of kicks with a nice big chain on.

Where was this young boy getting all this money from? She quickly came to the conclusion that he had to be hustling. She rung up his total and told him it would be two hundred and fifty dollars. Without even flinching, Alton went into his pocket and pulled out a knot and counted quickly. She was in shock once more.

"Boy, how old are you and don't be talking about no 16!" She said holding the money in the air.

"I am 16," he said, smirking with his signature smirk.

"What school you go to?" She said smacking her teeth.

"Seminole."

"Then why I never seen you there? I graduated last year," she said with an 'I got you' look in her eyes. She knew she had him and was waiting on his next lie. Hustler or not she wasn't going to let him outsmart her.

"Alright I'm 14, but I'll be 15 in March," he said giving up.

"What's your name, little boy?" She said trying to intimidate him. Alton asked, "Why I gotta be a little boy?"

"Because you are, and where you get all that money from? And don't tell me you work for it because you're not old enough to have a job. Ain't no job paying that much no way," she said handing him his change. *Here she goes with that preacher shit,* Alton thought as he grabbed his bags and headed for the door. She followed behind him.

"Aren't you going to ask me my name?" She said like she was in need of attention. Alton just walked away, without looking at her and said, "Kesha, I know how to read."

She looked down at her name tag and smiled, watching his sexy young ass leave the store. Fuck waiting, she thought. She was going to get his young ass now. She heard about the party in Midway tonight, and she was going just to see him. She smiled to herself then helped the next customer.

Alton left the mall and headed back to Mary J house to park her car. As he was approaching the front door, he heard Mary J and her boyfriend arguing. The door swung open, and Dread looked at him with murder in his eyes. Alton proceeded to ask Mary J could he take a shower and change as if Dread stares didn't phase him. She told him to go ahead. Alton went in the restroom, took a shower and changed into his new clothes, when he heard Dread say, "You fuckin' dat lil' boy!" with a lot of anger in his voice.

Alton finished up and came out of the bathroom as Mary J was telling Dread that he was her little brother.

"But he got a dick between his legs!" Dread stated bitterly.

"Please leave if you gon' be accusing me of fucking my little brother." Mary J told him sourly.

Dread grabbed his keys and stormed out of the house slamming the door. Mary J looked at Alton smiling with lust in her eyes. She almost told Dread she was fucking him, but she couldn't because she didn't want to mess up her connect with him. She didn't want to admit it because her plan all along was to get Alton sprung but she was fucked up about that young nigga. The plan had reversed, and now Alton had her sprung!

"Why you gettin' all fly? Where you going?" She asked with an attitude.

"I'm going to the party tonight at the Center," Alton said calmly.

She looked at him and studied him and knew it wouldn't be long before Thelma got wind of him hustling. He was starting to get wide open.

"Well, you can drive my car because I'm going with Debra. I don't know if Thelma's going. But take some weed with you because people gon' want to smoke. Get money while you at the party," she said, trying to drop some game for the young nigga.

Alton grabbed the keys and walked out the door. He got in the car and went to Georgetown to see his girlfriend, Ayeshia. Since he had started hustling, he bought her all the little XO sets and kept her hair done. He saw her mother's car there, so he kept going. After riding across town and going through all the hoods, he headed back to Midway. *It was 11:30pm, and the party should be getting started, he thought.*

As he pulled into the parking lot, he seen all the dope boys were in attendance and women were everywhere. He rolled him a blunt and sat in the car. He didn't want to try to go in because he knew he wasn't old enough and he didn't want to get embarrassed at the door. So he just got out the car and sat on the hood. There were people all over the parking lot doing the same thing. Then he saw Debra and

Mary J ride by and park. Halfway through smoking his blunt two dudes approached him.

"You got some weed?" One of the dudes asked.

"Yea, wassup?" Alton responded.

"Let me spend $20 with you," the same dude said, handing him the money.

He served him and looked over at Mary J, and she nodded her head. He rolled him another blunt and people just kept coming up to him for the next 30 minutes to buy weed. As he sat there chilling, he saw Mary J walking towards him. Her hips and ass were everywhere in a short miniskirt.

"I'm finna go inside. If the police come put that weed in your drawers and try to come inside. Don't try to drive that car off. Walk to your mother's house if they don't let you in." She grabbed his dick and walked off smiling.

Alton quickly looked around to see if anyone saw her do that. He saw a crowd of dudes standing around a guy named Lil Gee's red Cadillac. Lil Gee looked right at him and started smiling. Alton smiled back because he knew he had seen Mary J grab his dick. Then he heard a girl's voice call his name. He didn't know any girls out there so he was wondering who it could be. They called it again, and he realized it came from a car 2 spots over. He heard them listening to music with the windows cracked.

"Come here," the girl yelled, but he didn't want to walk to the car not knowing who it was.

"I ain't gon' bite you. Come here boy," the girl said giggling. He still didn't recognize the voice. He walked over to the car, and they rolled the passenger's window down.

There were 2 girls in the front seat smiling at him, but he didn't know either one of them.

"So you talk to her?" The girl in the passenger seat asked.

"Who the fuck are you?" Alton said curiously.

"My lil sister wants you, she's in the back seat."

The back window rolled down, and he couldn't believe his eyes! It was Kesha, the girl who worked at Foot Locker.

"Get in and let me holla at chu," Kesha said as she opened the door. Alton got in the car.

"What's up?" Alton asked, shocked to see her.

"So you gonna be my little boyfriend or what?" Kesha asked while smirking. Both girls in the front were trying to pretend like they weren't listening. Alton looked at her, and she was looking good as fuck. Way better than she did with her work clothes on.

"Nah," he said in a straight tone.

"What chu mean? Oh, I see! That's your bitch that walked over there to you? Old ass Mary J!" Kesha said with a jealous tone. The other girls started laughing. He realized they must have seen Mary J grab his dick.

"Man, that girl like my sister," he quickly tried to clarify.

"Wow! Sisters don't grab on their brothers dick like that!" Kesha quickly shot back. He smiled knowing he was busted.

"So you gon' act like that?" Kesha said poking out her lips. She looked sexy as fuck pretending like she was mad.

"Why I gotta be yo' lil boyfriend? Ain't nothin' lil bout me. If we gon' do that, or be fucking with each other, I gotta be yo' nigga. Ain't no lil' shit, what I look like?" He checked her.

"Ok! Girl, you heard that! Kesha, I like this lil' nigga. I want you to be my brother-in-law, Alton." Kesha sister said.

Kesha was surprised at the level of authority this little boy spoke with. It turned her on.

"Ok then, give me your pager number," Kesha said humbly. He gave it to her and got out of the car.

As she was getting out the car everybody that was sitting around started walking toward the door of the Center that leads into the party. Everybody that was on Lil Gee car got up and moved as a click. That was how the Midway niggas operated. Showtime saw him and told him to come on.

Alton followed the click as they were walking and he looked at everyone in the crew and realized that he was the youngest. As they got to the door, Showtime directed Alton to get in the front of him. The music was blasting coming out of the place. As they got closer to the door, the bouncer stared at Alton, knowing he was underage. Alton thought he wouldn't be able to go in, but Showtime didn't have it.

"He with the West, this the youngest nigga in charge!" Showtime said pushing Alton forward. The dude at the door searched him and let him in.

There was smoke all over the place, and the girls were everywhere! He waited for the rest of the guys from their way to come in, and he followed them to a corner in the back.

A little time had gone by when he noticed Kesha walking towards him. It was a crowd of niggas surrounding him, but she walked boldly over to him and started talking to him in his ear over the music. Then she stood in front of him. All the older guys just looked at him. Alton didn't understand why they were looking at him. He didn't realize that Kesha was claiming him in front of everybody. That is what girls did when they didn't want other girls to talk to a guy they were interested in. At this point she didn't care how old he was, she wanted him. She liked the energy and vibe he gave off. Then suddenly, a fight broke out in front of him, and the music cut off. It looked like it was some niggas from Midway.

Alton kept his eyes on Showtime as he watched him swing on a dude knocking him down. Some of the girls he was with started kicking the man, then Showtime went to another nigga and hit him. Kesha was holding on to Alton's shirt for dear life. Then everybody started running for the door. You could hear screams as the lights came on. All hell was breaking loose! Everybody was running over each other trying to make it out the door.

It was a lot of commotion and chaos going on. After finally making it outside, Alton noticed everybody standing around as they watched a guy named Looney with a gun in his hand pointing it at another dude. You could hear a pin drop, there was complete silence.

"Shoot that fuck nigga," someone yelled in the crowd.

BOOM! A single shot rang out, and everyone started running towards their cars. Boom! Boom! Blat! Blat! Two different guns were heard going off, and Looney fell on his back. Another dude ran off holding his stomach. Shots started ringing out from everywhere. It was straight pandemonium. Alton had broken away from Kesha and ducked off by the nearest car he had seen. Cars were almost getting in crashes attempting to get out of the congested area. Alton heard more gunfire and police sirens in the background.

Alton had finally made it to Mary J's car after running trying his hardest not to get shot. Fumbling with the keys, he finally got the car door open and got in. He felt safe now until he heard more shots. The sounds kicked him into another gear. Even though he had cranked up the car he couldn't move, traffic was jammed. People were slamming their cars into each other trying to get away.

As he was making his way out the tight entrance, someone started beating on the window of the car frantically. This scared the shit out of him, and if it wasn't a car in front of him, he would have sped off.

Alton looked to see who it was and noticed that it was the guy named Looney. Alton had thought he was dead.

"Jit hurry up and open the door them crackers coming," Looney said frantically pulling on the door handle. Alton quickly leaned over and opened the door for him. Looney quickly jumped in the car and let the seat back with the gun still in his hand.

"Just drive and be easy jit," Looney said whispering.

The police had arrived and were walking by, shining their flashlights in all the cars looking for a suspect. One officer shined his light in a car that was in front of them, and the car sped off through the opening. It was Alton's time to go, but he was hesitant because he knew that Looney had a gun on him. Looney told Alton to go, and Alton sped off, bypassing the police. He made a left on 21st St. and was in the clear. Looney started laughing like something was funny as Alton looked over at him wondering was he shot.

"Jit, I shot that pussy nigga in the chest. I hope I killed that fuck nigga." Looney said in a laughing voice.

"I thought he shot you," Alton said amazed at how Looney was taking the whole thing in.

"Hell no, I fell on the ground, so he didn't shoot me, nigga. I'm from the West! That's what we do, bury niggas! Fuck them niggas from across town. We Desperado's out here," Looney said feeling himself talking to the youngster.

"Who was that?" Alton asked.

"That pussy ass nigga named Bumpy from the project's," Looney answered.

Alton had heard of him in school. That's who the kids from the projects always bragged about. He was supposed to be one of the biggest drug dealers from their side.

Alton just rode in silence thinking that if he were in school tomorrow that's all they would be talking about. "Drop me off on Sipes," Looney ordered. Looney then told him to go and park the car because Midway was hot due to all the shooting. Alton drove the car to Mary J house and parked it in the driveway. Once he got to the house he realized Dread was there, so he went inside and put the keys on the table. He heard Mary J and Dread talking, so he walked outside wanting to smoke a blunt but suddenly realized he didn't have a cigar.

While he was standing on the porch, he heard his pager go off. He didn't realize the number, but it had 911 behind it. He went back into the house to use Mary J's phone to call the number back.

"Who is this?" He said with authority in his voice.

"This Kesha. Where you at? And are you alright?" Asking him two questions before he could reply.

"Midway," Alton said quickly.

"I know Midway crazy boy, but where?" Kesha asked agitatedly.

"At my sister's house." Alton fired back.

"At your sister's house or Jenita White's house a.k.a Mary J?" Kesha shot back with a lot of attitude. Alton knew she must have seen the caller ID.

"Yeah, at Mary J's," Alton said knowing she knew where he was.

"Well let me come get you from that hoe house," she said insistently. Alton took the phone from his ear and stared at it.

"You heard me didn't you?" Kesha said.

"Yeah, I heard you. Do you know where it is?" Alton asked.

"Yeah, my sister and them be getting weed from her."

"Bring me some swisher sweet blunts from the store," Alton demanded.

"All right daddy, I'll be there in about 30 minutes," Kesha said hanging up.

Alton was about to stand up and walk out the door when he heard moans coming from Mary J room. "Do the young lad fuck you like this?" Dread asked. Alton heard Mary J moaning, but she wasn't screaming how he made her scream. He smiled and continued to walk out the door. He was glad he heard them fucking because she was starting to trip about him and his girlfriend Ayeshia. Now he had some leverage.

Alton sat on the hood of the car contemplating. He didn't care for Mary J and was starting to outgrow their relationship. He was getting bored, and the only reason he was still fucking with her was that she was his weed connect. Then his mind wandered somewhere else. He started thinking of ways to elevate his hustle. The weed money was doing something, but it wasn't doing enough. He was ready to get into the crack game. He felt he wasn't making enough money.

As he was sitting on the hood of the car deep in his thoughts, a car pulled up. It was the same blue Honda Civic from the party Kesha was in the back seat of. He walked to the car and got in and leaned his seat all the way back. Kesha smiled and handed him the blunts.

"Did I get the right kind of blunts daddy?" Kesha asked in a flirtatious tone.

"Yes," Alton said with a smile on his face.

Fifteen minutes later, Kesha pulled up to some apartments by the Riverfront in downtown Sanford. After parking the car, she got out, and Alton followed her. As they walked inside Kesha's apartment, Kesha said, "I hope I don't get you into too much trouble staying outside all night?"

Alton didn't say anything because he knew he wasn't going home tonight. He knew the wrath his parents would let off once they found out that he was at a party and could have possibly got shot. But he would cross that bridge when he got to it.

"So, Mr. Mosley I see you got a few girls that you fuck with," Kesha said, sitting on a couch beside him with one leg under her clutching a pillow. Alton had no idea that in the few hours they got acquainted Kesha had done her P.S.I work. She found out that he was a Mosley and that he was the baby of three boys. She graduated with his brother Buck and knew his other brother Billy. She also had found out that Alton was the young boy fucking with her little god sister, Ayeshia. She knew he was the one that bought Ayeshia all those nice things that she had.

"What you mean by girls? You said that plural." Alton looked confused.

"Well, I seen you driving Mary J car and she was watching you all night at the party. And I know about Ayeshia too, your little boo. Alton, the player!" Kesha said with a sarcastic twist to it. Alton was just smiling and looking at her. This was a small ass world, he thought. How she found out all that so fast?

"So you're not going to answer?" She said looking at him. She knew he was shy, so she liked teasing him just so she could hear him speak with his raspy voice.

"If you know all this then why you asking me?" Alton fired back, rolling his blunt.

"I just wanted to see if you would lie." Kesha fought back.

"Naw, I fuck with Ayeshia and Mary J is like my sister. That other shit just started with Mary J. We just started fucking." Alton said nervously, instantly feeling the urge to smoke.

"Can I fire this blunt up?" Alton asked holding up the blunt.

"Boy, this my apartment. Go ahead," she answered then explained. "As soon as I graduated I moved out my mom's house."

"How old are you anyway?" Alton asked hitting the blunt.

"Nineteen and I know age don't mean nothing to you since you're fucking old as Mary J," Kesha giggled.

Alton didn't say anything he just watched her ass jiggle as she bent over to pour food in the bowl for her cat. She looked back to see if he was watching.

"Come on little boy, let's go take a shower."

Kesha had a one bedroom apartment with a bathroom connected to the bedroom. A picture was on the dresser with her and some dude in it. Alton followed her to the restroom and watched her take off her clothes. Kesha looked back at Alton and said "What you gon' do, just sit there and watch me? Or you gon' get in?"

Alton took his clothes off as Kesha eyed him. Her eyes began to wander, and she looked between his legs at his dick and immediately got aroused. *Alton was hung like a horse,* she thought. Now she knew why Ayeshia and Mary J was on him.

Alton followed her into the shower, and she immediately started to lather him up. She started off from his chest and then to his back and then worked her way down to his dick. She grabbed at it erratically and began to stroke it. She was in shock by the length and girth of his dick. It was the biggest she ever saw. She started feeling guilty about how young he was, but it didn't matter at this point.

She quickly leaned up against his chest and told him to bathe her. He lathered her up and rubbed her all over her body. When he got between her legs, Kesha moaned out with pleasure. She cut the water off then exited the shower with him following her. She grabbed two towels and handed him one to dry off.

As they walked inside the bedroom, Alton's pager was going off. He was wondering who was paging him this early in the morning. He knew it wasn't Ayeshia because she didn't have a phone. As he was reading the screen, it went off again.

"Whoever paging you, they blowing you up," she said smiling.

"I don't know," Alton said trying to figure out for his self.

"Well, you can use the phone," Kesha said, as she reached over and handed him the cordless phone.

Alton looked at the screen and realized it was Mary J. He thought to himself, *Dread must be gone so now she wants to call me.* Then the pager went off again.

"You better call those people back!" Kesha said smiling even harder, testing him.

"They straight," Alton replied.

Kesha put her Victoria Secret lotion on then laid in the bed naked. She knew she smelled good and knew he wanted her but she wasn't going to give him none tonight. She wanted to see where his head was at, plus before he got with her, he would have to leave Mary J alone. She could tolerate

Ayeshia for now but not Mary J. She was very jealous and wanted him all to herself. Besides, Mary J was grown so she knew she would be controlling and consuming a lot of his time. Kesha wasn't having that, *I would be the only one doing that, she thought to herself.*

Alton laid on his back in the bed and Kesha threw one of her legs across his. She laid on his chest then started to spark a conversation with him. Then she started to question and quiz him. She was asking him all types of questions like, why did he fuck with Mary J and did he want to fuck with her followed by a series of other questions. She told him that he wasn't getting no pussy until she knew he was serious. Kesha realized she liked him a lot. Then his pager went off again.

"Call them back now or I will," Kesha rolled off of him grabbing the phone. She took the pager off the nightstand and looked at the number then realized it was the number he called from earlier, Mary J's house. She dialed the number on the screen.

"Don't call that number!" Alton said reaching for the phone.

"Yeah," Kesha said into the phone.

"Who is this?" Mary J fired back."

"Did you page someone?" Kesha asked rolling her eyes.

"Where's Alton?" Mary J demanded.

"Laying his fine ass up in my bed," Kesha said quickly looking for an argument.

"Who the fuck is this?" Mary J said angrily.

"Don't worry about all that, just go to sleep cause he ain't coming over there tonight," Kesha said laughing into the phone.

Alton tried to grab the phone from her, but she slapped his hand down and stared at him coldly. "Bitch that's my brother, hoe." Mary J shot back.

"Brother my ass! So now you're grabbing your brother's dick huh?" Mary J didn't say anything she was wondering who this could be. She knew she grabbed his dick in the parking lot at the party. But who could have seen that? Then she thought about NiSole's little sister Kesha and how she was all in front of him at the party like they were together.

"Oh this Kesha," Mary J said with a smile in her voice, happy that she figured it out.

"The one and only," Kesha said glad that Mary J figured it out also.

"So he fucking with your little-tired ass," Mary J said trying to offend Kesha.

"Bitch please, he upgraded. You're too old for him, and you know you got too many miles on that pussy hoe." Then Kesha hung up the phone and turned his pager off.

"Man why you did that? Alton asked her.

"Because you're fucking with me now," Kesha said without hesitation.

"Man you don't know what that bitch doing for me. That's who I be getting my weed from." Then at that moment, he realized that he said too much.

"Oh well you gotta find someone else to get it from," Kesha said rolling her neck.

Alton was angry at what Kesha did, but for some reason he liked it. He liked all the attitude and the jealous shit she had going on. He was tired of feeling like Mary J's boy toy. Kesha laid back on his chest and rubbed him all over his body. She made him feel grown. He had never stayed the night with a girl before then he thought about what he would tell his parents. His sister Vickie would cover for him if things went left. With those thoughts, he drifted off to sleep.

He woke up with Kesha kissing on him. "You want some breakfast daddy?" Kesha cooed softly in his ear.

"You got some cereal?" He said.

"Cereal," Kesha asked sarcastically.

She couldn't help but smile and giggle realizing that he was still a little boy in some ways. He started smiling too realizing what she was thinking. "Alright you can fix me some breakfast, do you have an extra toothbrush?" She told him where to get the toothbrush from then started to fix breakfast.

Alton sat in the front room and turned on the television then started watching cartoons as he smoked a blunt. She put his plate of food on her kitchen table.

"So who's the nigga in that picture with you?" Alton asked continuing to eat his food. "That's Corey. I don't talk to him no more."

"Well, why you got his picture up then."

"Well, we just broke up a couple of weeks ago." Alton didn't say anything else, he just continued eating. After they finished eating she told him she had to go to work and asked him where he wanted to go. He told her to take him to Midway. She got dressed in her work uniform then walked towards him and wrapped her arms around his waist.

"So are you gonna be my boyfriend little boy?" She said knowing the little boy thing agitated him. He looked down at her and started thinking about Ayeshia. Ayeshia, all of a sudden, felt too young for him. So he asked Kesha, "What about Ayeshia?" She thought about her little god sister and knew this nigga was too much for her. She would allow him to play with her for a little while longer because she knew once she fucked him Alton would want to be with her.

"You can keep her for now." Kesha leaned in to kiss him, and he kissed her back. He was a really good kisser. But then he pulled away from her.

"What about your boyfriend?" "That ain't my boyfriend, he crazy. He be hitting on me," she said with a fearful look in her eyes. Alton thought about what she said for a second, then he said to himself *fuck that nigga, this my bitch now.*

"Yeah, but you gotta chill with that little boy shit."

"OK, I'll just call you daddy then," she said smiling.

"So I'm daddy?"

"Yes," she answered. Then on that note, they left her apartment and got into her little Honda and headed to Midway. He told her to drop him off at his sister Vickie's house.

As he pulled up, he saw his sister Thelma outside talking to Vickie. He told Kesha to page him when she got off work. She said OK then he got out the car and walked towards the house.

"Boy why you ain't go home last night? They told me you was at that party. You know yo' young ass had no business out there with them niggas. They was shooting out there too! You gonna drive momma and daddy crazy." Thelma said staring at him.

"Man I was just chilling. I was going home, but then I just stayed at my girlfriend house" he said to his sister.

"I told momma and them you stayed at my house and watched Mike for me."

"Alright," Alton said then asked her.

"Did you talk to Trucker? When are you going to go see him?"

"I'm going this weekend once I get me some money," Thelma replied.

"How much money you need, I got some," Alton said.

Thelma just looked at him, thinking about *how much she should ask for.* She had heard he was slanging weed, but she didn't know what he was worth. She figured he was making a little something to buy himself some shoes and stuff. She thought Trucker brought him the chain, so she wasn't going to ask for too much.

"Fifty dollars," she said.

"That's it?" Alton questioned. She misjudged him but quickly recovered with an excuse. " Well that's just for gas, but I gotta buy him something to eat when I get there. Plus he wants me to stay for the weekend and get a room. But I ain't got that type of money." Thelma said, throwing the bait.

Alton calculated in his head really quick. He reached in his pocket and pulled out his money while both of his sisters watched. He counted out two hundred and fifty dollars. "Is this enough?" He questioned. Thelma looked at the money, then back at her little brother, then back at the money. She couldn't believe her little brother had this type of money. Teke, her old boyfriend, told her jit was going to be a problem. Now she believed him. He also was the one telling her he was messing with weed too.

She looked at him again before she took the money and no longer seen a little boy or her little brother. She saw a young nigga that was smarter than the average jit his age. Alton was full of ambition. Thelma wasn't going to ask where he got the money from, she already knew. Alton gave her the money for several reasons. One, he didn't want her to keep looking at him as a kid when she knew what time it was. Two, because it was to help Trucker, his brother-in-law. He had love for Trucker because he showed him the ropes to the game. And three, to keep his parents off his back. His parents listened to Thelma.

"Tell mama and them I'm still at your house," he told Thelma. She caught on quick. "Alright" she shot back quickly, eagerly accepting the contract. She now had another resource she could get money from.

Alton walked into the house and started conversing with Vickie's boyfriend, Gipp. They rolled up some weed and started smoking, and Gipp mentioned that his homeboy.

Trab was coming home from doing a bid, and they were going to link up tomorrow. After the blunt was finished, Gipp told Alton to ride with him across town.

As they walked outside, Alton made sure he had the blunt in his hand. He wanted to make sure Thelma saw it. She just looked and didn't say anything. They got into Vickie's car and pulled off. Alton told Gipp to stop by his girlfriend Ayeshia's house.

They pulled up at the house, and Alton got out the car and went inside. Ayeshia was braiding someone's hair and asked, "Why haven't you returned any of my calls?"

"I've been busy." Alton shot back.

"Too busy to take five minutes to call," Ayeshia said rolling her eyes.

"Yeah," Alton replied nonchalantly.

"Whatever Alton," Ayeshia said sucking her teeth.

Alton walked out the door annoyed from her questioning him. When he got back in the car, Gipp told him he was going back to Midway.

"Where you want me to drop you off at?" Gipp asked.

"Drop me off on Sipes," Alton said, still feeling annoyed by Ayeshia.

"Curtis is going to kill you!" Gipp said laughing.

As soon as they pulled up on Sipes Ave., Gipp parked the car then got out and ran towards a group of niggas that were crowding around an all-white Mustang. They were competing to try and sell the driver some crack cocaine, better known as rocks. Everyone was trying to make the sell, but Lil Gee came out on top.

Lil Gee walked away from the Mustang with the money in his hand and approached Alton smiling.

"I saw you last night too. You think you slick. You fucking Mary J?" He questioned. Alton didn't respond but just looked at him with a grin on his face. Lil Gee nodded and walked off knowing what it was by Alton's reaction. Alton sat on the hood of Vickie's car and watched white person after white person come up and down the strip.

Damn, I'm in the wrong business, he thought. Selling crack was where the real money was at, but he didn't know anything about crack cocaine. He would have to get someone to show him what it was all about. His thoughts were interrupted when Showtime walked up out the blue.

"What up lil nigga? Let me get ten dollars." Alton reached in his pocket and gave it to him.

"Daddy-Low!" Showtime yelled waving at another guy to come over. He pulled the guy to the side and gave him the money for the exchange of a piece of crack. Alton didn't know Showtime had asked for some money to buy crack. Showtime went behind the building to take a hit. A few minutes later he resurfaced bug-eyed and scratching his face. He walked over to Alton and started to bring up the events that happened at the Center.

"You see how I put it on them, niggas, last night lil bruh? Next time you better help! You from Midway so you better represent!" Showtime said glancing at Alton.

"Looney shot that fuck nigga Bumpy last night. Fucked him up pretty bad but he'll live," Showtime continued.

"Yeah, I know. I gave him a ride last night up here," Alton replied.

"I see you 'bout ready to jump off the porch. Ain't no money in that weed shit? You got to get you some hard, and I'll show you what to do with it," Showtime said while giving off the symptoms of being high.

Alton quickly said, "All right" and wondered how Showtime was reading his mind. Alton told Gipp he was gone and started walking to Mary J's house. Once he got there, he knocked on the door.

"Who is it?" Mary J asked.

Alton didn't say nothing. Mary J opened the door and just stared at him.

"I don't know what your pussy ass comin' round here for. Ain't nothing, tell that hoe to look out for you!" Mary J said slamming the door in his face. *Damn, I done fucked my connect up, Alton thought.*

The school was coming up, and Alton was running low on funds. He only had about twelve hundred dollars. What was he going to do? He still needed school clothes, plus he had daily expenses. He had intentions of being straight by the time school restarted. The only money he was making was when he was at Mary J's house because the school was out and he damn sure wasn't standing on no corner. Alton went into deep thought as he headed to Thelma's house.

A black Toyota pulled up on the side of him with tinted windows as he was walking. The passenger window rolled down. It was Teke.

"Curtis's baby boy, get in!" Teke said showing his signature smile. Alton got in the car, and they rolled off.

"Boy, I seen you at the party last night. Be careful out there in these streets," Teke said turning serious. Alton didn't see Teke at the party. He must have been in one of the cars in the parking lot.

"I hear you gettin' money now!" Teke said changing the conversation.

"Shit, I'm trying to. This weed shit to slow and I'm goin' to get me some hard in a minute," Alton said. He called the crack cocaine hard because he remembered that's what Showtime called it.

He tried to throw it out there just to figure Teke out and Teke bit the bait. He looked at his little brother-in-law and seen that Alton was serious. Damn jit out here! It's too late to try and stop him. I got to show him the ropes, thought Teke. "Let me know when you ready," Teke shot at him.

"Alright, but first I gotta handle somethin then I'll let you know," Alton said.

They smoked a few blunts in route to Teke's house. When they finally arrived, Teke backed his car into the yard. As they sat in the car, Alton watched as different cars kept pulling up to the house. They would get out and walk to the car and Teke would serve them. No sooner than he would make a serve another car would pull up.

A white Chevy Caprice pulled up, and two dudes got out. Alton recognized one of the guys immediately from school but didn't know the other one. The one that he recognized was a nigga named Terry, but everyone knew him as Squeaky.

People in school always clowned on him about how dirty he was, but he didn't look dirty anymore. Teke got out the car and told Alton to do the same. The other dude with Terry approached Teke and said, "Nigga you gon' be ready next week to put that hoe down or what?"

"Nigga, is you gon' be ready?" Teke shot back.

"Nigga we ready now!" Terry added looking at Alton. Teke and the other guy went into the backyard to look at the dogs that he had in the pens.

"Damn boy, I haven't seen you in a while. What chu been up to?" Alton asked.

"Man I just been coolin', getting this money," Terry said in a slow voice pulling out a fat knot and a pill bottle full of hard.

"Damn that's what you fucking with? I've been getting money too, but I been fucking with weed." Alton said. Terry just started laughing.

"Man ain't no money in weed you better get you some cane," Terry said. They talked back-and-forth about school hoes and who was getting money. Then the dude that Terry came with walked back up front and told Terry that it was time to go. They got in the car and left.

"You know jit?" Teke asked Alton.

"Yeah, I go to school with him."

"That's Little Dannie's little brother, he getting' money," Teke continued.

Alton didn't say anything, he just knew it was his time to get some real money. Suddenly, his pager went off interrupting his train of thought. It was Kesha. He told Teke to let him use the phone and dialed Kesha's number.

"Hey daddy, I've been thinking about you all day. You ready to get this pussy tonight?" She said waiting for his reply.

"Here you go with dem games again. What's so special 'bout tonight? You could have gave it to me last night."

"Because nigga I ain't wanna give it to you last night. Now, are you coming over or what?" Kesha said in a feisty tone.

"Yeah," Alton said calmly.

"You're not going to get in trouble with yo' people are you?" She said in a joking manner.

"Naw."

"Well I'm going to cook for you, just call me when you're on yo' way," Kesha said before hanging up.

Alton went back outside and chilled for a minute.

"Aye, you feel like taking me to this bitch house?" Alton asked.

"Yea, where she live at?" Teke replied smiling at Alton.

"She lives on the Riverfront in those apartments," Alton replied.

"You ain't gon' fuck nothing."

"Shit I betchu I'ma get dat pussy," Alton shot back, thinking about the conversation between him and Kesha.

"Well let me get you on this drink, let's go to the liquor store," Teke stated.

"I don't drink."

"You do now so come on!" Teke cranked up the music pulling out the yard. UGK blasted from the speakers.

Mama put me out, I was only fourteen, so I started selling crack cocaine and morphine...

Teke bought a bottle of Hennessy and fixed him and Alton a cup. As they rolled around the city Teke dropped real game on him about dealing with the crack game. Alton didn't talk, he just listened. Teke knew he was out here now, so he vowed to stay in the shadows and watch his back. Alton turned the music down as his pager went off. He saw it was Kesha. Damn. It had only been two hours since he talked to her and he had four pages from her. He gave Teke the directions on where to go as they headed to Kesha's house.

"How much I got to spend to get some hard?" Alton slurred. That's what Teke was waiting on. He didn't know how deep his pockets were so he started out low.

"Shit, I'll look out if you spend a hundred dollars. That way you can double up and make two." Alton started laughing feeling the effects of the alcohol.

"Man, I ain't trying to spend just a hunnit dollars. Shit, I spend more than that on weed. I'm trying to get me some real money. Alton slurred again. Teke's mind started racing. *How much did this little nigga have?* He realized he was sleeping on jit. He knew he was fucking Mary J, but he didn't think he had his mind on real money. Then again he hadn't been around jit in a while since his sister started fucking with Trucker.

"Well, what you wanna spend? How much dope you trying to get?" Teke asked a series of questions, but even though Alton was feeling tipsy from the alcohol, he wasn't about to reveal his hand to Teke about what he was doing with Mary J.

"I got fifteen hundred, but I gotta get my school clothes. So I was thinking about spending five hundred on hard and a grand on school clothes." Alton added up the twelve hundred he had with the quarter pound of the weed making it fifteen hundred. Teke couldn't believe what the little nigga said. *How the fuck did this lil nigga manage to get that type of money?* Damn this jit was the truth.

"When you gon' be ready?" "Give me a day or two," Alton told Teke where to turn as they pulled into the apartment complex. Teke immediately recognized the little blue Honda Civic out front. A young dude that he knew from the projects used to come around and brag about how he fucked with a bitch name Kesha and that it was her car. Corey was fucked up about her and Teke knew they always were fighting but he didn't understand how Alton got into the mix. Teke wanted to put his little brother-in-law on the game because he knew that Midway and the projects didn't get along and he refused to have them beefing over a bitch.

He wanted Alton to be on his shit.

"Man you know she fuck with some nigga name Corey. That bitch who drives that car right there." Teke said pointing at the blue Honda Civic. "Watch that nigga cause he crazy about that bitch."

"She say she don't fuck with him no more," Alton said with a confused look, still feeling a little tipsy.

"Man let me tell you something about these street bitches! They gon' always tell the new nigga that. Don't trust no hoe." Teke dropped game on the young nigga talking about his own relationships.

"Get my pager number and call me when you want me to come get you."Teke gave him some dap and watched his lil brother-in-law get out the car and go inside the apartment. Speaking out loud to himself he said, *Curtis Mosley's baby boy.*

Kesha opened the door and let Alton into the apartment. He was dizzy from the alcohol. "Why you didn't answer when you saw me paging you?" Kesha said with her hand on her hip standing in the doorway in front of him.

"I was riding with someone, and I couldn't stop, so I just came straight here." He sat on the couch and laid his head back trying to gather his thoughts.

"What's wrong with you?" Kesha noticed something wrong with him from the way he sat down. He looked drunk.

"Nothing, where the food at?" Alton asked slurring. She went into the kitchen and brought him his plate of food and watched him say his grace. He began to eat while she watched TV.

"You've been drinking?"

"Yeah, I had a cup."

"You brought your school clothes yet?"

"No, I was going to go get them in a couple of days."

"Let me dress you and go with you to pick out your things."

"Alright."

"How much money were you going to spend?"

"Well, I'm going to spend a thousand now and get more later."

"Boy you don't gotta spend no thousand dollars, just get you a week's worth of stuff."

She didn't want him spending a thousand dollars on clothes. *That was just crazy,* thought Kesha.

"Fuck that, that's what I'm spending," slurred Alton.

"Alright, daddy."

He finished eating and felt better. He leaned back and relaxed. "Take your clothes off," Alton demanded. She looked at him with a scowl on her face but complied with Alton's demand. As she stood in front of him, he admired every curve of her body. She had thighs like she ran track.

"Scoot over," Kesha said. She sat down on the couch and put her back on the arm of the couch. Then started playing with her pussy looking directly at him.

"Look at me, daddy." Her pussy was fat and shaved bald. "You like what you see?"

"Yeah," Alton said with a hoarse voice drooling at the mouth.

"Bring me that dick then," Kesha ordered biting her lip sexily. He undressed then set back down stroking his dick.

"Where your condom at?"

"I don't have one."

"Well, you not getting no pussy. I'm not about to get pregnant by a fourteen-year-old." Kesha spoke but then realized her mistake.

"Here you go with that again. Well, I'll go get one. Shit, I thought maybe you had one. Don't you use them with the ole boy, your man?" Alton shot back at her for using his age against him.

"I told you I don't fuck with him no more," Kesha said rolling her eyes. "That's not what I heard, but whatever."

"Well, you heard wrong," Kesha said as she got dressed putting her clothes on looking for her keys. The alcohol had taken effect on Alton. He put his boxers back on and just laid back down.

By the time she got back, he was asleep. She walked over to him and picked his pants up off the floor. He had four hundred dollars in his pockets. She counted it then put it back. She folded his pants and shirt then put them in the dresser drawer that was empty. She had just dropped Corey's things off at his mom's yesterday. She hoped he didn't come over and try to run the boy off. She liked him, fuck Corey! Corey liked to beat on her, and he was stingy with his money. Alton wasn't that way even though she hadn't asked him for nothing. She felt like he would give it to her if she did ask.

She undressed then looked down at him and smiled, *This little nigga had it going on,* she thought. She was going to put it down before someone else did. She was really going to fuck this little nigga. Kesha knew he was getting pussy, but right now she was about to fuck him. She knelt down in front of him and reached her hand into the hole in his boxers and grabbed hold of his dick. He didn't move. Then she took his dick in her mouth and sucked on him until he grew hard. After she got him good and hard, he finally stirred and opened his eyes. He looked down at her and locked eyes with her as she tried to take the whole thing in her mouth. It was like she was trying to suck the life out of him. Her head game was mean! She made a lot of slurping sounds as she sucked his dick.

"Take them boxers off," she ordered while stroking him. Alton slid the boxers off, and Kesha hurriedly straddled him. She placed his hands on her ass and Alton squeezed it as he dropped lower on the couch tilting his dick upward. Kesha leaned forward placing her hands behind his head. She started to ride Alton very hard and fast breathing heavily.

"Slap my ass daddy! Squeeze my ass!" Kesha moaned with ecstasy. Alton slapped her ass then grabbed both ass cheeks apart pulling Kesha down hard and fast, meeting her rhythm.

"Like that?" Alton asked.

"Just like that, daddy. I'm going to cum all over your dick. Make me clean it up after daddy," she said breathing heavily.

"Come on daddy's dick," Alton said scooting low so he could get deeper. Kesha pumped harder and faster holding his head close to her breast.

"Fuck, I'm cumming!!" Alton shouted at Kesha. Alton continued to hold her ass spread apart pumping her from the bottom until he came all in Kesha.

"Now get your ass down there and clean that dick up," Alton said out of breath. Kesha obediently jumped off his dick and sucked it until it was dry. She led him to the bedroom where they fell asleep.

Once morning came, they were back at it again. This time she took him in the shower and held the shower rod and let Alton pound her from the back. He came in her again. They dried off, got out the shower and cuddled until it was time for her to go to work.

"Listen I'ma give you the money when you get off work to get my clothes. Don't be getting me no gay shit." Alton stated jumping back on the topic of his school attire.

"What you're not gonna go with me?"

"Nah I gotta handle some things."

"Anything specific?"

"Nah just make sure I'm straight," Alton said while grabbing the phone to page Teke. He waited a few minutes, but he never called back. Kesha was dressed and ready for work.

"What you gonna do? I gotta go to work. You want me to drop you off somewhere because I know you don't want to stay here."

"Yeah."

As they were walking out the door Teke was pulling up. "Oh I'm straight, that's my ride right there."

"Alright here," she said handing him a key to her house. "And don't lose it, you know how you little boys are," Kesha said smiling.

"I wasn't no little boy last night was I?" Alton said returning the smile.

"You sure wasn't daddy." Then she watched him get in the car and pull off. "You didn't hit it, lil nigga?" Teke said with a smile. "Do a bear wipe his ass and shit in the woods? Curtis's baby boy beat that ass all night and this morning." Alton said then let the seat back. "Drop me off at the park though, so I can get this cash together."

"Alright." Teke dropped him off at the park then Alton walked around the corner to his house. When he walked through the front door of the house and looked to the left, his father was laying in his usual spot on the couch smoking a cigarette watching the door. "What up dad?" Mr. Curtis didn't say anything back he just looked at him and smoked his cigarette. Alton kept walking to his room. He shut the door then went to his stash and got all his money and weed and walked out the side door so his father wouldn't see him leave. He jumped on his bike and headed to Teke's house.

Teke was sitting on the car smoking a blunt when Alton arrived. He passed the blunt to Alton and rolled another one before heading into the house. Teke walked to the table and pointed at a tan, cookie shaped, a piece of crack.

"That's for five hundred right there!" Teke said to Alton.

"Alright," Alton said. He looked at it and was excited to be dealing with crack now. He knew he was about to make more money than he made selling weed. He went inside his pocket and pulled out the five hundred and gave it to Teke.

"Let me show you what you got and cut it up for you. This will be my first and last time showing you. Alton watched as Teke expertly cut the cookie in half with a sharp razor blade. Then cut the half in half. He marked it with the razor then snap it where he marked it.

"Always squeeze the work as hard as you can before you buy it. This is called a straight drop. This what you want, if it ain't hard, it ain't good." Alton nodded his head listening to Teke as he continued to draw lines on the triangle piece of cookie. He separated the little pieces into fives. He had twelve piles of five with two rocks left. "These are twenties," Teke told him pointing at the cut up rocks.

"Alright," Alton said looking at what he bought with his five hundred dollars.

"You got twelve hundred dollars' worth. Watch who you be serving this shit to. There's all types of undercovers out there. Follow Showtime, he's going to show you who's who and what's what. Walk light and keep your eyes open. And I gotta get you some heat." Teke said looking into Alton's eyes. He saw the ambition. He saw the hunger. The eye of the tiger.

Teke scooped up the pieces of crack and put them in the bottle and told him to be careful. "Alright, you can go on Sipes. I got people up there watching your back that's gon' show you the ropes." Alton dapped him up then got on his new bike and rode off happy to be getting ready to sell real drugs.

As he got on Sipes Ave., he noticed a few niggas standing on the corner but didn't recognize them. He continued riding and posted up by a pay phone not knowing what to do. There was a couple of guys up there, but they didn't speak to him. They just kept talking amongst each other. Suddenly, Looney looked at him and said, "Jit you got some of that weed on you?"

"Yeah."

"What you got another dude asked?"

"Jit got that Mary J," Looney said. They put their money together and spent fifty dollars. He sold them the weed and fired up a blunt. No one seemed to notice or care why he was up there. Everybody that wanted weed Looney sent them to Alton. He was selling the weed observing and watching the other guys run and serve the drivers. He took mental notes of the cars. The color and familiar sounds they made. If they were a male or female driver and waited to see the same car twice. After about five hours of hanging on Sipes Ave., he still hadn't sold a piece of crack yet, and he was out of weed. Showtime walked up on him towering over him scratching his face as usual. "Come on let's go on the other end." Showtime took off, and Alton followed. It had been a whole day, and Alton hadn't sold one piece of crack. Showtime said the real money came after 5 o'clock when everyone got off work. After smoking blunt after blunt, five thirty then six o'clock rolled around and just like Showtime said, the money started coming. "Jit there goes one now coming in the white truck," Showtime said pointing. Alton took off running in the direction of the truck. "What's up, what you want?" Alton asked fumbling for the pill bottle. "Let me get a hundred," the bald white man said, clinching the money in his fist. Alton quickly emptied five twenty's in his hand and gave it to him.

The white dude put it in his mouth to taste it. After being satisfied, he gave Alton the hundred dollar bill.

Alton walked back to where Showtime was standing smiling like a kid who just lost his virginity. "Always block the window jit in case someone else run up behind you," Showtime said, showing Alton how to box out just like basketball. "And always lean in the car in case one wants to snatch from you. Therefore you can get the keys out and keep from getting ran over," Showtime continued.

"Shit, I do the rest. There goes another one in the little red car. Hurry up them niggas coming!" Showtime said to Alton, noticing three other boys were running to the car, but Alton was too quick for them. When he got a hold of the serve, he made sixty dollars.

One after another, they came back to back and before 10 o'clock Alton had made five hundred dollars. "Alright jit, you done pretty well for today. Now go home before it's too late and give me one of those rocks." Alton dumped a rock in his hand and gave it to Showtime then got his bike and went home. After Alton made it home, his pager was constantly going off. Kesha kept paging him. He returned her call and told her how to get to his mom house.

Alton had already snuck out the window and was waiting on the corner when Kesha pulled up. He got in the car and laid the seat back as they drove to her apartment. Kesha had already fixed dinner and had his plate ready. After eating dinner, Kesha wanted to watch a movie, but Alton's mind was on the money. He wanted more and loved the rush it gave him.

Alton asked Kesha to use the car. "Where are you going?" She asked, snapping her neck to look at him. "Please don't ask me a thousand questions all the time," Alton said staring at her.

"Well let me suck your dick daddy before you go. Mama always said keep a man's stomach full and his dick empty," Kesha said as she walked towards him dropping to her knees. Kesha sucked his dick like the vet she was, and once Alton came in her mouth, she continued to suck it, draining him. Then she slapped the dick on her tongue making Alton snatch his dick away. He pulled up his pants and got the car keys and headed back to Midway.

After he parked the car on Sipes Ave. and Jimmy Hamp, he sat on the hood of the car. Showtime came from behind the rooming house that sat next to Jimmy Hamp scratching his face. "Where your work at?" Showtime asked knowing the answers already. "Right here in my pocket."

"Don't ever keep no drugs in your pocket this time of night. The police don't play fair at this hour. Always put it down and cover it up where you the only person to know where it's at. Always keep your eyes on you' sac. This is called the Graveyard Shift. Everything is dead, and when you out here by yourself, you get to do what you want to do. This is when you get to cut heads." Showtime said scratching at the skin on his face.

Two white women pulled up in a white Explorer. "Hey, you guys got anything?" The one on the passenger side said. "Yeah," Showtime said. "Well she wants a hundred, and I want a hundred. So that's two hundred," the passenger said smiling. Alton hurriedly ran to his stash spot. Showtime followed behind him.

"Give me five twenty's, one hundred dollars' worth," Showtime said knowing he could cut the heads. "But she said she wanted two hundred Alton stated questioning Showtime's method. "I know," Showtime said smiling.

Showtime got the five pieces and broke them into half making ten and walked to the car. He dropped the ten pieces in the passenger's hand, and she gave him two hundred dollars. Showtime walked back to Alton and gave him a hundred and eighty dollars and kept twenty for himself. Then he told Alton to give him a twenty out of the bottle. Alton did as he was told. "Did you see what I just did?"

"Yeah," Alton said. Showtime continued, "See late night when you're the only one out you can do what you want to do and give them what you want to give them. Most of the time with no competition out, you can give them anything, and they'll go for it. Let's go to the store," Showtime said.

As they headed to the store on Highway 46, Showtime dropped game on Alton, and he listened. Showtime saw the hunger in his eyes and knew that Alton was going to change the game.

Showtime backed the car up in the cut at the rooming house then cut the lights out. He pulled out a crack pipe which was made out of an antenna off the hood of a car stuffed with a brillo pad. He placed a twenty piece of crack inside of it then placed fire to the end of it. Alton watched as Showtime melted the piece of crack then placed the pipe with the rubber on it between his lips and started to run the fire up-and-down the pipe made of the antenna. As the pipe started to sizzle, Alton watched Showtime eyes grow wide from the light of the fire in the dark car. He looked right at Alton. After inhaling the smoke and holding it in, he blew it out slowly and said, "I usually rob little muthafucker's like you straight off the porch to let you know who Show is. But I like you, and I see the tiger in your eyes. What would you do if I took everything you got right now and run you off my block?" Showtime eyes stared into Alton's double the normal size from the blast he just took from the crack. Alton looked him directly in the eyes without blinking. "I'll kill you," Alton said starring coldly at Showtime only seeing the whites in his eyes.

A shiver went through Showtime's body. Looking into the youngster's eyes, Showtime liked what he saw. Fearless. He knew the kid was dead serious and one day would take over the city. So he decided then and there to play fair with this one and protect him from the cruel underworld. "That's right jit never let no one take nothing from you. It's a sign of weakness, and it will start a domino effect. If you go and let a nigga take what you hustle for, you might as well not hustle. Your new name is Terrible T cause you gonna be terrible I can see it." Alton and Showtime stayed up through the night. He called it an 'all night flight.'

Before the sun broke, Showtime had sold all Alton's drugs. Alton dropped him off in a drug hole in Midway called the Duck Hole. Showtime had made himself a good hundred dollars' worth of crack, so he didn't need anymore. Once he got out of the car, he asked Alton for twenty dollars, but Alton gave him fifty. Showtime had made Alton five hundred extra from cutting heads. Alton respected his mind, game, and wisdom. Showtime accepted the money and looked deep into his eyes. He knew this jit was going to go far. He just wanted to be alive to witness it. Jit respected the game, and he made a promise to himself to never cross him. He dapped Alton up, got out the car and watched him drive off.

Walking in the crack house ready to extort and rob, Showtime thought to himself, No more Mr. Nice Guy.

Alton went back to Kesha's apartment, using the key she gave him to let himself in. He counted up all his cash. He had twenty-six hundred total including the money he already had. He felt good knowing there was more to come. He showered then crawled into bed next to Kesha. She stirred at the movement and woke up. "I see you came home daddy," she said in a sleepy voice.

"Oh, this is home now?" "Might as well be, you haven't been staying at your mom's house." He thought about what she said and realized he wasn't interacting with his family. He was growing up in the streets. He wondered if his parents knew. Alton quickly brushed the thoughts from his mind. "Daddy put that dick in me," Kesha said rubbing her butt up against Alton. He did as he was told and fucked her from the side until the sun came up.

Alton heard laughter coming from the living room and women talking. He put on his boxers then sat up in the bed and listened. It was two other female voices he heard besides Kesha. He decided to put his clothes on and tell Kesha he needed to go to Midway but didn't see his clothes nowhere in sight. He went to the door and called Kesha. "Yes, daddy?" She answered. He heard snickering in the background through the door. "Where is my clothes?"

"I'm washing them, but I bought you something yesterday." She came into the room and handed him a bag with new clothes in it and started kissing and hugging all over him. Alton couldn't help but blush knowing her friends were right on the other side of the door. "I made you breakfast, but you wouldn't get up. It's two o'clock, you've been knocked out."

"Who is that out there?"

"My sister and sister-in-law."

"I need to use the car today. You gon' let me use it?" Alton asked.

"You just gonna take my little car, of course, you can use it. You're my daddy aren't you?" Kesha said with a sexy smile.

"Oh, I'm daddy now?" Kesha play slapped him and went back into the living room. Alton got dressed and rolled him a blunt then walked into the living room. "There goes my baby brother-in-law," Kesha loud mouth sister said. Alton instantly started blushing remembering the first night he met her. "What's up, sis?"

"You got this hoe sprung. All she can talk about is Alton this and Alton that. You ain't little now, huh bruh?" She said with a huge smile waiting for his reply. "Your sister still seem to think so." Kesha looked at him rolling her eyes, knowing he was falling into her sister game. *Let me change the subject,* she thought.

"Bae, you still want me to get your clothes?" She asked, bringing his food to him out of the microwave. "Yeah."

"You gonna give me some money too?" Alton was startled that she asked him that in front of people but he quickly replied *yea, how much?* Both girls were looking from her to him. "Two hundred will be good." The other two girls watched him closely for his reply as he went into his pocket and pulled out his cash. He quickly counted thirteen hundred and handed it to her. "Three hundred for you and a thousand for my clothes,"Alton stated, knowing the girls were watching the transaction.

They both had lust in their eyes when they looked at him. He knew they envied Kesha. "Bitch I told you that little nigga was the one," Kesha's sister said. "Shut up hoe!" Kesha said smiling. Alton just smirked watching the two. "Thank you, daddy!" Kesha sat on his lap kissing and touching on him, playing in his hair. He was shy, so he told her to stop. She acted like she was mad. "I can touch you, you my man." He smiled then fired up his blunt and headed for the door. "See you later." Everybody seemed sad to see him go. After walking out the door, he stood there and listened for a second. He heard them laughing and giggling about how Kesha was going to go to jail for statutory rape. He heard Kesha talking about how big his dick was, and he just smiled and walked to the car.

Showtime was at Teke's house giving him play by play of what happened last night. Teke was smiling from ear to ear for several reasons. One, jit was going to come up fast. So if Alton came up fast, that meant more money for him. Two, he pushed a plate off on him for five which only went for four hundred. The quality wasn't that good, but he moved it all which meant he was ready to re-up again.

As Teke replayed what Showtime told him in his head. He knew Alton was going to take over Sipes Ave. real quick and with that came beef. Alton would have to prove himself and Teke was ready to help him prepare himself.

Teke hit the blunt and told Showtime to watch out for Alton when he was on the block. Also to keep him away from the crowd and continue to show him the ropes. He told Showtime it won't be long before Mr. Curtis found out and Showtime replied, "Well Mr. Curtis is going to have to watch out for that one. He's already terrible.

Alton reed up with Teke and bought double the amount from the last time. He spent all day with Showtime again, but this time there were other guys out. Showtime made Alton park and walk on the other end of Sipes and Midway Ave. He showed him how to put the bottle down. "Hold at least five twenty pieces in your hand so if you had to throw it, you won't lose your whole bomb of crack. Showtime said, "I'd rather throw five twenty pieces freely and risk losing it in the dirt and the police finding that than your whole bomb."

The money started coming on Showtime and Alton's end of Sipes, and so did the crowd. After the crowd came, the shit talking began. The older guys had bottles of Hennessy out, shooting dice and snorting cocaine. The younger ones smoked blunts back to back.

Alton seen the kid named Corkey hanging around the crowd. He and Alton were the youngest two on the scene. No one seemed to notice Alton had a pill bottle full of cocaine. "Bet twenty more!" Dirty said shaking the dice in his hand looking at the guy they called C-Murder.

"Bet." C-Murder said, dropping a twenty dollar bill on the ground. Four, five, six showed up on the three dice. Dirty collected his money and continued to talk shit. Alton saw one of the white dudes coming up the back road and quickly sprinted to the red car and dived in, boxing out like Showtime told him to do. "Let me get a hundred," The white guy said holding his money away from Alton. Alton quickly dropped the five pieces of crack in the white dudes hand which he quickly transferred to his mouth. Then gave the hundred dollar bill to Alton.

Alton walked back around the dice game, and everybody seemed to be smiling, so he smiled too. "Curtis is going to kill your ass boy," The guy name Big J said. Alton kept walking to the side of the rooming house to get more crack out of the bottle. After running after cars for three to four hours,

Alton's pager started buzzing. He walked to the pay phone and called Kesha back.

"Hello," Kesha said in a bubbly voice.

"What's up?" Alton replied back in his raspy voice.

"Daddy I got your things."

"You do?"

"Yes, you gonna look so good," Kesha said with a smile bursting through the phone.

"Well I'll be there later," Alton said. Kesha pouted then told him bye. The crowd began to get thick on Sipes Ave.

All around Jimmy Hamp girls were parked around corners in cars smoking and drinking.

"What's up little bad ass nigga?" Dirty said.

"Just chilling," Alton responded.

Dirty stayed on 21st St. across from Thelma house. He was originally from New Jersey but went back-and-forth up until 5 years ago when Florida became his permanent home. He hung out with Trab off Dixie Ave. and was one of the original 21st St. boys.

Dirty passed him the blunt and told him to be careful. He also let Alton know that he was going to stay out late night to the sun came up.

Showtime and the kid Corkey set in the corner and watched them talking.

Lil Timmy walked up. "I see you out here," he said.

"Yeah, trying to get me some money." Alton shot back.

"Ain't nothing wrong with that?" Alton passed him the blunt realizing Lil Timmy had on a sweater in the summertime, and he never pulled his right hand out the pocket in the middle.

"You got you some fire?" Timmy asked.

"Naw not yet, I need some," Alton said.

Alton was raised around guns and was used to them. His daddy made sure of this. While Billy was the hunter and better marksman, they both were familiar with guns. They'd been shooting guns since they were five years old.

"If I run across another one I'll grab it for you. You're just gonna have to shoot me back my money." Timmy said. "Bet," Alton replied.

Showtime and Corkey walked up. "Let's go to the store, and Lil Timmy leave that damn pistol," Showtime said.

Showtime started the car with Alton in the front, Corkey and Timmy sat in the back. After leaving the store from buying snacks, Showtime dropped Lil Timmy and Corkey off, and Alton had Showtime take him to Kesha apartment. He told Showtime to come get him at ten PM sharp.

Alton stuck his key in the keyhole and walked inside. Kesha was sitting on the couch with her shirt on from the night before. "Hey, daddy!" She said excitedly. "What's up, baby?" Alton said strolling over to the couch. He sat down and proceeded to take his money out his pocket. Kesha sat behind him and took off his shirt. Alton counted up his money and laid back on Kesha while she rubbed him down. "So you wanna see your things?"

"Yeah," he replied. She got up, got the bags and brought them out the room to Alton. She begins to pull outfits from everywhere. Nike, Jordan, Polo, Tommy Hilfiger, Nautica, and Perry Ellis. Then she pulled out matching hats and colognes. Alton never would've thought the money could go that far. He was happy with what he saw because he knew he would be the freshest in school. Then he thought about it, he must get his money back and then some. "What you think?" Kesha said smiling holding her hand out gesturing to the clothes. "I love all this shit, thank you!"

"Bae, you gonna look so good in school."

"I know right!"

"And don't try anything slick, I got my cousins watching you!" Alton immediately started smiling. He wondered who her cousins were.

"You hear me boy?" Kesha continued.

"Yeah man!" Alton said. He couldn't hold back his grin.

"Now let me show you what those little girls can't do. Put your dick in my mouth!" Kesha said, kneeling in front of him.

That night Kesha sucked and fucked Alton to sleep. Alton stirred when he heard a knock at the front door. Kesha immediately got scared because she figured it was Corey. She laid in a daze. Earlier, she had stopped by his mother's house to pick up her things, and he was there! When she went into the house, he followed her and made her have sex with him. It was bittersweet, although she hated him, she loved the sex. She tried to act mad in the end but fell victim to pleasure. After he was done fucking her, he said he was coming home, but she told him she had changed the locks and not to come by because she wasn't going to be there.

Kesha laid in the bed hoping it would go away. Knock, knock, knock. The sound came from the door again. Alton's eyes popped open, and he began to climb out of bed. Kesha grabbed him. "Let them go." He looked at the fear in her face and paid it no mind. He went to the door and opened it. It was Showtime.

"Jit you ready?" Showtime said staring down at Alton. "Yeah, give me a second." Alton went back to the room and put on his things. Kesha just watched him and asked, "Who was that?"

"My big homie," Alton answered. "Oh," is all Kesha said, barely over a whisper.

"I'm going back on the block, and I'll bring your car early in the morning, then you can drop me off," Alton said without waiting for an answer, then walked out the door and left with Showtime.

Lil Timmy was still in the car, but Corkey wasn't. They parked back up on Sipes Ave. Earlier that day the police ran everyone off. Showtime, Lil Timmy, and Alton were the only ones on the corner that night. The money started coming, and Showtime taught Alton the split game with Lil Timmy. He told him the same went for Corkey.

"Therefore you can make shit a little easier. Sometime he'll beat you out and vice versa. Then Showtime continued, "Y'all the only ones out so you might as well take advantage of it and just take y'all time. I'm going to see y'all in the morning," he said, walking down Sipes Ave. to the rooming house ran by Slapp.

After dropping little Timmy off, Alton parked the car at the park at the Center and walked around the corner on

Dixie Ave. to his parent's house. Billy was in the yard with his shirt off washing his car, a 1972 Ford Galaxy, cream color with peanut butter insides. It was really clean with some deep dish 30's and lows.

"What's up little brother? See you ain't been home a few nights!" Billy said, smiling showing his dimples. Billy was sixteen and wasn't into drugs or being a wide open thug. He was slow to the streets. He liked cars, hunting, fishing, girls, and sex. Billy was humble. If Alton was a natural genius, then Billy was a taught one. Alike, but different. Billy was the jokester of the family and his daddy's favorite son. He was named after two people very important and special to his daddy that were both later killed to the violence in the streets of Midway.

Billy always had money and more than one hustle. Curtis groomed Billy from the womb. He was the definition of a hustler. He had so many ways to get money. He'll beat you at basketball for money, kill more rabbits than you, catch more fish than you, and then sell them to the old people. He washed cars with Spanish Joe, sold wild game that he caught and killed, and ironed clothes at Mary's house. Curtis drilled all his children to keep money in their pocket. But especially Billy. Billy was his favorite boy.

Billy was dark and handsome, but you could tell him, and Alton were brothers. His hair was good but not as good as Alton's. He had a broad chest because he lifted weights to work on his physique. His face was rounder, while Alton's was sharp.

"You know Trab out? Got out last night, he got a little size on him," Billy said, continuing to wash his car. "Oh yeah, that's what time it is," Alton said.

"Mom and them heard you selling drugs in the streets. Daddy said he gon' kill you if and when he catches you, and he gon' call the police and put you in jail!" Billy said cleaning his rims.

"Man, a nigga, ain't with this poor shit, a nigga ain't got no money. People be laughing at a nigga and shit, but daddy makes sure you're straight though." Alton said, leaning up against another car. Billy remained silent and kept washing his car. Alton walked into the house to speak to momma, but Buck had taken her to the store or something. No one was home but his dad and Mark. Mark came outside with him, and they talked shit and shot some basketball on the basketball court his father had put on the side of the house.

"Grandma went school shopping for us with Buck, and she said we better be here when she got back," Billy was laughing because he passed the stage where mama bought him clothes and picked them out. She was just getting the basics. They were only at the Dollar General and Goodwill stages. You only got one pair of shoes all year. If you wanted more, you better hustle. Well, hustling they did! Curtis made sure everybody hustled or had one, its survivor tactics. But Billy had branched out in the real world applying his hustle. Alton chose to hustle by getting in the game.

"Man I'm in the front seat in the morning," Alton said smiling at his brother. Billy just kept washing his car like he didn't hear him. He probably would have to have a scuffle or two about the front seat. He liked to see his little brother fight. The boy was good with his hands. Then out of nowhere, Trab walked around the corner with Renzo.

Renzo was Mary's son, Alton's sister's boy. He was three years younger than Alton. "What's up lil bruh?" Trab said drinking a soda from the candy lady.

"Chilling, damn you got big!" Alton said looking at Trab. Then he quickly snatched the pickled egg from Renzo and ate one and Renzo chased him around the car before Alton gave him a dollar to go get more.

"Yeah man them crackers finally let a nigga go," Trab said. Alton dug into his pocket and pulled out a knot of money in front of Trab and Billy and gave Trab one hundred and fifty dollars. Then pulled his pill bottle out and gave him ten big dimes, which was really twenties. "Damn lil bruh bet that up," Trab said dapping him up. "Ain't no pressure dog, a nigga out here?"

"I see," Trab said, shoving the dope and money in his pocket. Since no one was home, Alton, Billy, Mark, and Trab smoked a blunt in their front yard while Renzo watched on. Alton called Kesha and told her to catch a ride to Midway and bring him his clothes. He was around his boy Trab who was like his other brother and was staying in for tonight. Also, school started in the morning.

While standing in front and on the side of Billy's car on Dixie Ave, a brown Mazda came around the corner and hit the brakes right in front of them. It was Ayeshia with three more girls in the car. She looked at Alton then swerved around them and hit the gas. *What was that all about,* thought the other boys. Alton kind of knew what it was about because he hadn't called or returned any of Ayeshia's phone calls and he knew she was mad at him. The streets had grabbed him by the throat, and Ayeshia was a little girl to him. But little did he know Ayeshia had been making moves of her own. She was sliding with the boy, Terry from Bookertown, and had moved on too. She was driving one of Terry's customer cars.

Kesha and her sister pulled up seconds later, and Alton walked over to the car while she got out and handed them the bags. Alton called his nephew Renzo over to help.

Alton was leaning in the car when Renzo came out of the house from taking the last bag in. He turned around and noticed Ayeshia was in the Mazda. He tried to signal Alton, but he had already peeped game. Alton looked from Ayeshia to Kesha knowing they both knew. And felt worst knowing they both knew each other. "Alton, that's your girlfriend?" Ayeshia asked and stated.

"Something like that," Alton said, barely over a whisper.

"Cool," Ayeshia said and hit the gas.

"Damn she finally know now!" Kesha said.

"Yeah."

"You know she like my little sister, I done broke her lil heart," Kesha said, really not giving a fuck.

"You want me to stay with her then?" Alton asked, trying to see where her head was,

"Shit, she'll get over it. You're my daddy." Kesha said hugging him and made him blush.

After talking with Kesha a little, he told her he'll be over after school tomorrow, and she went to the park to get her car and went home.

"Damn little bruh I see you got them hoes. What the hell you got going on Dixie?" Trab said, shaking his head.

"Nigga this the dog pound," Alton said.

"Everything going on back here," Mark said. Billy just shook his head smiling showing his dimples.

Time had gone by, and they decided it was time to go in. After hearing mama fuss all night about school clothes and supplies, they finally went in their room and called it a night.

Both, Billy and Alton woke up early and excited about school. They got dressed and showing off their shoes and clothes to each other. When they got to school, they flirted with all the girls. Billy flaunted with his car and keys and Alton stunted with his clothes and shoes. They were the shit. When school was out, they drove back home to Midway.

Alton grabbed his pill bottle and went up to 21st St. towards Uptown. He noticed it was different walking on Sipes Ave. in the daytime than at night. Everyone hung at the store or the Bodega on Highway 46 and Midway Ave in the daytime. It was owned by an oriental couple who allowed the drug dealers and wine heads to linger and loiter around. Highway 46 was a major highway that led to Interstate 95. So a lot of the truckers stopped and bought large quantities of drugs. There was an auction across the street so a lot of people will stop at the little store and would buy drugs or get robbed. Alton came to this store all the time with his father to buy his pops cigarettes.

A lot of people would come from the Whiskie Rivers, a bar and liquor store owned by whites on the corner of Highway 46 and Beardoll Ave. That's when the money started coming! One white person after another. Not including all the black people that constantly came. "Boy, there go, Mr. Curtis!" Someone yelled out. Alton quickly ducked behind a car and waited until his father made a right on Midway Ave then rode out of sight.

Everybody was bugging because they all went through it, trying to duck their relatives when they first came out. Daddy-Low was the one who warned Alton that Mr. Curtis was in route. He was a really big kid. 6"4, 240 - 250 lbs, with twelve gold teeth. A real ugly motherfucker who came from a family of fighters and hustlers. He had an *'I don't give a fuck attitude.'* Rumor had it, Daddy-Low controlled the block for the younger cats. He was the one knocking them out on the block and had the biggest piece of cut up crack. He also kept a pistol on him.

"Curtis is gonna kill you!" Lil Gee said snickering back-and-forth with Daddy-Low. Alton just smiled and leaned against a gate. The same cars that came on Sipes Ave. in the night time started coming on Midway Ave. off of Highway 46. Guys were running right in the middle of the highway. All up and down Highway 46 flagging cars right in front of the fire station. The police would park at the fire station and watch the activity as if they didn't care. They were tired of blitzing the block. Everybody either ran, walked off or walked into the store and hid their drugs. And the orientals would come outside and argue with the police for running their money away.

"Jit, how old you is?" Daddy-Low asked.

"Fourteen," Alton said.

"Shit you know how old he is, you was fucking the man, damn sister!" Lil Gee said then walked away smiling. "Man don't listen to that stupid ass nigga, let me see that work you got," Daddy-Low said smiling.

Alton showed him the pill bottle and the texture inside it. "Shit, you ain't gone never come up buying that. Who you bought that from, Fonso?"

Daddy-Low asked.

Fonso was known for having bad quality drugs in the hood but would give you a lot. Alton didn't really know the different qualities of dope until Daddy-Low pulled his sac out of his pocket.

"This is what you call straight drop," he said while taking one of his twenties out and showing it to Alton. He told him to squeeze it as hard as he could and throw it in the air. When Alton hesitated, he threw another piece in the air out of the bottle.

"That's what you want jit, you don't want nothing to break. And you want it as hard as possible. Yeah, you'll get more of that bullshit but we talking quality here." Daddy-Low explained.

Lil Gee just sat on the corner studying Alton, counting his pockets and wondering what he was worth. He figured he would holla at Meat and start trying to serve the jit some weight while Alton didn't know nothing.

"Thinking of how to rob jit blind huh?" Banjo said to Lil Gee. They were partners directly up under Meat. Meat had beat the murder charge and came home.

"Shit, if I can beat you and Daddy-Low to the punch," snickered Lil Gee.

"Nah I got that from Teke," said Alton.

"Man Teke don't sell no hard like that! Next time you're ready to get some let me show you who to holla at." Daddy-Low said.

"That's what's up," Alton said. "It's gonna be smaller, but the customers are going to come straight to you,"Daddy-Low said, looking at a crackhead coming his way.

"Daddy-Low let me get a fifty." The black thin looking woman said as Daddy-Low served her 3 and a 1/2 of the pieces out of his sac. She was smiling as she took it and walked away.

There was someone who backed in the cut in a blue Porsche, watching while all the activity flows back and forth. He was fat and had a lot of gold chains around his neck with solid gold bangles and Cuban bracelets on his wrist. Every time he rode through the block in one of his Porsche's, everyone would say, "There goes Boot!"

Alton sold all the drugs that evening and walked home back towards Dixie Ave. Sean was just leaving with his mom and Alton overheard his sister, Gracy yelling at Sean for smoking weed. She continued yelling about sending Sean to West Palm Beach to live with his dad.

Night came, and once everyone was sleep, Alton stole his daddy's keys. He pushed the car out the yard down the street and cranked it up to head to Sipes Ave. He parked the car and hustled to 4AM and then put the car back how he found it. It gave him an hour to sleep before it was time to go to school.

After the second week of school, Alton was tired of it already. He made up his mind that school was not for him. The block demanded his attention.

He got his bike and rode to the New Store. Big Peewee was gambling with another OG named Stack.

"Bet a hundred and hundred more!" Stack yelled before the dice flew out of Big Peewee's hand.

"I call that!" The dice rolled out of Big Peewee's hand, and three deuces popped up.

"Trips," Big Peewee whispered, shocked that he had won as he collected his winnings.

Alton was riding down the highway, flagging cars out of nowhere when he spotted his father. Alton quickly turned his bike down Midway Ave, and his father was right on his trail in another car with tinted windows. Alton was nervous because he still had the pill bottle in his pocket full of crack. Big Chief's bumper was literally 6 feet away from the back of Alton's bicycle wheel. Every time Alton looked back to see where his dad was, his dad gave him direct eye contact, pointing at him telling him to go home because he was caught.

Billy was sitting outside in his car on the phone when the scene occurred in front of him.

"What the fuck?" Billy said, instantly smiling. Alton just looked at his brother like *It's about to go down!*

"Stay right there fish mouth motherfucka!" Big Chief said.

Alton got off the bike and moved towards his father.

"Thought I wasn't gon' catch you, boy, I know everything son! A young dog is for running and an old one for trailing. Learn the difference. I'ma old dog! Empty your pockets!" Curtis knew he had drugs on him because he had got into another car and watched as Alton served crack cocaine all day at the New Store behind tinted windows.

Alton's mind raced, wondering how he was going to pull this off. He emptied his pockets slowly into Big Chief's right hand. His money, his change, some gum, dental floss and a few numbers he wrote down. He never brought out the pill bottle.

Curtis watched everything slow as Alton gave him everything. He still didn't see the brown medicine bottle with the white top.

"Is that it?"

"Yes, Sir," Alton said, trembling.

Mr. Curtis wasn't fooled. He seen the imprint in his pocket and Billy did too. He was hoping his little brother didn't have anything else on him, but his body language said he had more. Big Chief grabbed Alton and pulled him towards him with his left hand and lifted him off his feet. Suddenly, the old gray head man no longer existed, only the street legend everyone talked about.

Big Chief went in Alton's pocket with his right hand and pulled out the pill bottle and a bag of weed. Curtis placed both items along with everything else that he took from Alton down on the car.

Curtis cocked back his right hand openly, expecting the boy to bitch up and run or try to protect his face. But instead, Alton poked out his chest and looked at his father square in his eyes, fearless!

Mr. Curtis saw a lot of things at that moment before he brought his right open palm down over Alton's left eye, cheek and jaw. He expected him to fall and go limp, but he forgot he was holding him up with his left hand. The boy turned up, and when they locked eyes again, Curtis saw himself in the boy and respected his mind.

In the American culture, this was a 14-year-old boy. But in his Indian culture, this was a 14-year-old man. From that moment, Curtis respected him, but he did what he had to do. He kicked him out to the wolves to see if he could survive.

They stared at each other for a few seconds with Alton's hands balled into a fist, thinking he could take the old man. Billy immediately stepped up on the side of his father, ready to take the battle for his dad but Big Chief was 10 steps ahead as usual. Curtis had his pistol, a .38 special with the hammer cocked back, pointing at Alton's chest.

"That's right motherfucka! Swing so I can kill you," meaning every word. Before Curtis let anyone disrespect him, he would kill them. He was big on respect.

Alton sensed defeat. It was two against one and one aimed. His shoulders slouched down, and his head dropped as he turned into the fourteen-year-old he truly was. Curtis wanted to hug his son, but he knew what he must do, and he made the right decision. He knew he had to back his son's decision, but he wouldn't allow it in his house.

"Getcho' shit and get off my property since you wanna be grown. Everything I bought, leave it!" Mr. Curtis said as he placed his gun back in his pocket and walked into the house.

Everyone breathed a sigh of relief, happy for Alton. Billy and Alton stared each other down for the show of loyalty. Billy was loyal to his father, but brothers were always supposed to be there for his brother. That day their relationship changed.

Alton belonged to the streets, and they had him. He got on his bike and rode out the yard, towards 21st St.. Billy pulled up on the side of him with his things.

"Where you want me to take your stuff?" Billy said, never looking at him.

"Vickie's," Alton said, refusing to look at his brother as well.

Alton pulled up on a drug dealer they called Slapp. He owned the rooming houses on Sipes and 21st St. Money flowed all day and night. Nothing but crackheads, pimping, and prostitution.

"What's up jit? What the lick read?" Slapp said, sensing something was wrong with the youngster.

"Man, I need a room," Alton said.

"How much money you got?" Slapp replied.

"How much I need?" asked Alton.

Slapp realized it was true that he was on the street slanging drugs. He decided to let Alton hang around and make some money.

"You slanging? 'Cus if you is that's gon' be extra. I got hourly, daily, and weekly rates." Slapp told Alton.

"What about monthly?" Alton asked.

Slapp was a little startled. "Jit, I usually charge $200 for the whole week, but you can shoot me $500 for the whole month. You got that?" Slapp asked, watching Alton's eyes to see what he knew and how far along in the game he was.

"I got that and how much you want for that car you advertising right there?" Slapp looked from the car and back to Alton. What the hell he had been missing, he thought. He wanted $700 for the car, but he'd take $500 from the kid.

And he knew he didn't have the full grand. He could sense Mr. Curtis kicked him out because he had been there.

"Five hundred for you," Slapp said.

"Okay. I'ma come holla at you when I'm ready." Alton said.

"Okay, one more thing!" Slapp said trying to find ways to make more money.

"What?" Alton asked.

"If you serving down here, you cop threw me and only me!"

"Alright!" Slapp walked off to the fat dude in the Porsche everybody called Boot. He had the window down twirling a toothpick.

Alton roamed the streets of Midway all night until 3 in the morning. He went on Dixie, knocked on his window. Mark opened up immediately, and Alton climbed in.

"Whats up, Unc?" Mark said with sadness in his eyes.

"Coolin', just came to get something," Alton said, pulling both carpets up grabbing an envelope with the money in it. Then he went inside some old boots that his brother, Leroy got killed in and grabbed another cookie of crack he had. Altogether he had thirty-five hundred dollars, and his dad took at least seven hundred. He pulled off a hundred and gave it to Mark.

"Thank you, Unc!"

"No pressure!" Alton replied.

"Where you going?" Mark questioned as if he wanted to tag along.

"I'll be around trust me! Hit my pager if you need anything!"

"I will."

"I'm gone," Alton said and climbed back out the window. Alton shut the window and walked around the front yard and got in the car and fell asleep.

He woke up at the sound of the rooster crowing in the backyard. He rode his bike up 21st St. and cut through a path on his way to Uptown and ran into a jit named Dunney. Occasionally, Alton would hit him and his little brother upside the head and then give them twenty dollars a piece. They were his third cousins, and he liked them.

After standing on Sipes and Midway Ave with the kids until the sun came up, they were off to school. He walked to the New Store and stood on the corner waiting for the store to open. He was the first person out.

After serving someone, he leaned against a fence and put the crack back into his bottle. He heard someone say, "The early bird gets the worm!" Alton looked back and saw it was Showtime.

"Damn what's up? Where you been?" Alton asked.

"A little here and a little there," Showtime replied.

The truth was he was coming from a seven-day binge. He had pulled a nice lick and people were looking for him, so he had to stay out of dodge.

"Let's get something to eat, look like you need it," Alton stated as they walked in the oriental store. They ordered breakfast, and Showtime kicked a little game to one of the workers. After the order was finished, they grabbed the food and left.

"I heard you got kicked out the house," Showtime said out of the blue.

"Yea, but ain't no pressure. I'm straight," Alton shot back.

"You seen Teke?" Showtime said changing the conversation.

"Naw I ain't fucking with him no way, that's that bullshit!" Alton said looking at Showtime to confirm.

Showtime caught on quick and knew it was better to keep it real with the youngster on the come up than to keep lying to him. "Yea it is, you can get a better quality and deal somewhere else," Showtime said.

"Where?" Alton said looking directly at Showtime.

Showtime thought of a scheme in his mind of how he could introduce Alton to all the other niggas selling hard, and they'd give him a cut, but then that plan slowly vanished because of his loyalty to Alton. He was really fucking with this young nigga. "What about that nigga they call Boot?"

"Boot! Hell yea," Alton smiled because he knew that having Boot as a connect was a must. Just as they were about to get up and head to Main St., Showtime yelled, "Boot!" This time he was driving a Land Rover and not the Porsche he usually rode in.

Alton and Showtime walked over to the parking lot where Boot was, "You go stand against the wall while I go talk to him!" Showtime ordered.

"What's up, Show?" Boot said as Showtime was approaching the car.

"You see that lil' nigga over there?" Showtime said while looking back at Alton. "That's my little brother, Curtis Mosley's son. He ready, but he needs that glass. That straight drop! I don't know what he got to spend but he trying to fuck wit chu'. Break me off nigga!" Showtime said grinning.

Boot looked at him then back to Alton. Then back to Showtime, "Look, man, I ain't responsible for what he do with it. He get caught, he on his own!"

"Man, jit a soldier!" Showtime replied.

"Shit he better be, and a warrior too when Mr. Curtis get through with him!" They both laughed as Boot hopped out the truck and went into the store.

He bought an orange juice, and two Swisher Sweet blunts, came out of the store and stood right next to Alton. Little did Alton know, this was the king of Midway and most of Sanford.

For a few minutes, neither said nothing. Boot drunk his orange juice and reached in his briefs and pulled out the loudest smelling weed that Alton ever smelled.

"That's you boy!" Boot said tossing Alton an ounce of weed. And then handing him the two blunts he bought in the store.

"Shit. Bet that up!" Alton stated.

"You tryin to see me?" Boot asked.

"Yea," Alton stated, looking towards the road, never showing eye contact.

"A little bit of money or a lot?"

"A little bit," Alton replied.

Boot wasn't really concerned about how much money he had because he had been watching Alton for a few months. He knew he was about to jump in the streets and now was that time.

"Get in the truck boy!" Boot said. Alton got in the truck and bent a few corners with Boot.

"How much do you want to spend?" Boot asked Alton. He thought Alton was going to say one hundred or two, but the kid surprised him.

"I got fifteen hundred," Alton said while looking straight ahead. Boot had to hide the joy on his face and straighten the truck up at the same time.

"Alright, I can work with that," he said.

"Bet!" Alton replied.

"Listen, I don't give deals. I want every dollar of mines, but I like you jit. You are special!" Boot paused then continued, "The whole circle goes for four hunnit, and you are a hunnit short, but I'ma give it to you anyways so you can get four of 'em! Where you gotta get the money from?" Boot said curiously.

"I got it on me," Alton said. Boot looked shocked again.

"Listen, never keep that much money on you."

"I don't usually, but my daddy kicked me out, so I got that on me," Alton stated looking ahead.

"Where are you staying now?" Boot asked trying to hide the fact that he was concerned.

"I'ma be at my sister's on Washington St. until I rent this room from Slapp at the rooming house," Alton said.

Boot smiled to himself. This lil nigga was making all the right connections. He was going to come up in no time. Slapp was one of his loyal customers who bought a quarter key weekly of crack.

"But he told me I must buy from him if I plan on serving anything while I'm down there," Alton continued.

Boot understood the game, but Slapp worked for him, so he wasn't having any of that. Boot continued driving and pulled up to one of his dope holes in the back of Midway. He went in and grabbed a shoe box and got back in the truck and then pulled off.

Alton gave the money to Boot in exchange for the four circles of hard. They drove off and went to Vickie's house. When they pulled up, Boot told Alton to go in the house and put the drugs up and come back to talk to him. Alton did what he was told.

Alton got back in the truck and listened to Boot kick game. When they pulled up to the rooming house, Slapp was standing around while people moved about. When Slapp saw the Land Rover, he recognized it was Boot and started to approach the truck. Once he saw someone was in the front passenger side, he walked to the back and got in.

"From my understanding, you was going to rent this youngster a room?" Boot asked. Slapp hesitated to give his answer because he was trying to figure out how Alton got in the truck with Boot. He then finally replied, "Yea."

"Alright, rent him the room but don't worry about who he copping from! He can come direct. Look out for him Slapp!" Boot looked at him directly in his eyes through the mirror.

"I got em'!" Slapp replied.

"Good."

"When was you going to want the money for the room?" Alton asked Slapp, looking back at him.

"Shit, when you make it!"

"I already got it," Alton stated as Boot chuckled to himself.

"Give it to me then." Alton reached in his pocket and gave Slapp a wad of cash. Slapp quickly flipped through the money and said "A grand!"

"Yea."

"How you wanna do this?" Slapp asked Alton.

"You said five for the car and five for the month," Alton said as Slapp nodded his head. "Well, I want the car, and the rest is for the month," Alton continued.

Slapp thought to himself quickly, trying to figure out how he was going to utilize Alton in his spot. Nothing came to mind at that moment, but Slapp knew he was going to make a pretty penny off of him somehow.

"You gotta get your own lock for the room, and if something in your room come up missing, I'm not responsible!" Slapp got out the car and walked towards the rooming house.

Boot backed out and took Alton back to Vickie's house. "Fuck with me jit!" Boot said as Alton got out the car and walked towards the house.

When he finally got into the house, Vickie was cooking her daughter something to eat.

"What's up lil brother, fire that smoke up. I know you got it!" Vickie said, throwing him a black box she usually rolled her weed up in. After he finished rolling the weed, he played with his niece for a little then asked Vickie to bring him the box he had brought to her earlier that day.

When she brought him back the package, Alton opened it up and examined the four cookies he had got from Freddie Sole aka Boot. They were beige to brown and almost about a half an inch thick. He laid one down on the glass, and it sounded as if the glass had hit the glass.

Alton grabbed the phone and called Kesha. When he got no answer, he decided to page her to see if she'd hit him back. He then directed his attention back to the cookie sitting on the table. Alton started to cut the dope the same way Teke had taught him then placed it in a separate bottle.

Then he paged Ayeshia, and she called back immediately. "Who is this?" she said.

"Alton!"

"What chu want?" Ayeshia said with an attitude.

"I was just calling to check up on you," Alton said smirking.

"Well I'm fine, don't check up on me! You need to be worried about yo' old lady, Kesha!" Ayeshia said smiling into the phone.

"You know I didn't know that was like your big sister?"

"Well, its okay now!"

"I'm coming over there," Alton stated waiting on a response.

"No, you're not! I got company," Ayeshia smiled knowing that what she said would get under his skin. No one was with her now, but she knew Terry was coming later.

"I'm on my way!" Alton said and hung up not giving her a chance to respond.

Ayeshia freshened up because she knew Alton wasn't playing when he said he was on his way. Although she couldn't stand him, she loved and cared for him.

Alton hid the three cookies and the pill bottle he had in the attic. He then got on his bike and headed to the rooming house. On his way, he stole a tag off a car that was parked on the side of the road.

When he got to the rooming house, he saw Slapp standing around. When he spotted Alton, he walked into the rooming house and brought out the title to the car and the keys to a brown, 1982 Buick Century. Alton screwed on the stolen tag and drove to the nearest gas station. After he pumped the gas, he headed to Ayeshia's house in Georgetown.

He parked the car around the corner and walked to Ayeshia's house. When he knocked on the door, Ayeshia opened the door playing, "What?" she asked with an attitude. Alton pushed past her and went inside.

Alton walked around the house to make sure she didn't have company like she said she did. When they finally got settled into her room, they both questioned each other about what was going on since Alton started avoiding her. They started play fighting then one thing led to another they started fucking. Alton was on top of her pounding her pussy. As Alton felt himself cumming, a horn started beeping.

"Get up, that's my momma!" Ayeshia said pushing Alton up. He hurriedly pulled his pants up and told Ayeshia to page him and just like that he was gone. Ayeshia thought to herself, good because she had known it was Terry and she didn't want to get caught.

Alton ran out the back door which came out to the back door of the Elks bar. He walked to his car and got in. Something told him to ride by Ayeshia's house to make sure she was good. When he did, he saw Terry from Bookertown holding the door open for Ayeshia to get in the back seat of a car.

Now Alton knew who she was fucking with, but it wasn't no pressure. He had already moved on. He stopped by the Auto Part store and bought some tint then decided to swing by Kesha's apartment. Alton hadn't seen her since he started school and wanted to make sure she was good.

He pulled up in the parking lot and walked to the door. When he stuck his key in, it didn't work. He tried a different key, and that one didn't work. As he was walking from the door, it swung open.

"Who you looking for?" a dude coming from Kesha's apartment asked.

"Whoever stay here!" Alton shot back with an attitude.

Hold on jit!" The guy said, stepping back inside smiling. After a few seconds passed, the door swung back open, and Kesha walked out with a swollen eye.

"Damn, what happened to your face?" Alton said looking at Corey, as he just smiled back with a tank top on.

"Don't worry about my face Alton. That's my boyfriend, Corey right there. We are back together and could you please not come over here no more!" Kesha told Alton while looking at the ground.

Alton looked from her to the nigga, and even though she said what she said, she didn't mean it.

"Cool!" Alton said as he turned around and started walking towards his car.

"You just gon' let the lil fuck nigga slide?" someone said. Alton heard a different voice and turned around.

"Fuck nigga, you make me leave!" Alton spoke with authority and had a look of murder in his eyes. He saw fear in Kesha's face when he responded. Out of the blue more dudes started to come out of her house.

"You ain't said nothing!" One of the dudes said as he started walking toward Alton. He didn't recognize any of them, but one and his name was Anton. Alton knew him from school.

"He's just a lil boy!" Kesha said catching herself looking at Alton as he walked towards the one who was more aggressive.

"Taz, leave that boy alone!" Kesha yelled out.

Now it made sense to Alton because the same dude, Taz, is who they talked about in school. He was supposed to be the *pressure,* but Alton didn't see none of that. He wasn't big, but he had a crazy look in his eyes even when he was smiling.

A car whipped into the apartments and a guy with an afro jumped out, "What's going on?" the guy said.

Damn Perky. This ain't got shit to do with you!" Taz said.

"Jit get in the car. You are outnumbered!" Perky said.

Perky was Kesha's brother. He was from Georgetown up and coming in the game. For some reason, Alton listened to Perky and got in the car, pulled off and headed to Midway.

He thought to himself, *Damn, I just seen Ayeisha with Terry and now this bitch back with Corey. Hoes ain't shit!*

Alton pulled his car in Vickie's yard and backed in. He smoked him a blunt and watched the traffic from Mary J's house come and go. He knew he was done with school and was now in the streets. He gave his self to the block and decided then and there it was time to come up in the game.

Alton hopped on his bike and went uptown. When he got on Sipes Ave., he saw Little Timmy on the corner by himself.

"What's up bruh?" Alton said, pulling up on him.

"Chillin', I got that for you!" Little Timmy said looking into his eyes.

"Perfect timing!" Alton was glad Little Timmy had the gun for him. He realized no one was going to protect him in the streets but him.

"How much?"

"One fifty," Little Timmy quickly responded.

"Soon as I make a play I'll give it to you."

They sat on the end of Sipes Ave., and two other kids joined them. One named E.J and the other one name was Robert. A few minutes later, a dude named Caskey pulled up on his bicycle. All the younger kids were on this side of Sipes Ave., and the older dudes were on the other end.

After standing up for a couple hours and giving Little Timmy his money, Alton was out of product and needed to bring out the dope he had bought from Boot. Showtime walked upright as Alton made the decision to go get his stash from the house.

"How everything went with Boot?" Showtime asked.

"Shit, I bought four cookies from him!"

Showtime couldn't believe his ears. He knew the kid was on his way and was glad he was a part of it.

"Give me a hunnit dollars!" Showtime said scratching his face as he continued, "I'll pay you back on the first!" Alton reached in his pocket and gave Showtime the money.

As they were walking into Jimmy Hamp, someone shouted: "There go Show right there!" As they turned around, they saw a heavyset man holding a pool stick angrily.

Walking towards them, he yelled, "Fuck nigga, I finally got your pussy ass! You want to steal from me!" The man raised the stick to hit Showtime in the head.

Showtime weaved the stick in the nick of time, but the wild man charged him. Showtime was known in Midway for having hands despite him being a crackhead. The man never gave Showtime time to get himself together. He kept striking at Showtime and connected every time.

He fell on top of Showtime and sat on his chest as he pounded his fist like a silverback gorilla.

"The police coming!" Someone yelled, pulling the man off of Showtime.

Alton went and stood over Showtime. He was out of it but slowly coming back to his consciousness.

"Alton, watch round two! Motherfucker wouldn't let me put that jab on him. Give me a second!" Showtime said as blood ran from his mouth.

Before he could straighten up, two police officers walked on the scene with their flashlights.

Smokey and Andrews were their names. Andrews was a white guy with a crew cut and Smokey was a black guy who was considered an Uncle Tom type of nigga. They were two police officers assigned to Midway and were trying to make a name for themselves.

"James Campbell, there you are!" Andrews said. "You have an outstanding warrant!" Smokey added as they lifted Showtime up and placed him in the police cruiser.

Damn, that was crazy, Alton thought. Showtime was someone Alton had become accustomed to, and now that he was gone he was out here by himself, but Alton knew the show must go on! At that moment, Alton realized that he had become too dependent on Showtime to make things happen for him. He told himself from now on he would have to manage the block on his own. Even though he was young, Alton set big goals for himself. He was determined to make sure that every block he touched, he'd take over it.

Alton waited until the police car pulled off and went and got in his car. He went to Vickie's house to grab the dope that he had copped from Boot. Alton put the dope in a new pill bottle and made sure he grabbed his gun. He walked to the corner of Sipes and King Rd. with a made up mind that from that moment this was his block!

CHAPTER 4

MARRIED TO THE STREETS

Alton hung on the corner of Sipes and Midway Ave with 5 young kids around his age. This had become his new crew. None of them had been on the block more than a year, and we're all trying to make names for themselves. All of them had the same mindset to get money but were different in many ways. There was Little Timmy who was the one who had been off the porch the longest. After he shot his dad in the head, the streets were literally his home. Then there was EJ. He was short and stocky built and was more the comedian type. He didn't smoke weed or anything, but he kept us laughing. His dad was a single father because his mother had passed away. He was similar to Alton's dad in the sense that he was very strict.

James was another youngster on the block. He was a fat boy who was known in the neighborhood for being a fighter.

His dad was a man named Do Do who had a well-respected name as a hard worker because he fixed everyone in the neighborhood's lawn mower.

Then there was Corkey, who was some kin to Alton. Alton's father had a daughter outside of his marriage, and her name was Phebe. She was Corkey's aunt and Alton's sister. Corkey was the youngest out of the kids on the block.

Also, there was Robert from 20th St., who had just got out of the program. His daddy was a boss and was considered the hood's weed man, but he also hustled on the side selling guns. He was responsible for supplying the neighborhood with the heat. Robert was spoiled because he was his father's only son.

All these kids had something in common. They were all the youngest making moves in Midway. All the old heads talked about them and would wager on who was going to make the cut, who would boss up and who would be shit eaters. Alton was the freshest on the block but took the forefront as the leader of the pack.

It was a normal day for Alton and Corkey as they walked to Jimmy Hamp. It was a familiar scenery to both of them. You had the usual OG's posted up, drinking, smoking, and trying to holla at the younger girls who occasionally passed them.

Out of nowhere, there was a female's voice that caught Corkey's attention.

"What the fuck you doing up here? You ain't grown. Bring yo' ass here! I know you out here slanging that shit!"

It was Corkey's mom, Ms. Sharran. They lived right behind Jimmy Hamp on the next street. She had already had suspicions of him and was determined to get her son back on the right track. She continued to rant and rave about how she was not having a drug dealer for a son. Alton felt bad for Corkey because he knew that he was embarrassed. For one, she was loud as fuck and two, she had the nerve to have on a house robe. Ms. Sharran continued to march behind Corky yelling and cursing as they headed towards their house. Everyone was humored by the scene.

"You've got to fight for your right to be a thug! Huh, Lil Alton? If somebody can break Mr. Curtis you a bad motherfucka. You better show yo lil dog how it goes," said Stack in a raspy cocaine voice.

Alton just started smiling, thinking to himself that all the real bosses knew who he was. He knew he had their respect. He turned his attention to a car pulling up at the other end of the road. He darted up to the car and sold the man some dope.

Sipes and King Ave was where the guys that were a little older than him hung. C-Murder, Big Jay, Daddy-Low, Lil Gee, Bango, Benzo, Barbarian, Kenny King and a few others. They had a little more experience when it came to getting money, but there was always some sort of fighting going on where they hung. There was no love on their end.

Night after night Alton stayed out and hugged the block. Time was causing him to become more advanced. He developed a system by dividing his day into shifts. First one at the New Store in the early morning hours, Sipes Ave in the evening, and the rooming house until the sun came up. He slept whenever and wherever he was. Alton had become addicted to the streets. He would sleep in his car, the rooming house, Vickie's house, pretty much whenever his body would shut down from exhaustion. Other hustlers would often ask him when he slept and he would always respond, "I don't sleep, I take cat naps!"

"Get up jit!" Alton was waking up by someone yelling through the crack of the door at his rooming house. Grabbing his 9mm, Alton yelled in a sleepy, grouchy voice, "What?" The dream killer spoke, "This Clev." Clev was Slapp's yard man. He brought Alton all the late night money. Alton was pissed that his cat nap was being disturbed. "What the fuck you want?"

"Open the door," Clev pleaded.

Alton swung open the door aggravated. "What's up?" Immediately he noticed a look of fear and shock on Clev's face.

"Hollywood's dead!" Alton's facial expression quickly went from irritated to a look of concern.

"What do you mean she's dead? I've been serving her all night."

Hollywood was a woman who was known as the hood's superstar smoker. She was a female version of Showtime in the eyes of Alton. She was also one of the ones who had shown Alton the ropes. Hollywood had just ripped someone off for seven grand and was spending it all night with Alton. She had been on a binge for 14 days straight and was literally walking dead.

"I think she O.D'd," Clev said emphatically. Alton walked out of his room down the hall to Hollywood's room, and there was another crackhead standing at the door crying. Alton walked into the room and walked over to Hollywood, careful not to touch anything. She laid there with her crack pipe in her hand. He could tell she was dead by the color of her skin.

"Y'all get out of here! Clev you stay and call Slapp." Alton ordered. After the other smokers cleared the hallway, Alton told Clev to check Hollywood's pocket. Clev reached in her pockets knowing there was nothing in there because they had already taken everything before Alton had arrived.

Slapp came walking through the door with a look of shock on his face. "What happened? He asked Alton. All Alton could do was tell him what had been told to him. Slapp told Alton he could go and he would get everything in the room situated. After straightening up a little, he called the police and coroner to come to pick up Hollywood's body.

Alton stood on the corner of Sipes and 21st St. talking to Dirty and watching the scene. Dirty was envious of Alton because Slapp allowed Alton to hustle down there but wouldn't allow him. After listening to Dirty complain for an hour, Alton walked on Washington where his car was parked and sat in the driver's seat. He pulled out his money and begin to do inventory. After counting every bill, he wound up with $4800. Almost five grand, he thought. Not bad considering that he had only been on the streets for two months.

Alton started missing his family, but the money he was making was too good to him. He had adopted a new family. The streets were his Daddy and Momma. The guys in the street had become his brothers. The people of Uptown had become his family too. Alton was on the rise, and everyone that was someone from Midway could see it too. Vickie came outside on the phone and Alton asked her to use it for a second. He paged Boot and put the code in the pager to let him know he was ready and that he was on Washington St.

Vickie walked up to Alton with her hand out, and he gave her $50. She walked away happy, headed towards Mary J next door to get some weed.

Alton went back to the car to sit down and count his money again. As he got to four thousand, there was a sudden knock on the window. He looked up, and it was Mary J. He let the window down, and she looked at him staring, so he just stared back at her. "What's up?" Alton said breaking the ice. She didn't reply right away because her eyes were glued to the stacks resting on his laps.

"You tell me," she replied in a flirtatious voice. For a minute they just stared at each other thinking about what they used to have.

"You got something in there to smoke?" Mary J asked.

"You wanna buy some weed to smoke, or you wanna smoke one with me out of your personal stash," Alton replied.

"You know I got the shit I'm slanging, but I keep me some personal shit," she shot back definitely.

"I'm waiting on somebody so let's smoke out here." Mary J looked around wondering when Dread was coming. Shit fuck this, she thought. I'm not going to fuck this up.

"Open the door!"

Alton opened the passenger door, and she got in. Mary J reached in her bra and pulled out the loudest smelling weed that he ever smelled.

"Damn that shit loud!" Alton expressed.

"This shit is called Crippy. It ain't hit the streets yet and its really expensive. People don't want to pay for it because its $20 a gram." Mary J rolled the blunt, and as she was about to fire it up, a blue Porsche pulled up in front of Alton's car. It was Freddie Sole better known as Boot.

"Hold on for a second." Alton got out the car with her and got on the passenger's side of the Porsche.

"What's up jit?" Boot said.

"Shit, I'm trying to get six of 'em."

"Alright, its gon' be about an hour, I got to slide somewhere and handle something. That's cool?" The whole time Boot was looking in Alton's car trying to figure out who he had in it.

"Make it an hour and a half," Alton said smiling looking from his car to Boot.

"Bet jit!" Alton got out of the car and headed back to his car with Mary J. She had already fired up the blunt and passed it to him as soon as he sat down.

"Oh, so you fucking with Freddie Sole?"

"Yea," Alton said hitting the blunt once more.

"Damn you trying to come up, huh?"

"Tryin' to?" Alton said coughing up his lungs and breaking out in a sweat. Mary J instantly started laughing. "Easy with that jit."

"Man let me see that!" She handed him her personal stash of crippy. It was so sticky that you could smash it against his windshield.

"Who car is this you got me in?" Mary J asked as she opened the door and held her leg out, brushing the cigar guts off her lap from the joint she just had rolled. Then she shut the door back.

"Who behind the wheel?" He looked at her and noticed she had the same look in her eyes from when she seduced him the first time.

The streets had aged him and women were not his weakness. Within the last 3 months, he had countless women, and Mary J had become just a number.

They passed the blunt back and forth in silence listening to the radio. "You want to come inside?" she asked.

"For what?" Alton replied looking straight forward. She just started smiling, immediately turned on by his demeanor.

"You know what for."

"No I don't, tell me," Alton said pretending to be clueless.

"Why are you doing this to me?"

"What am I doing?"

"Let me see your hand." Mary J insisted. He looked at her, then gave her his right hand. She grabbed it and opened her legs to make her skirt raise up. While looking at him the whole time, she placed his hands between her legs. She had no panties on, and her pussy was shaved bald.

"You see how wet you make me?" she said seductively, placing his fingers inside her.

"Where Dread at?" Alton asked, not really caring for the answer but just wanted to see what she would say.

"He ain't coming back for a while. Come put it on me, I know you miss it." Alton wanted to refuse, but the lust in him wouldn't allow it. She pushed his fingers in deeper.

"You can have that crippy," she said smirking.

"What you trying to buy me now?"

"Naw nigga, but just remember that was my dick first!"

"You ain't never lied!" Alton said smirking.

Alton followed Mary J in her house with his pistol on him. He wasn't going for Dread slick talking ass today.

Mary J had fucked him hard and fast, and he did the same to her. The lust was there, and they both had missed it. After they were finished, she rubbed Alton down, and he fell asleep.

A horn blew, and Mary J immediately got relieved. Freddie Sole was outside." Bae, wake up!" She said, waking Alton up. She was happy she had heard the beeping because Dread probably was on his way. How would she be able to explain Alton being here this time?

Alton hopped up, put on his clothes and walked out of the door. Freddie rolled down the window and handed him a box.

"I thought your sister lived next door," Freddie said, laughing as he punched the gas. Alton just smiled knowing Boot had figured out he was fucking Mary J.

"You gon' smoke one with me before you slide?" Mary J asked.

"Yea," Alton said with his door opened, examining the work Boot had just dropped off. Mary J was breaking her neck to see how much quantity of drugs Freddie had given him. Even though she was slanging weed, she was no stranger to the crack game. She was deep in these streets.

Once she saw the six cookies of hard, she knew that he was on his way and Boot had him under his wing. At this point, her ultimate motive was to get back good with Alton.

"Damn you doing it like that? You don' came up on a bitch," Mary J said, staring at him to see his response.

"Not yet." Bingo, Mary J thought to herself. For him to be so young, Alton was still humble and hungry. She knew he was about to take over the game.

They smoked the blunt. She asked if she'd page him would he call her back. He said, sure and went back to Vickie's house.

Alton gave his sister five cookies and told her to put them up. He cut one of the cookies down and counted seven hundred instead of the grand he normally counted. He made sure his pieces of dope were bigger than the competition.

He left Vickie's and headed towards Sipes Ave. He parked in a field behind Sipes and walked to the block. Corkey walked up on him and said his uncle Showtime had just got out and his mom picked him up. Alton couldn't help but smile thinking about the last time they were together when Showtime got knocked out talking about around 2.

"Where he at?" Alton asked.

"He around Teke's way," Corkey said.

"Come on, let's go!" They got in Alton's car and went on Byrd and Gamby St. to Teke's house. Showtime was in the front yard with Teke when they pulled up. When they got out of the car, they heard Showtime say, "Let me hold somethin', you too badass rascals, before I take everything!" Playing with two of his favorites. They both went in their pockets and blessed him. He never looked at the money, he just shoved it into his pocket while drinking a beer.

"I'm hearing good things about you too. I hear y'all don' took over my block. Well, I guess my fee goes up. Ain't nobody finna be puttin' down on my streets and ain't gon' pay a fee," Showtime said jokingly.

"I'm rested up now, boy! I'm ready for round 2. That's my second stop after I go to see my wife, Darlin. Show you how The Show gets down. I'm gon' beat the fuck outta him. Make him go get his pistol. Shit, he can't even kill me with that! Teke you better tell 'em. I got nine lives like a cat!" Showtime said.

"Shit, you been shot seven times already! You only got two more left then," Teke added while laughing.

"Ain't nobody gon' get two in a row. I'm hard to kill I tell you!" Showtime shot back.

"Go 'round there fucking with Darlin, she just might do it to you!" Teke replied laughing.

"If she do it, I won't be mad," Showtime said as he took another sip of his beer.

They laughed some more and talked shit to one another for a minute. Then got back in the car and left.

Night had fallen, and Alton and Little Timmy were standing on the corner of Jitway and Sipes Ave, smoking a blunt. Robert, Corkey, and James were rolling dice and talking shit amongst each other when suddenly they heard gunshots.

"Boom! Boom! The shots rang off again. Then it was dead silent. All five of the youngsters started walking towards the sound of the gunfire.

"She killed him, she killed him!" The rock head Kathy said, running towards them.

"Killed who?" Alton grabbed her in her hysterical trance.

"Showtime, my baby Showtime!" Kathy said crying.

"Who killed him?" Corkey said.

"Darlin, crazy ass!" As Kathy said Darlin's name, the rain started to pour suddenly.

Timmy, James, and Robert had no connection to Showtime, so they begin to walk back towards Sipes Ave as Alton and Corkey walked towards Darlin's house.

Once they arrived, they saw police cruisers turning off the highway and coming up to the crime scene. With no hesitation, Corkey and Alton walked up to the yard towards the porch where Showtime's body laid lifeless. Half of his body was on the porch, the other half laid slumped on the stairs.

When they got closer, it all became a reality to both, Corkey and Alton. The two bullet wounds to his chest were as big as a fist, and his eyes were wide open. The sight alone was horrifying to Alton and Corkey's young eyes. The rain started to pour even harder into Showtimes face.

They didn't hear the door crack open because they both were still in shock. Darlin stood in the doorway behind them smoking a cigarette with a bathrobe on. She was still holding the double barrel shotgun in her hand that killed Showtime.

"Yall motherfuckers get off my porch!" Darlin said coldly.

"Why'd you kill my uncle?" Corkey said.

"You want to join him?" Darlin said pointing the shotgun slyly at Corkey and Alton with a deadly stare in her eyes.

You could see the lights from the cruiser pull up. As Alton and Corkey walked off, Officer Andrews walked towards the crime scene.

"Are you Darlin Campbell?" He asked with his hand on the butt of his pistol.

"Yes, I am. The one and only!" Darlin stated with sarcasm in her voice. She took a puff of her cigarette and blew the smoke into Officer Andrews's face.

"Could you give me the weapon you used to kill your husband with?"

"No problem," Darlin said as she opened the door and reached behind to pull out the shotgun.

The officer opened a bag that he was holding and secured the weapon. He then asked her to follow him to the car to begin questioning.

By this time the neighbors and family of Showtime and Darlin begin to show up along with more police officers. The crowd started to grow as one of the officers started to put up the yellow tape.

Alton and Corkey heard people whispering how this wasn't the first time that Darlin had killed her husband. And how her mother and her grandmother had killed their husbands as well. They had no tolerance when it came to men putting their hands on them. Darlin's whole family were men killers and were known to get away with it.

Darlin silently smoked her cigarettes and answered all the questions the homicide detectives asked her. Yes, she was married. Yes, she had a restraining order and injunction. And yes, he beat her regularly. So, from the look of it and the way the crowd was murmuring, she wasn't going to jail.

Alton and Corkey just shook their head. *Damn! Showtime just got out of the county and was dead hours later. Life was crazy,* thought Alton. He had lost two people in the last month that he had real love for. First Hollywood and now Showtime.

Corkey and Alton walked back to the block and told the others what they had seen. Everybody knew it was a matter of time before Showtime got killed. He lived by the gun, and as the saying goes, *you live by the sword, you die by it.*

Alton, Robert, Corkey and Lil Timmy rode around in Alton's Buick Century catching plays and panty chasing as they like to call it. Everybody was making money.

Alton thought about getting his teeth done. He wanted gold all over them. Robert already had his top teeth done, and Alton thought it was dope.

The streets had changed them. It was 2 am, and they were still hanging on the block. A white dude named Rambo had been coming through the Ave robbing the drug dealers. Sometimes he would spend four or five hundred and then sometimes he would stick a.45 handgun to their head and tell them to jump out the truck while it was moving.

He came from off Sipes Ave this time. Everybody watched as he cruised through, passing the first set of guys on King Rd. Then he made a right on Jitway Ave and stopped right in front of Alton. Alton heard the guys yelling, but his mind went blank as he stared at the dude, who they called Rambo.

"Let me get two hundred jit?" Rambo said.

Alton's finger was curled under the trigger in his sweater he was wearing. Something about the way Rambo looked at him, Alton didn't like.

Alton pulled the 9mm out of his pocket, pointed it at Rambo and squeezed the trigger!

"Boom! Boom! Boom!"

Rambo leaned down in the nick of time. If he hadn't, he would have got hit in the head by the kid with the sweater on. God dammit, you little bad motherfucker, Rambo thought as he leaned down and smashed on the gas.

Rambo's head was down, still driving as he heard more shots.

"Boom! Boom! Boom! Boom! Boom! Boom! Boom!"

"Motherfucker trying to kill me!" Rambo said turning on Broadway and driving fast towards Highway 46.

Alton was chasing the truck continuously letting rounds loose at Rambo's truck. He was trying to kill the cracker.

"Damn jit, you crazy as fuck!" Daddy-Low said.

"That's good for that pussy ass cracka," C-Murder added.

"Young desperado," Big Peewee said.

Alton was still in a trance from what he had just done. His gun was empty. He felt good, and he loved the sound of gunfire.

"Got damn that nigger done fucking shot me," Rambo said to himself, punching his truck up Highway 46. He knew it was clean, through and through. He had been in the Army and was shot on numerous occasions, so he knew it was clean. He made it to his spot and grabbed some wild turkey alcohol and a clean needle and attempted to sew it up. Then he took some painkillers, laughing the entire time.

"That little fucking nigger tried to kill me," he said laughing hysterically, "I'ma never forget him. I'm going through there and spraying any and everything moving. He continued to laugh, bandaging up his arm.

Alton was chilling on Washington St. when he saw a new van with tinted windows pull up next to him.

"Nigga comes on and ride with daddy," Smurf said with no one in the passenger seat.

Alton jumped in the van and looked in the back. God damn, he thought to himself. The whole Midway and Crawford Drive was in the van. Lil Gee, Big Lee, Booney, and Looney, Daddy-Low, C-Murder, E.J, Lewis and Cake Boy. Alton noticed one lonely girl in the back who was butt ass naked.

If you weren't from Midway, you wouldn't understand. It was spring break, and everyone had rooms at the Budget Inn on Highway 17-92. Spring Break to them was about going to the pool, running down on enemies and running trains on girls who had come from out of town to have fun.

Smurf pulled up to the Paint and Body Shop, and one of the painters named Hanson came out. Daddy-Low got out, along with Lil Gee and Booney. All three of them had cars at Hanson's shop and had come up there to pay for them. They were trying to catch all the events that happened during spring break. Once they were paid off, they all hopped back in the van.

Alton knew he was accepted by the hood. This was his family. He was from Midway. The wild, wild, west. And he was a young Desperado. He felt good!

He was chilling with his new family, and they finally accepted him and let him in. He decided then and there that he was going to get his grill right so he could look like money when the West pulled the whips out on the events.

CHAPTER 5

YOUNG DESPERADO, GRILL

The older guys on Sipes were known as the Desperados. Daddy-Low, C-Murder, Donglong, Big Jay, Looney, Outlaw, Big Lee, Big Man, and a few others. Alton had gained a reputation, and it was known that he was going to bust his gun.

Alton decided to get his grill right. Standing uptown, he saw the guy named Bango he worked directly up under Meat through the scene.

"What it do Alton? Smoke one." Alton jumped in the passenger side of the car and rolled up a blunt.

"When you gon' grab you a whip, everybody know you got that cash. The hoes ain't gon' come until you got you a whip, or your grill right. They want to know you're getting it in," Bango said planting the seed in Alton's head.

"Soon."

"When you ready I got one for you!" Bango said pulling up to the Paint and Body Shop.

Bango, Daddy-Low, Meat, and Outlaw got out of the car and walked up to Hanson, who directed each of them to their fully loaded and freshly painted vehicles.

"We gon' kill 'em for spring break," Bango said, as two men walked up to him.

"I see yall boys tryin to mount up on us," the taller one said.

"Yall ain't ready tho'. Tell your boss man, Meat," the shorter one said.

"Versace, you ain't ready for Meat!" Bango said smiling.

"We gon' see."

"And I got you and Gee," the taller one said.

"You think so Yellow?"

"Know so!" Yellow replied as he walked away.

"Who dey is?" Alton asked.

"That's Earl and Talven, but they call themselves Versace and Yellow. Them boys getting it in! They from Goldsboro."

Alton had heard about them before, but this was the first time he could put a face to a name.

"Yea I think I'm ready to cop me a whip," Alton said.

"When?" Bango replied. That was music to his ears.

"ASAP!"

"Alright, I got a clean ass Delta '88, just like Daddy-Low. It'll fit you," Bango said with a grin. Little did he know, anything fit him. Bango was wondering where he was going to get the extra money to get his baby out of the shop.

"But first take me to the dentist where you got your grill from," Alton said.

"You gon' get some?"

"Yea."

"How many? You can't just get one or two. You got to get a wall!" Bango said smiling.

"I'm getting a twelve pack!" Alton said.

Bango counted up almost two grand. He didn't want him to get a grill because he felt like it was going to fuck him up from selling Alton the car.

"You sure," he asked, hoping that Alton changed his mind.

"Let's go to Midway!"

They made a few stops and headed straight to Midway. Alton grabbed his stash and jumped back in the car with Bango. Bango was so anxious to get his hands on the money that he stopped by his spot so he could show Alton the car.

"That's you right there!" Bango said gassing him up to cash out with him. He threw Alton the keys and Alton got out to inspect the car. He fell in love!

"How much?"

"I want fifteen, but give me a grand," Bango said hoping he didn't say that it was too much.

"Bet!"

Alton went between his sweater in the middle pocket and pulled out seven grand, gave Bango his money and put the money back in his sweater. Bango couldn't believe that this young kid was caked up like that. He had more money than him.

"Take me to the dentist!" Alton said smiling because he knew he had shocked him. Bango still couldn't speak.

Bango took Alton to Elkcam Dental in Volusia County. They drove around and found a crackhead to lie and say he was the father so that he could sign the papers. Alton paid them eighteen hundred and dropped twelve gold teeth. Six on the bottom and six on the top.

"Man them hoes gon' go crazy! You going to the bar tonight?" Bango said.

"Man I ain't never been there, you think they gon' let me in?"

"Man we gon' get you in!"

"Yea, then!" Alton replied excitedly.

"Well let's go to the mall!"

As they headed to the mall, everybody was hype. Alton felt like the man. A new car, a fresh twelve pack, and he had a pocket full of money. There was no way he would turn back now.

CHAPTER 6

A MAN AMONGST BOYS

"So you mean to tell me lil Alton, Thelma's lil brother, the one who started hustling six months ago showed you seven grand? Bought the Delt, dropped twelve in his mouth and still had racks left?" Meat said.

"Yea fucked me up. Jit getting it in!" Bango replied.

"Damn, he ain't bullshittin'!" Lil Gee said silently. Benzo, Meat's poorest hustler just sat back growing hatred for the kid because he knew he couldn't get right.

Meat sat back and started thinking to himself, *it's time to bring lil Alton on board.* He knew he was going to be a star. A trap star that is. Meat knew he was copping from Boot and Boot prices was hard to beat unless he was selling him powder. He also knew he started with Teke.

"One of yall bring him to me!" Meat said as he came up with a plan.

After leaving the car wash on Highway 46, getting his ride cleaned, Alton and Corkey went to Midway and turned on Center St. There were police lights everywhere, so they crossed over and parked so that they could walk to the scene.

"What happened?" Alton asked Lil Gee.

"Man, Lil Ant from Midway just killed C-Murder!" Lil Gee replied.

"How and why?"

Gee started to explain how Ant's mom smoked crack cocaine and Benzo and C- Murder had smacked her up. Ant waited on the side of C-Murder's house, and when he came home, he shot him five times and tried to slit his throat.

Alton couldn't believe that he was dead. He was one of the ones from Uptown that Alton actually liked. He was Jimmy Hamp's other son. Everybody was overwhelmed. Everywhere you looked you saw tears.

"The sheet just moved! The sheet just moved!" C-Murder's sister said while crying hysterically. One of the officers looked back, and sure enough, the sheet was moving.

"Holy shit!" The officer said as his face turned red.

"My brother ain't dead! Get him some fucking help!"

The paramedics rushed C-Murder to the hospital, and from the word on the street he was admitted to the intensive care unit.

Back on Sipes, niggas were getting ready to go to the Deluxe Bar in Goldsboro. Everybody was looking at Alton's teeth and counting up the money. It was decided upon without question that Alton was nominated as rookie of the year. With Corkey in second place.

All the other drug dealers were trying to reel him into getting on their team. Fonso who was laid back stepped to him.

"Jit come on and ride with me."

"You think they gon' let me in?"

"If they don't, ain't none of us going in!" Big Pee-Wee said.

Alton started smiling.

They finally arrived, got out and walked towards the door. It was all types of females out tonight. He recognized a few of them from being at his sister's house and others he had met when he hung out with his older brother Buck.

"Alton! Boy, you know you too young to get in here," one of the girls said shaking her head.

"This ain't no lil Alton, this young Grill. The youngest Desperado from the wild, wild, west!" Big Peewee said.

"Yep, our lil big homie. He run the hood!" Fonso said. Alton just smiled showing off his new grill.

"Damn that jit grilled the fuck up. Who he is?" One chick said, standing bowlegged.

"Girl, that's Thelma's lil brother," her friend said.

"Come on Al, you know this boy too young to get in here," the bouncer said.

"Jit show 'em what time it is!" Big Pewee said smiling. Alton pulled out his knot of cash and asked, "How much extra I gotta pay?"

Alton then pulled off a fifty dollar bill and told the bouncer that it was for him. Everyone in the line was shocked as they stood quietly. Everyone wanted to know who he was.

The bouncer lets him in with a grin, as he put the money in his pocket with no hesitation. "Stay out of sight, lil nigga!"

Midway grabbed the corner of the club, ordered countless bottles and started showing their ass. Slick Bo was the DJ tonight, and he played all the jams. When he played *Wild, Wild, West by Kool Moe D,* the entire Midway went crazy!

Several eyes were on Alton, but he didn't notice it because he was having a blast. As he walked to the restroom someone grabbed his shirt. He turned quickly, and he was face-to-face with Kesha! They stared at each other at what seemed like an eternity. Neither spoke. She was with her sister and her sister-in-law. Alton smiled at her, then spoke to her sister and pulled away. Kesha was furious, she felt like she had been dissed.

"Bitch you seen my lil brother-in-law. Jit turnt the fuck up! His whole mouth grilled up. You don' let him get away. Yo' stupid ass chasing Corey!" Kesha sister said while smacking her lips.

"Bitch shut the fuck up," Kesha said, but she knew her sister was right. Little did she know, there sister-in-law,

Shika was plotting and devising a plan to trap the young hood star. She had already been doing her research.

The Midway Boyz started moving towards the picture booth where the Project Boyz were. Midway Boyz paid the picture man and took numerous of pictures, and all eyes were on them.

The whole Midway formed a wall around Alton while he kneeled for a picture. He knew everyone was looking, so he pulled out all his money and laid it on the ground. He threw up a (W) with his left hand and pointed his right hand like a pistol at the crowd and the cameraman. Of course, he didn't forget to show his grill. The entire Midway loved it, and all the females wanted to know who he was! Kesha was mad! The alcohol had taken control of her emotions. She wanted her man back. She approached him later and begged and pleaded for him to take her back but Alton just continued to tell her no and walked around the club getting numbers from other females.

Once they got on the other side of the bar. Alton recognized the boy Taz, Corey, and Anton with a few more from their clique. Little did Alton know, he had become public enemy number one with the young project guns.

Out of nowhere, Big Peewee struck the biggest one in the head with a bottle! And Big Jay came through the crowd and hit Taz in the face. They immediately started fighting. Alton didn't waste no time. He wanted Corey's head!

He lined Corey up and hit him with a cross, directly on the chin and dropped him. When he followed up, there was nothing in sight because Corey was on the ground. Alton still was on the go! He went to the next one who was Anton.

Alton threw a flurry of blows and dropped him as well! The music stopped because shots had started to fire. Without hesitation, everyone started running to the door. Teke grabbed Alton by the shirt and literally snatched him out the club. While running to Teke's car, Alton still could hear shots ranging out. Once he made it to the car, Teke handed Alton a Glock.40 and told him, don't play no games.

They pulled out the bar and headed towards 13th St. When they got to 13th St., they spotted Taz, Corey and his crew standing in the front of Dread Bar. Teke wasted no time and bent the corner.

"I'm gon' let you out, run up on them fuck niggas and give them the business. I'ma pull up and you gon' dive in, and we gon' shoot back to the west!" Teke told him the play. He really wanted to see where his heart was at.

He let Grill out on 14th St. and pulled off. Grill walked through the dark side of Dread Bar where Taz and his crew was standing. When he got a little closer, he heard someone scream. He didn't hesitate.

"Boom! Boom! Boom! Boom! Boom!" Taz returned fire as his friends ran. Grill crouched down behind a car, ran on the other side and started shooting back.

"Boom! Boom! Boom!"

"Ugh, I'm hit!" Someone yelled.

Grill's gun was out of bullets. He looked around and seen Teke's car pulling up. He got low and ran towards the car with his gun in his hand. Bullets flew by his head, but Grill didn't flinch. A van pulled up that he had recognized from Midway and opened fire on Dread Bar. Teke's back door opened, and Grill dived in.

"Curtis baby boy! Young Desperado! Boy, you a beast!" Teke was hype.

That night Grill stayed at Vickie's house. Once he got settled, he rolled a blunt and reminisced on how much fun he had at the Bar. He thought about how he had busted at them niggas, and the thought made him chuckle. Grill, Alton thought while looking in the mirror. He liked the name and decided to stick with it.

CHAPTER 7

BEEF

"You know that lil fuck nigga was Kesha's lil boyfriend she called herself talking to," Taz said.

"He got to see me, straight up!" Corey said.

"Man yall just mad because that nigga dropped both of yall," Taz said laughing at Corey and Anton.

"Oh yea, lil fuck nigga got them hands. Shit, I been knew that" Anton chimed in while rubbing his eye.

"Then he jumped out bussing up at Dread's and Freddie Lee got shot in the side but he straight though. I like the lil fuck nigga!" Taz said.

"That nigga gotta see me!" Corey said again. His pride was hurt because he got knocked out in front of his girl.

"Wherever you see him at, you better fade him on sight!" Taz said with authority. Corey knew that Taz wasn't playing by the tone of his voice, but he also knew that he would make him jump out anywhere and fight the boy.

"And he gettin money now, you seen his grill?" Anton said.

CHAPTER 8

FAMILY REUNION AND YOU OWE ME ONE

Meat sat on his sofa smiling as Bango told him play by play of what happened at the Deluxe Bar. He loved it, especially when Bango told him that Grill got out on 13th St., crept through the dark and emptied the clip on the whole compound. Meat loved that gangsta, shoot 'em up, bang bang shit. He knew he couldn't fight, but he had three bodies and knew he was a beast with his trigger finger. Grill started to grow on Meat. He wanted a young nigga who was "bout it" because none of his crew would shoot.

The streets were talking. Mainly about Young Grill. He had the juice, and the hoes were looking for him. The jugs knew he had straight drop and his enemies wanted to get at him. Grill was laid up at the Budget Inn. His pager was full of numbers, but he didn't return no calls.

Teke loved what his brother-in-law did as he kept smiling replaying how Grill busted at them niggas with no hesitation. Teke found out that he had to turn himself in but before he did he needed something done. Grill was the perfect one for the job. He only had to do thirty-six months, but he was a scumbag to the fullest. He had been plotting for a minute, but now he had the perfect plan. He was going to stick up his connect before he turned himself in. But first, he needed to find Grill.

Corkey had just bought him a Delta '88 like the one Grill had bought. He decided to slide to the Budget Inn and pick up his homeboy. He filled Grill in on what the streets were saying as they were heading to Sipes Ave. It was Friday, and the hood was jumping as usual. The money was coming, and Grill was getting off his rocks.

"Somebody wanna meet you," Lil Gee said.

"Who?"

The window came down from the car that Gee was standing at. "Me!"

Grill peeked his head in the car and recognized her immediately. The unknown woman came out to be Kesha's sister-in-law. The one who was at the club the night all that shit went down.

"What's good?" he asked.

"You tell me shit," she said,

"Don't you mess with Kesha's brother, Perky?" Grill asked. She just smiled.

"Something like that. Don't you fuck with Kesha?"

"Not no more."

"How old are you?"

"Fifteen!"

"Damn you a young tender," she said smiling with lust in her eyes. Grill looked up and seen one of the white dudes that bought dope and struck off running. When he finished making the play, he came back to the car and finished the conversation he was having with Shika.

In the midst of the conversation, a familiar car pulled up. It was his sister Thelma. He stopped the conversation and walked to the car as Thelma dropped her window.

"Boy, look at you. Got all that damn gold in your mouth. Daddy gon' kill you!" She said laughing. "Get in!"

Grill sat in the car and played with his nephew Mike in the back seat.

"Momma them worried about you. They heard you got gold teeth and you was in a shootout the other night. They want to see you."

"Shit, Daddy them kicked me out. I'm straight. I can take care of myself."

"Well Daddy ain't ask about you," she lied, "Momma wanna see you."

"Man, I ain't fucking with them."

"Oh, you going!" She said smiling while driving to Dixie Ave.

When she pulled up to the familiar street, it all seemed strange to him. Grill hadn't been home in six months. Billy, Trab, Mark, and Sean was standing in the front of the house. Grill studied all of them, they seemed so young to him now.

"What's up lil bruh?" Trab said grabbing his head, showing him his four gold teeth.

"Chillin' man!"

"Unc, what's up?" Sean said while smiling, eyes looking like he had just smoked a blunt. That was Grill's, main man. "When you got back?" Grill asked him.

"Man, bout two days ago. I had to hitchhike a ride from Palm Beach!"

Everybody started laughing.

Grill walked in the house, and his mother was in the front room sitting in her lazy boy, while the kids ran around the house.

"Hey, there baby!" Grill's mother said. Before he could reply, his dad interrupted everything. He was laying on the couch and watching the front door. It was clear that he was already damn near drunk.

"Fishmouth motherfucka, you made a lie out of me!" His father said slurring every word. The entire house got quiet at the sound of the comment.

"What I told you? If you get them gold teeth, I was gon' knock them, bitches, out!" Grill instantly shut his mouth. "I paid all that damn money for them wire things to straighten yo mouth, and you go and put gold on 'em?" Grill didn't say anything. He just looked at his mother who was at an angle where his father couldn't see. She was telling him to remain silent.

"I hear you getting in shoot outs! You know if you pull a gun you better use it. Don't play no games. I rather see you in prison than see you dead." Mr. Curtis started crying thinking about his son, Leroy. He was afraid that he was going to lose another one to the streets, so the next best thing to do was to show him how it goes.

"Irene, go get my toolbox," Mr. Curtis said in his drunken slur, "And tell Leroy to come in the house with the rest of them."

Mrs. Irene brought out the toolbox. Billy, Trab, Mark, Sean, and even Mary's son Renzo was in the house.

"Yall women get out of here while I talk to my boys," Mr. Curtis said.

He broke down the word family. How you should ride for each other at all cost. A family that prays together stayed together. And before you leave one on the scene. You die with them right there. You eat with each other. Fight with each other. And die with each other.

He opened the toolbox and gave Grill the same pill bottle he had taken from him. Then he lifted the toolbox and pulled out two.38 Revolvers.

"Pick which one you want!" Grill picked up the black one and examined it. He didn't want to tell his dad no, so he took the gun.

"Leroy you get the other one and Trab I'ma buy you one. Don't you let nothin' happen to each other? Especially my baby," he said crying, thinking about his son Leroy who got murdered. He missed him so much that he called Billy, Leroy. Billy looked just like him. Curtis had literally cloned Leroy. They even had the same birthday. He pulled out a bottle of Seagrams and poured him a drank.

"Y'all are men! Pour your own troubles."

Grill poured him a drink from the bottle first, and the rest followed him. Renzo just watched. They all watched how Curtis threw his shot back, and they did just that.

The boys talked back and forth about their lives and what each other had missed since Grill had been gone. Billy told him how he had lost his job and got a chick pregnant.

"I almost forgot," Mr. Curtis went in his wallet and pulled out seven hundred dollars. "I took this from you that day, it's the same seven hundred."

Grill just smiled at his father and flipped through the money. He pondered for a second and handed it over to Billy because he knew he needed it.

His father loved every moment of it. Two brothers reunited. He knew they would need each other. He didn't have too long. Maybe five years before he met the man above, so he vowed that he'd teach them as much as possible. Also, he would make sure there was no beef between them. He closed his eyes feeling overwhelmed.

Grill's mother came from the back room and hugged her son. She told him to come home because she missed him. She cooked him something to eat, and he hung out with his family on Dixie!

Grill jumped in the Ford Galaxy with Billy and went and got his Delta '88 and parked it in his mother's yard. He still was getting money on Sipes Ave and Uptown, but he was Downtown Dixie and 21st St. all day every day!

While pulling up on Washington St., Teke pulled up and told him he needed him tomorrow to slide somewhere with him. He told Teke, no pressure.

Grill slept in the car on Dixie that night because him, Trab, and Sean hung out to the wee hours of the morning smoking blunt after blunt. Sean had told him that he wasn't going back to West Palm Beach, so Grill gave Sean and Trab the pill bottle with the bullshit crack rock.

The following morning, word had spread that Boot had been grabbed by the FEDs. He had been caught with 5 kilos and 21 guns. He was done. Grill slid to Teke's spot to see what he was talking about. They got in the car and headed towards Orange County to a city called Eatonville, better known as Chocolate City.

"Now listen. When I slide in, you hold the road down. If you hear shots, don't panic; just make sure you cover me. It's gon' be a car pull up while I'm inside, three of them are going to be in the car Two are going inside the house, and the other one is going to stay in the car. That's your man and everybody else that breathe wrong out there. You hear me, lil nigga?" Teke asked as serious as possible.

When he looked in Grill's eyes, he saw no fear. He knew he had the right person for the job. Teke used to have Showtime hit licks with him. Damn, he missed that nigga.

They pulled up to a house with one car in the parking lot and a screened in porch. Teke grabbed his bag out the backseat and cocked his .40 Caliber. He slammed around in the Mac 11 and placed it back in the book bag with the money.

"Jit when I get out, crack your door too. Don't worry, the damn light don't work." Grill watched Teke as he got out the car and walked up to the dark porch. When the light came on a door opened, and Teke walked right inside.

"Who we going to serve this too, that black motherfucker I don't trust?" The driver of the vehicle said, in his Haitian accent.

"He's okay man. His name is Teke," the passenger said.

"I swear I don't trust him, he wants to rob us!"

"And if he do. We kill him and his whole family. Simple!"

Grill saw a black Rodeo truck pull up. He quickly laid his seat back as he threw his black hoodie over his head. He put a round in the chamber and leaned against the door.

There was a Haitian in the backseat of the car with a round in the chamber of an AK 47 ready for action. You could tell he was an immigrant, a real vagabond. You could tell he was good at using the Russian AK by the way he was holding it. You could look at that nigga and see he wasn't fucking off. He was hungry and was looking for a come up with his cousins.

Teke sat on the sofa with his backpack between his legs alert. He heard the car pull up and he immediately took deep breathes. He knew he would have to be quick because it was three against one. He had won these types of battles before, but he always had someone more experienced with him. But fuck it, he was committed.

"Teke, I think they outside," the other Haitian said.

"Bet, I got somewhere to be, " Teke said unzipping his bag.

Grill squeezed his Glock for dear life once he seen the Haitians disappear inside the house. He wasn't scared, he was anxious.

"Hey, my friend Teke," the taller Haitian said coming through the door greeting Teke holding the duffle bag.

"Whats good Musway," Teke said eyes locked on the shorter one whose eyes never left him.

"One brick, and five pounds," the taller Haitian said taking out the kilo of dope.

Teke wanted to grab the mac first, but the one who had the weapon was to his left. Teke would have had to shoot across his body but he was left-handed, and his hand was on the Glock so he could hit him easily. But the Haitian who owned the house was standing to his right. He was sure he was strapped too, but Teke didn't give a damn.

Teke unzipped his book bag with his right hand and pulled out a five-thousand-dollar stack first, and everybody seemed to be at ease. That's all Teke needed. The taller Haitian seen the movement but he was too late. Teke dropped the money on the table with his right hand and came up with the Glock with his left. The taller one tried to reach, but Teke shot him in the throat with the first shot, "Boom!"

The Haitian in the back seat of the Rodeo swung the door open and came out with the AK 47 extended. He was crouched low in a stance like he knew what he was doing.

Grill watched him before he made his move as the shots continued. "Boom, Boom, Boom!"

Teke shot the taller one in his chest twice after hitting him in his throat. He grabbed the Mac out all in the same motion.

The Haitian was making his way toward the porch when Grill eased out of the car crouched low with his pistol extended. The dude whose house it was fired two shots but Teke was a pro. "Braaaaaat," the Mac sounded off on full auto, ripping across his chest.

"Teke, my friend, why you do this huh?" The shorter Haitian said attempting to grab his gun, but Teke was way too swift. The Haitian knew he was about to die, so he cursed Teke in Creole and put a spell on him. Teke hit him right between his eyes and grabbed both bags.

"Boom, boom, boom!" The Haitian outside let off shots as Teke tried to come out the door. Teke backed up quickly and realized he needed to find a new way out. He knew that AK 47 was spitting at him and for a second, he wondered if the Haitian had already killed Grill. But no need to think soft now, he must escape. He hit the back window, and as he hit the window, he heard the Glock spit.

Grill crept around the car parked in front of the house. The Haitian had just shot three rounds at Teke trying to exit. Grill crept as quietly as possible towards the screen porch trying to get a good shot. When he got about ten or fifteen feet from it, he kicked something catching the Haitians attention. When Grill heard the noise he made, he instantly opened fire. "Boom, boom, boom, boom, boom!"

Teke smiled hearing the Glock go off. The Haitian felt the impact of the first shot on his shoulder. He tried to straighten up, but his attacker kept going. He heard the second shot followed by an immediate pain in his chest and torso. He fell back, squeezing the trigger.

Grill ran up on him and fired two more times. "Boom, Boom!"

"You got me!" the Haitian said trying to speak English. Grill just stood over him, ready to go in the house but he heard footsteps and spun around. "Easy," Teke said looking the kid in his eyes. He walked up on Grill and the dying Haitian. "Finish him!"

Grill put a bullet in his head and just like that he was a killer. "Take their truck and meet me in Midway at the abandoned building," Teke said as the sirens started to get closer in the background.

Grill parked the car on Beardoll Ave. in the abandoned building parking lot. He searched the car and came up with a kilo, bag of money and two more assault rifles. He wondered did Teke know the money and the kilo was in the truck. He decided to separate the kilo from the money and bust the money in half.

"What was in the truck?"

"Money and guns."

"Where it's at?" Teke asked.

"I threw it behind the building."

"Get it and let's dump the car."

Grill went behind the building and grabbed the smaller bundle of money. He left the kilo and another bundle of cash and followed Teke in the Rodeo. They drove across the bridge to Volusia County and dumped the truck. When they got back to Midway, they went to Vickie's house and parked in her yard. Grill gave Teke the money and Teke flipped through five grand and reached under his seat and gave him a quarter kilo and two pounds.

"Grill!" He said smiling, knowing he created an animal tonight. "Be easy lil bruh, I gotta go make this lil bid in two days. Thirty-six months! Don't trust any niggas or hoes. And never hesitate. Hesitation gets you killed!"

"Bet," Grill dapped him up and got out of the car.

Teke pulled off, and Grill saw his brake lights turn on Midway Ave. He knocked on Mary J's door, and she opened it up.

"What up?" Mary J said smiling seeing him.

"Take me somewhere real quick."

"Let's go!" Mary J said quickly. She was in the bar the other night and had heard what he had done on 13th St. She was fucked up about his young ass.

Grill leaned back in the seat and directed her to Beardoll Ave. He jumped out and ran behind the building and grabbed the bag. He was happy that everything was still there. He smiled and jumped back in the car with her.

"Who at your house?"

"Nobody!" She was glad because she wanted to see what was in that bag.

Grill grabbed the bag and the assault rifles and went into Mary J's house. He went back to Vickie's house and grabbed all the money he had there and the one cookie he had left.

When Grill got back to Mary J's, he sat at her table and pulled out the quarter kilo that Teke had gave him and the five grand. He recounted the money and then counted his own money he got off hustling which was eight more grand. Altogether he had thirteen grand.

Mary J's eyes were about to bust. He pulled the two pounds of weed out, and her eyes grew like saucers. He looked in them and smiled.

"See what's that's about, roll up!" Mary J did as she was told.

"This Dro."

"What's that?" She played with the buds, "Well it isn't crippy, but it isn't regular weed either, it's in between. It doesn't have seeds and its smokin'. You got the best in the business," she said looking at the bags.

"Nah, you got the best in the business. How much you make off a pound?"

"Fifteen hundred, but this I can make two grand."

"Okay, give me two grand when you get it and keep the other pound for yourself."

She loved that she could push this off as crip. Twenty dollars a gram, she thought to herself. Dread had just cut her off too, she needed this come up.

"Ok," she said excitedly.

Grill then went in the other bag and counted the other money. It was ten grand. He pushed that to the side with the other thirteen grand and pulled out the brick. He put it next to the quarter kilo. He just smiled.

Mary J couldn't believe that Grill had all this money and cocaine. He had come up from nowhere, and now he was the nigga in the streets. She was going to try her best to stay in his life.

"Come on, take me somewhere."

"Let's slide," Mary J was eager to take Grill anywhere and do whatever he said. Grill grabbed the money, the quarter kilo, and the assault rifles, walked next door and hid it in the attic at his sister's house.

"Let's go."

"You drive," she said, as she threw him the keys.

Grill turned on Washington St. and made a right on Beardoll Ave. He then made a left on Highway 46, which took you to Interstate 95, towards Brevard County. He was headed to Titusville.

CHAPTER 9

NEVER BE THE SAME .

Titusville, Florida is where most of the Mosley's resided. That's where Grill's father first wife lived. Most of Grill's brothers and sisters still lived there, and all were killers, drug dealers, pimps, or prostitutes. In other words, they were considered low lives in the eyes of society. But in the streets, they were natural born hustlers.

Grill didn't know what to do with a kilo of cocaine, so he decided to take it to Titusville to sale it to his relatives and get the cash off it. He smoked back to back blunts on the way there with Mary J. Once they arrived, he pulled up to his niece house who was a well-known drug dealer in Titusville. Her name was Margret, but the streets called her Metal Mouth because she had a mouth full of gold. She was the true definition of a boss bitch.

Metal Mouth was a killer, drug dealer, a madam, pimp and all the above. She did anything to get the almighty dollar. Grill loved her because when she came to Sanford when he was younger, she would get his dick sucked by her girls and gave him joints of weed to smoke. He was only nine at the time.

As he pulled up and parked in her yard. She came outside. "Who that is?"

Metal mouth came to the car with some short ass shorts on with all her ass hanging out.

"This Unc!" Grill said getting out the car.

"Unc who?" Metal Mouth said approaching the car.

"Grill!" Metal Mouth face instantly broke out into a grin, showing all her teeth.

"Look at my little uncle, what's good?"

"Chillin." Grill smiled back showing his grill.

"Damn Unc you don' growed up. You all grilled up and shit."

"Yea," Grill said nonchalantly.

"What brings you this way?" Metal Mouth said eyeing Mary J. "Let's go in the house and let me talk to you." Grill told her. "Tell your chick to come in." She leads the way in the house.

Once in the house, Grill saw all kind of females laying around. Metal Mouth introduced him as her uncle, and all of them started to be flirtatious with him. She then led him to the back room.

"What's really good, Unc?" She said looking serious.

"Check me out. I had to sack some shit in Orlando. I still got the pistol, and I need to get rid of it. And how much is an ounce of soft going for?"

"You killed him?"

"Yea," Metal Mouth brain started working quickly.

"You had somebody with you? That hoe wasn't with you was she?" She said, thinking about how she was going to have to kill the hoe out there to make sure it was no witnesses. "Nah, she don't know what happened."

"Where the gun?"

"Right here." He took it out his pants.

As they stood there a breaking news report flashed across the television. *"Breaking news. This is eyewitness news reporting live in Orange County, Florida. In the city of Eatonville, police responded to a call that was made after a shooting occurred. Multiple shots were fired, and nearby neighbors called the police. Once arriving on the scene, Police found three dead bodies inside the house. And one outside on the porch. All of them were Haitian immigrants. One was identified, and the other three had no identification on them. Neighbors say shots were fired, and the shooting went on for over five minutes. No one saw anything. Neighbors say it was a known drug house. If you have any information regarding these murders, please call 1-800-Crime Stoppers with the information. This is Denise, reporting live with Channel 9 News."*

Metal Mouth looked from her uncle to the TV screen and seen his face and knew that he was responsible. She couldn't believe he was that cold, but she knew the blood. She also knew that he had to have help with him, knowing that she vowed to coach him on what to do.

"How many people were with you?"

"One."

"Who?" Grill hesitated for a while then slowly said the words. Teke. Metal Mouth should have known it had to be somebody ruthless. He had turned her lil uncle out. Teke was about his business, and she was glad to hear it was with him and not some kids.

"First we got to get rid of that gun."

"Alright."

"And an ounce goes for six hundred." Grill quickly counted in his head. He knew it was thirty-six ounces in a kilo and that was fifty-four hundred for a quarter. He rounded it off to twenty thousand a brick. He figured he would get rid of it for twenty thousand.

"Let me go outside, I'll be right back." He grabbed the brick out the car and came back into the room where Metal mouth was. "I need to get rid of this," he said smiling.

"Bingo," Metal Mouth said taking the brick out his hand.

"What chu' got?"

"I'ma give you seventeen thousand, right now!" she said hoping he took it. She was paying twenty-one thousand. "Where it at?" They both started smiling showing their grill. Metal Mouth cut into the kilo, playing with the texture of cocaine.

"Fish scale too!" She said.

"What?" Grill asked. "You see the scales in it?" She showed him the quality of the work. Grill knew nothing about cocaine. He only knew about crack. Metal Mouth helped him throw the gun in the ocean near Cocoa Beach and gave him the money.

Driving back to Sanford, Grill did a quick count in his head of what he was worth. The seventeen grand he'd got from Metal Mouth with what he had put him at forty grand. Plus he had a quarter of a kilo of cocaine, which he needed to find someone to cook up for him. Mary J owed him two thousand. He was about to get back to his hustling shit. He didn't want to go with Teke, but he felt like he owed him, so that was the only reason he went along. He wasn't into robbery, he just helped his big homie out, and Teke blessed him. That's how he chose to look at it.

That night he stayed with Mary J with his pistol on the nightstand. If Dread came home, he would have been in for a surprise. He tossed and turned all night thinking about the Haitian he had killed.

CHAPTER 10

NO TURNING BACK

Grill stood on Sipes Ave. with his pistol in his pocket, kicking it with his homeboys, Corkey, Robert who they started to call, Ratty, and Young Thug, who had just come home. His nephew, Sean had come through Sipes Ave in a stolen car with two hundred dollars looking for drugs.

Grill gave him a double up of the product Boot had given him and told him to be easy. He was in the streets now. He gave Young Thug a few pieces of crack and two hundred dollars to get on his feet. His father pulled up on him in his car.

"What's up Pops?" Grill said walking to the car.

"Get in." Grill got in the car with no hesitation, and his father pulled off. They ended up at the Whiskey Rivers Liquor Store.

"You want something to drink Pops?"

"Yea," his dad said as he reached for his wallet.

"I got it!" Grill hopped out of the car and went into the store and told them to give him a fifth of Hennessy. The people who owned the store knew him since he was a kid and sold him liquor with cups and blunts.

He got back in the car with his dad, and they pulled up to Vickie's house on Washington St. They fixed their drinks and drunk as Mr. Curtis spoke game. The game he had never heard before. He ate it up.

"And son, don't play with no nigga and don't run with the crowd. Don't trust nobody, the only person you can truly trust is Leroy." Grill knew he was talking about Billy. "And don't keep all your eggs in one basket, put some up for a rainy day," his daddy said.

"Hold on Pops." Grill went into the house to his stash and grabbed all the money out then got back in the car with his dad.

"This is a nice drank son." His dad liked the Hennessy.

"You like that?" Grill said throwing the bag of money in his father's lap. His father looked in the bag and couldn't believe his eyes. He had to do a double take.

"Put that up for me," Grill said smiling to his dad, knowing the effect it had on the old man.

"How much is this?"

"Count it up and see," Grill said smiling.

"This a lot of money son, you've got to know the value of a dollar."

"Take me back on Sipes." His father dropped him off and told him to be careful.

While posted on Sipes Ave. like a light pole, a car pulled up. "Get in!" The voice said. It was the girl Shika, Kesha's sister-in-law.

Grill got in the car, and Shika pulled off. "Damn you hard to catch up with," she said smiling.

"That's a good thing," he said smiling back. Shika knew she had to come at this lil nigga straightforward. "I'm going to be straight up with you. I'm fucked up about you."

"Oh, yea?" Grill just smiled.

"So what we gon' do," she said. "I'm in the car, ain't I?" Grill replied.

She just smiled to herself, thinking how she was going to show him why they called her Freaky Shika.

Shika drove around the city smoking with Grill behind tinted windows. Her pager kept going off, and they pulled over to use the pay phone. She went to the crackers house that kept calling and served them. She was making a lot of money. Hell, more money than Grill and his boys. He really didn't know anything about her but seeing that made him want to get to know her. They ate at Red Lobster, smoked and rode around listening to the new album Four Hundred Degrees by Juvenile.

"Take me back to Midway, I got some things to handle."

"Ok," Shika said obediently. Before going back to Midway, Shika stopped at the Handy way to get gas. While Shika was walking back to the car, another car pulled up on the side of them. "Freaky Shika," the voice said. Shika turned her head and looked towards the voice, and the door opened. Taz got out with no shirt on, but the windows were up in the car so he couldn't see Grill. Grill noticed she looked uncomfortable when Taz approached her. She continued to pump the gas.

"Boy stop! I got somebody in the car with me!" She said smiling.

"I don't give a fuck," Taz said living up to his name The Devil. Grill slammed one in the head quite as possible and pointed it towards the driver's door.

"Let me see what lame you got in here anyways."

"Boy don't go in my car!" Shika tried to stop him, but Taz swung the door open staring down the barrel of Grill 9mm.

For a split second, neither of them moved or blinked. Taz broke the silence. "Damn jit, you gon' kill me?"

"Seems like it, don't it?" Grill snarled. Taz started smiling.

"This lil nigga bout it, bout it!"

"So what its gon' be?" Grill asked him. Taz continued to smile staring death right in the eyes. "Jit the hoe working in the store on the camera, and if you shoot me, she gon' tell. I ain't strapped no way!" Taz continued to smile, growing hatred but liking the young nigga at the same time. He hated him for catching him slipping but loved his heart. Right then and there a love-hate relationship built between the two.

"You caught me slipping this time," he said with a smile on his face. Taz boldly reached for the blunt out the ashtray and put it in his mouth as he walked away.

"Bout time you fuck with a real nigga!" He said grabbing him a handful of pussy and walking back to his car laughing loud as hell.

Grill just watched him do that and pulled off. For some strange reason, Grill liked Taz. He reminded him of Teke, and he had the strangest look in his eyes. It was like he feared nothing or no one.

Shika opened the door and got in the car and just stood there. She saw the gun in his hands, and it spooked her.

"Boy, I didn't know you had that on you," Shika said scared as hell.

"It's a lot you don't know. Take me back to the West!" Grill said leaning back. Shika was mad at Taz because he fucked up her chance with the jit. Perky was in jail, and Whiteboy Toby was in prison. She wanted him to be her boyfriend.

As she pulled up to Sipes Ave, Grill got out the car and didn't tell her bye or anything. Lil Gee saw Shika drop Grill-off. He knew that he could get in the kid's pockets through his cousin, Shika. Lil Gee walked up on Grill.

I saw you gettin' yo slick ass out that car," Lil Gee said with a smile. Grill just smiled back at him. Remembering what his father said, *never trust nobody that smiled all the time. Niggas used their smile to make you feel relaxed. Treat it like a weapon.*

"Meat wanna holla at you, we know you was fuckin' with Boot. Who you fuckin' with now?" Lil Gee asked, ready to reel him in.

"Shit, I'm straight right now. What's up with the coke tho? I'm tryin' to cross over."

Bingo, thought Lil Gee, just what Meat was thinking. "Shit I know where to get it from. Meat got it!" Grill was thinking he already had some, but he needed somebody to cook it up.

"You know how to cook it up?"

"Nah, but you can pay Meat, Big Peewee, or Stack to do it!"

"Come scoop me up later, and we can go holla at Meat."

"Shit you gon' slide with us to Daytona for Spring Break?"

"Hell yea, come get me!"

"You know that's my cousin, Shika. You better get her. She got Whiteboy Toby beeper. She getting' money."

So that explains it, thought Grill. *That's where she gettin' all this money from.*

CHAPTER 11

THE GAME IS TO BE SOLD, NOT TOLD

"So, you told him that we got coke?" said Meat, rubbing his chin sitting in the back seat of the car. While Lil Gee was driving and Bango was in the passenger seat. Backed in at the Jimmy Hamp with the windows down.

"Yea he ready to meet you."

"Man, that lil nigga getting' it in!" Bango replied as Big Peewee and Stack passed the hundred dollar bill back and forth amongst each other while they snorted cocaine and talked more about Grill, was standing next to the car.

Stack was Teke's cook and was an OG on the streets. Stack was from Fort Lauderdale. He was known for bringing a lot of game to Central Florida. Midway to be exact. He was also known for bringing the parlay game from Miami to Lauderdale, to Sanford. It was hard pieces of crack from down south where cocaine was plentiful. You could pop them three different times and make sixty dollars for what you got for ten dollars down south. Before no one really knew how to cook dope in Midway. They would go down south and spend five to ten grand on parlays and triple their money. Ninety percent of the drug game in Midway was controlled by Jimmy Hamp, known as the God Father, but he got popped in '92. Boot was up next, but he got jammed by the FEDs, and after him, it was Young Trap Stars who was getting parlays from Miami or Lauderdale.

Stack was down here as a teenager. He had relatives who were in the Midway area, so he was back and forth. His brother and cousins were killers. They all had bodies and was known as the Bad Crew.

Stack had two addictions that stopped him from getting to the top. His coke habit and his gambling habit. Stack was a trendsetter, but he was letting that go to waste. He would be up for days snorting cocaine in gambling houses, losing thousands of dollars. Sometimes he would win, but most of the time he lost. The streets took the game that he brought to Midway and used it against him by doing it better.

He was down to his last two hundred dollars, and he knew he had to find a come up quick or Twigga, the love of his life, was going to leave him. Bills were due, and he was broke.

He stuck his finger on one side of his nose, pulling out snot and cocaine, placing it in the other nostril. The collagen was gone from his nose because of all the cocaine he used. He sat back in the seat and thought of a plan.

Big Peewee, like Stack, was far from a flat-footed hustler. He'd rather gamble, rob and partake in white collar crime to get a quick dollar. He was the son of Manuel, a great man in the Midway community.

Big Peewee was only in the car because he was at Stack house trying to get his half of ounce that Stack had cooked up for him. But since he had been around Stack, he was losing. Stack had tricked him into pulling out some of the coke he had sold him yesterday for them to get high. He told him not to worry, that he'll make up for the grams he had snorted. Stack wasn't lying because the coke that they had was clean. You could see the rainbow colors in it and when you turned the rock over you still had cocaine in your hand.

"You ready for me to cook that shit?" Stack asked, mind focused on a quick scheme to get the bills paid and extra if pulled off right. He had to execute his plan properly. He went into his zone.

"Been ready!" Big Peewee said. He was mad as hell but feeling good for the moment off the high the coke had brought him. He was going to hate getting rid of the coke, but he had to have something to hustle. He decided to go through with his plan. He only had one hundred dollars to his name, and that was the bill they were snorting the cocaine out of. And Stack charged fifty dollars to cook a half ounce.

Stack took him inside of the house on Center St., on the corner. He told Big Peewee to wait in the living room, which Big Peewee never did. Stack got his ingredients and put it together. He was doing extra things in the kitchen to throw Big Peewee off his trail, but Big Peewee watched him closely.

Big Peewee was intimidating by being in a small house with anyone. After Stack cooked the cookie, he told Big Peewee to get in the car and ride.

Grill was standing at the rooming house getting his Buick washed when the two kids walked up on him. Dunney and Vario.

"What's up with yall badasses?" Grill asked. The younger of the two spoke first, "We just chillin'."

The older one was all in Grill's mouth counting his gold teeth as Grill spoke, "Let us get some money?" The older one asked. Grill went in his pocket and pulled out a knot and gave them a hundred dollar bill to split. The older one said, "Man what I'm gon' do with that? I want some real money."

"Jit you better chill yo lil ass out."

"He got some of that stuff you be selling," the younger one said.

"Want to see?" The older one named Dunney said.

"Yea," Grill said quickly.

Dunney went in his sack and pulled out a dime baggy, that was usually used for carrying weed. He had ten pieces of crack rock. And they were real!

"Where you get this from?" Grill said examining the quality.

"Fonso." Grill wanted to say something, but he caught himself. Who was he to warn someone of the game? He was a youngster himself.

"Be careful with that jit and don't just serve anyone. When you ready to get something else holla at me." Then and there Grill decided to take Dunney and his brother under his wing.

As the brothers walked down the street, Grill saw the white Grand Cherokee Jeep pull into the rooming house. It was Stack. He came to look for Grill but didn't have to look far because he was right there. Stack thought to himself about his plan to get his bills paid. His plan included Grill. He knew Grill had coke, the same fish scale he was snorting.

He was Teke's cook, and he had cooked most of the cocaine for Teke the other night. Then seeing on the news, the Haitians were murdered he knew Teke had done it and he told him that Grill was with him. Teke had already told him to look out when Grill was ready to have the dope cooked.

Stack had heard the youngster was good with his gun and knew from the news of the murders that it was more than a one-man show. No one would go with Teke to pull such a thing but Showtime, and he was dead. No one would go with Teke because they knew that he'd leave everybody that was with him and get out of dodge. It had to be someone he truly cared about for him not to do that. Then he thought about Thelma. Teke loved Thelma, and he had been grooming her little brother. He knew that it was a great possibility that the killer was Grill!

His plan was to pick at the youngster and pick the sack off him. Stack was a firm believer that the finesse game was the best game.

"Man, what we gon' do? Just sit up here in this hot ass hole 'til the police come?" Big Peewee asked taking a hit from the coke.

Stack fired the blunt up, inhaled then exhaled. He thought *This was his last shot at gettin' the money before he was kicked out.* He must trick the jit. Stack got out the jeep and started walking toward Grill standing there watching his car get washed.

"Youngster, what's up?" Stack said approaching him.

"Nothin' just chillin," Grill replied, eyeing him.

"You ready to step it up or what?" Stack asked while hitting the blunt.

"What chu mean?" Grill fired back. Stack thought for a second how much should he reveal, then he decided to go slow.

"Teke told me you was gon' holla at me when you was ready."

"Ready for what?" Stack thought quickly. The jit was toying with him. He wasn't giving free information.

"Well, I guess you ain't ready. He said you wanted me to cook something for you." Stack said looking directly at Grill.

Grill looked directly back, wondering how much Stack knew and debating on an answer. Finally, he looked long enough and replied.

Stack could tell by the look that Grill had, that he was Teke's partner. Now he had a different outlook on the kid. He knew he was dealing with a killer and someone who would go far. He would charge the kid now, but not that much because he knew what goes up, must come down.

"How much you gon' charge me?" Stack let out a sigh of relief.

"Fifty dollars a cookie. Each cookie is fourteen grams. Half of an ounce." Grill quickly counted nine hundred dollars, but his real money would come from the cocaine he would steal from Grill in his face. He hid the smile that was forming at the corner of his lips. Stack was back.

"Well you need to get right, because I'm hittin' the road early in the morning and I'ma be gon' for a week," Stack said, placing urgency in the situation.

"Come get me off Washington in thirty minutes."

"Bet!" Stack walked off singing, *Its Been A Long Time Coming But Change Gone Come by Sam Cooke.*

Stack opened the truck door, and the first thing that came out of Big Peewee's mouth was, "What you tricked jit into?" His eyes were big. "Mind your business," Stack said continuing to hum the Sam Cooke song. After stopping by Jimmy Hamp to get blunts, Stack saw Shika.

"Whats up Freaky Shika?" Stack asked.

"You tell me," Shika replied.

"Got some straight drop I know you looking for," Stack said while digging in his nose.

"Everybody say they got that, then it be that water whip bullshit," Shika said angrily.

Stack was already counting the money up he would make in the next few hours. He knew he could take the nine ounces and make half of a kilo with all right quality and risk an altercation with Grill. Or he could stretch an extra cookie out of each ounce and make them straight drop. He could make two nine gram cookies and keep ten grams for himself. That would be ninety grams for himself.

If he worked his wrist properly, that would bring him twelve cookies. At five hundred a piece that was a little over five grand. He whistled to himself. Since Freddie Sole was gone, the weight money was flowing.

"Come to my spot in an hour,"

"Make it two hours, I gotta run somewhere."

"Come to the back door."

Stack drove on Washington St. and pulled in Vickie's yard where he saw Grill sitting on the hood. Big Peewee just looked on as Grill got in the back seat and Stack pulled off.

They pulled up to Stack's house that he shared with Twiggy. He told Big Peewee and Grill to come in and pointed to a couch where he wanted both to sit. Stack went into the kitchen, ripped a paper napkin off the rack, poured the water out of the bowl he had the cookie of crack sitting in, then poured cold water on top of the cookie of crack in the bowl. The cookie was hard as a rock and made a clinking sound as it wiggled free of the grip it had on the bowl from turning from a solid to a liquid, then back to a solid. Stack smiled as he used a bent piece of the hanger to lift the cookie out of the bowl. He measured the size and weight with his eyes. He knew that it was really good coke. It was thick and hard all the way through. "Big Peewee," Stack called in his raspy voice.

Big Peewee was already making his way to the kitchen to observe Stack's handy work. Big Peewee stood over the counter and examined the cookie of crack. He was satisfied with the size. Now, he only had to steal a few customers from his neighbors to get rid of it. Stack handed him the cookie on a napkin and escorted him to the door.

"Damn why you rushing me, you still got the bill?" Big Peewee said wanting to stay to see what Stack was up too and what Grill had in the bag.

"This ain't no hang out spot. Our business is finished," Stack said holding the door open.

"What about the bill?" Big Peewee said prolonging. Stack pulled out the bill and told him to take a hit and snatched it back afterward.

"What about the bill itself, that's a hundred."

"I owe you one," Stack said holding the door.

Big Peewee walked in front of Grill on his way out the door. "This what a half an ounce cookie look like," he said showing Grill the cookie. Hoping to block Stack from the slick shit.

Stack smiled as Grill examined the cookie, knowing it wasn't nearly a half an ounce and knowing he could make all Grill's cookies look like that.

"Man get out my shit!" Stack said pushing Big Peewee out the door.

Grill reached in his pocket and pulled out the nine hundred dollars and handed them to Stack. As Stack walked pass him, he turned the TV on and handed Grill the remote. "We gon' be here all night, so make yourself comfortable. I got to cook your shit and mines. Roll a blunt!"

Stack limped to the kitchen, removing all his bowls, scale, and cooking utensils.

"Bring the work!" Grill brought the book bag to the counter. Stack pulled the bag of coke out and placed it on the counter. He needed to keep Grill's eyes off him so that he could do his thing.

"Listen the floor in the kitchen ain't steady, and it will make the cookie come out wrong. Sit in the living room." Grill not peeping game did what he was told and fired up a blunt.

Stack went to work. Separating the coke into nine grams, pouring them in their separate bowls, dumping the baking soda on top of them and placing the water on one at a time.

He placed them in the microwave for three minutes, then removed them. He beat the substance in the bowl, with the bent clothes hanger to get it to form into a cookie. The clinking sound went on for hours.

Grill heard the sound so much that it put him to sleep. That's exactly what Stack hoped for. *Two for him, One for me.* He made all nine-gram cookies. Thirty to be exact. Eighteen for Gill and twelve for himself. He was pleased with his handy work.

Some of the cookies started to dry, so he removed them out of the bowl and placed them on napkins. After the eighteenth cookie dried, he started to roll a blunt. He eyed the sleeping youngster.

He liked him, and he knew he would go far. He knew a lot, but he had a lot to learn. Like to never take your eye off the ball. The ball is the money. In due time, he would learn that. But for now, Stack would tax him for the knowledge he didn't know. Come with the game, thought Stack. He was old school. The game was to be sold, not told.

Grill stirred as he heard water running and splashing in the sink. Stack was pulling his last three out of the water. He limped to the youngster and passed him the blunt.

"What you finna do with all that work?"

"Grind it," Grill said.

"Get chu some clientale jit. Stay away from the weight game and remember that slow money is fa'sho money. Be careful what you do, it might come back on you," Stack said glaring at Grill. He just looked back trying to read between the lines, wondering how much Stack knew.

"Knock, knock, knock!" The sound at the door broke both their trance.

"Who is it?" Stack asked limping to the door. He was annoyed that the person had used the front door.

"Shika," the voice replied.

"Didn't I tell you to use the back door," Stack said swinging the door open.

"I thought this was the back door," Shika replied stepping in.

Stack shut the door behind her continuing to scold her. They walked into his kitchen like it was a restaurant. He turned to face her leaning over the counter.

"What's up, what chu' talking about?" asked Stack.

"Nobody don't want no bullshit, running my people off," Shika stated while looking at Grill on the couch as she walked passed him.

"You must be talking about them Goldsboro niggas who you be dealing with. Ain't nothing over here but straight drop being sold out this trap!" Stack shot back.

Shika looked in the kitchen and seen crack cocaine cookies everywhere. She had never seen so many. They were on the counters and in individual bags. He handed her one, and she examined it.

The texture was hard, and the surface was shining like glass. She remembered what Whiteboy Toby taught her. She immediately knew it was good. He always told her to buy as much as you can buy when it was good so you wouldn't run out.

"How much?" Shika said.

"Five hundred a piece."

"Give me four of them."

Four of them was music to Stack's ears. Tonight was going to be a good night. He was safe and out of the dog house.

Stack gathered up four cookies, while Shika counted the money. She handed him two grand.

The bedroom door swung open. Twiggy had heard a female's voice in her home, and she became curious. When she came out the door, she saw Shika handing Stack the money. When Twiggy got to the kitchen, she eyed Shika from head to toe with a disgusted look on her face. Shika had on coochie cutter shorts and a strapless shirt. Her ass hung out of her shorts, and her nipples were hard making it obvious that she didn't have on a bra. Shika just smiled even though she saw the anger in Twiggy's eyes.

"What the fuck you got people in the house for while you cook that shit?" Twiggy said looking at Shika.

"Woman, this is how I pay bills!"

"I don't give a fuck," Twiggy said continuing to look at Shika. Stack put the money in his pocket and called Grill to the kitchen.

"Jit come grab this," Stack said while gathering all his cookies together.

"Y'all get the fuck out of my house," Twiggy yelled. Stack just glared at her as he limped by her to get a shoebox for Grill to put the cookies inside.

Stack came back out of the room, gave Grill the shoe box and told him to put them inside. Grill quickly counted eighteen cookies and Stack asked him was he satisfied, and he was.

Grill hurriedly put the cookies in the shoe box, while Stack looked for his keys. He was coming down from the coke and couldn't remember where he put them.

Shika stood by the door waiting for Stack to come to unlock it and let her out. Twiggy continued to stare making everyone uncomfortable. Stack continued to flip things to look for his keys.

"Shika take Grill to where he gotta go," Stack said turning down a glare from his wife.

"Who is Grill?" Shika said smirking at Grill. Stack caught the look and knew he must have been on Shika's to do list. He smiled thinking of her freaky ass.

Twiggy caught the smile and Stack hurried up and said him.

"Crack, Crack gon' kill yo ass!" Stack said smiling referring to Shika's last boyfriend, Whiteboy Toby.

"Ain't gon' hurt what he don't know," Shika said as Twiggy let out an exaggerated breath.

"Come on Grill," Shika said, knowing she was getting under Twiggy's skin.

"Where to?" Shika asked smiling because she had him in her car again. Grill just looked at her, hating the fact that she was enjoying herself.

"Take me on Dixie."

"Where that's at?"

"I'll show you."

As they pulled up on Dixie Ave., Billy was sitting on the hood of his car with a white girl between his legs. Grill got out the car with his shoebox under his arms and walked towards Billy and the girl.

"What up bruh?" Grill asked.

"Just chillin," replied Billy as the white girl eyed him curiously.

"Who this is?" Grill asked nodding towards the white girl.

"This is Mary. She's pregnant!" Billy said smiling.

"Oh, yea?" Grill smiled.

"Mary this is my brother Alton, but the streets call him Grill," Billy said showing his dimples. Grill greeted Mary as his sister-in-law and listened to Billy as he filled him in on how he was moving. He talked about how he'd be as a father and that he was going to have to pay bills, even if he had to work two jobs.

Grill listened carefully, then told Billy to step on the porch with him. "Listen, I need you to put this up for me when your chick ain't looking. Put it in the trunk of my car and throw a towel over the box!" Grill said handing him the box as if he was the little brother.

"What's in it?" Asked Billy. Grill opened the box and showed him all the hard crack cocaine cookies in separate bags in the box.

"Damn! How much is that worth?" Billy asked. Grill instantly seen the hunger in his eyes but also seen the innocent look there too. He had a sick feeling in his stomach that the game was never for Billy.

He slowly said, "Five hundred a piece," regretting saying it.

"That's how much you sell them for?" Billy asked. You could tell he had no knowledge of the drug game, but he had a lot of common sense. Billy knew that this was a lot of drugs. At that moment, he had a new found respect for his brother. Billy wasn't in the drug game, but he wasn't lame either. It was in his blood. He had seen drugs and ran across a few stones himself, but he never saw anyone with this much. He knew then that his little brother was the man, standing on his own two feet on Sipes Ave, and had more dope than the big boys.

Then and there the roles reversed, and Grill became the big brother.

"That's how much you buy them for?"

"You cut them up into pieces, and you are supposed to make a grand," Grill said, looking at Billy do the figures.

"And how many is it?

"Eighteen," Grill said quickly. Billy quickly counted the numbers in his head.

"Nine grand you paid and eighteen grand you gon' make?" Billy said in astonishment.

"Something like that," Grill said smiling reaching in his pocket.

He pulled out a knot while Billy watched his every move. Grill quickly counted off five hundred and handed it to Billy, and he gladly accepted it.

"That's for you," Grill said as he took a cookie out of the shoe box, leaving seventeen in the box.

He then introduced Billy to Shika, moments after Shika got back in her car and they left.

CHAPTER 12

BONNIE AND CLYDE

"So that's where my in-laws stay?" Shika said flashing her trademark smile.

Grill just glared at her, hating the fact that Stack sent him with her and she thought that she knew what he was worth.

"You got a razor?" Grill asked. Shika reached in the ashtray and handed it to him, then she watched how he cut the cookie up.

"How much you got?" Shika said. Grill was able to squeeze twelve hundred out of his cookie. "Twelve!"

"Damn I only cut a grand, show me how to do that on my next one." Shika already had formulated a plan to get jit. Seduce him, fuck him good, and steal all his customers. She was the queen of backdooring. She was going to make Grill her new Midway buddy.

Grill caught the reply but didn't say anything. He didn't like the fact that she was well-known. He had no intentions of being around her for the next one.

"Take me on Sipes," Grill said leaning back in his seat with a bag full of cut up rocks.

Shika rolled her eyes and turned up the music, then pulled off. Once Grill saw she wasn't going on Sipes Ave., he turned the music down.

"I said take me on Sipes!"

"After I go where I need to go. I got people that's been on hold for two hours. You ain't the only one gettin' money. Everything doesn't just go your way."

Grill just smiled, and that's what Shika wanted to see. He was trying to play so gangsta, but she would break him. She loved the sight of his grin. The mixture of a little boy, but having a big boy grill that stated, *I'm ballin'*, turned her on.

Yes, she had become infatuated with him, and she would do anything to get him. She was willing to cross anybody, and he was her new boyfriend rather he knew it or not. After being in the car with Shika for three or four hours, Grill had a new-found respect for Shika. Every five to ten minutes her pager went off. She had customers lined up at the gas stations, restaurants, hotels, and alleyways. All waiting on her.

In four hours she easily made the two thousand dollars that she invested with Stack. Grill for some reason was embarrassed, and Shika sensed it. She decided to drop Grill off on Sipes Ave. Shika was wondering why his pager never went off and why he never needed her to take him somewhere. She wondered where he sold his drugs, she knew on Sipes, but she didn't think that shit was coming through.

"You gon' take me on Sipes. It's Friday, and it's the 1st, I gotta get out and get it," Grill said embarrassed.

"Going there now," Shika said laughingly.

CHAPTER 13

MY BLOCK

Pulling up on Sipes Ave the crowd was out, and more people were coming. Jimmy Hamp was live and in effect. Shika backed in and called her girlfriends over to her car. Grill eased out the car without being noticed.

Shika sent someone into Jimmy Hamp to buy drinks and blunts for them while they sat around their cars watching the traffic and the drug dealers work. Shika's eyes never ventured far from Grill.

He backed in the shadows and smoked a blunt while waiting for traffic to come through.

"Vroom, skirt!" Grill heard the screeching of car tires on the pavement. He took off towards the white truck and dived through the window.

"Two hundred!" The white dude said, holding his left hand out for the drugs and the money in his right. The passenger window was up, and his doors were locked.

Grill quickly caught the sale and walked back to Jimmy Hamp, while counting his money. No sooner than he left the road, another car came, and Grill quickly beat all the other sprinters to the car.

"One hundred," the female driver said. After serving her, another came.

"Fifty," Grill quickly caught him and was walking back to the spot he was at.

A lady approached and said, "Who got that glass? I want that glass." One drug dealer walked up on her, trying to sale her garbage.

"Nigga I'm trying to spend a hundred. I want straight drop and a deal," She said eying the crowd looking for Daddy-Low.

"Come here!" Grill said calling her in the light beside Shika and her crew.

"If it ain't straight drop. I don't want it!"

"This what you want?" Grill said dropping a piece on the hood of the car, letting the sound attract her.

Judy immediately recognized the sound and followed it.

"What you gon' let me get for the hundred?" Grill counted out seven of the big dimes. Judy hungrily accepted. "Do the same thing for another one!"

This time Grill went into his boxers and pulled what remained in his bag getting ready to count out seven more.

"Uh huh, what you want for that?" Judy asked, eyeing the golden colored crack rock which was known as butter from its color.

Grill quickly did a count in his head of what he had made. He rounded it off to about five hundred. He knew Judy hit a lick and he sensed it, so he wanted to get all the money. He took eight of the pieces out and told her to give him four hundred.

Judy went towards the dark and counted out four hundred from the twenty-seven hundred she clipped from the white man. Grill saw most of it and knew he must store out and keep her around to get it all. They exchanged crack for money and Judy hurriedly ran to the van awaiting her.

Shika watched everything from afar, counting Grill's pockets from long distance. She saw Kim and gave her the white bag full of blunts as she watched Grill walk to the pay phone. She saw him talk in the pay phone then hang up.

Grill went back to the spot in the dark and counted his earnings, totaling close to nine hundred. He just called his mother's house, and Billy was still there. He told his brother to bring him one more of those things on Sipes Ave.

Grill quickly sold the last pieces and was waiting on his brother. The money was starting to pick up, and the older boys were coming out.

Billy pulled up as Grill was growing impatient. Grill gave his brother the thousand dollars and told him to take it to Curtis. Billy gave him the cookie and Grill told him to stay by the phone. He might need another one.

Grill quickly cut the cookie down and posted back up like a light pole. He stood with a black hoodie, black dickies and a pair of black air max. Traffic was everywhere, and the money flowed in from all angles. Grill was quick on his feet and getting to most of the cars before anyone.

Corkey was right on his trail, and he had the same product as Grill. Black, white and Spanish smokers came on Sipes Ave to get crack. The money was booming, and it was a thousand dollar stroll.

Shika watched the exchange between Billy and Grill. She knew he was on his second cookie. She watched him work the ave. like a master of his craft. He would smile at her from time to time and let her know she wasn't the only one gettin' money.

Shika had a lot of respect for him after seeing him hustle and put it down on the block. The crowd was whispering, and everyone was watching a trap star perform, it was like he was on fire. Every soul came his way. No one could make anything.

All the walking smokers walked passed their regulars buyers and straight to Grill. The block was hot, and he wasn't aware of the stories from the other hustlers and the envy in their heart, but Shika was. She saw it, and she wanted to warn him. No one knew that she liked him or even knew him. Every time the drug dealers watched Grill's bag get low, they began to get relax.

Billy pulled up to Jimmy Hamp with a white girl and handed him something. It was like he had unlimited cocaine. All the OG's watched the show. Meat, Stack, Big Peewee, Big Man, and Fonso. It was without questions that this was Grill's block.

"That pussy nigga think he gon' make all the money?" Benzo said.

"Damn sho' look like it," another hustler said.

Judy was back in the van, and everybody heard about the money that Judy spent with him. Benzo had decided when she came back that she was going to spend with him or nobody. He was going to take the money if she didn't spend it with him.

Grill had just made three hundred off a fresh cookie when he saw Judy approach him. Her eyes were as big as saucers.

"Please tell me you got some mo' of that butter jit?" She said with hope in her eyes. Grill just smiled. Judy jumped up and down and ran towards Grill and began to kiss him on his cheek and neck. Grill pushed her off gently and wiped his cheek smiling.

All the other drug dealers approached Judy and tried to sell their product.

"I got my man, yall back the fuck up," Judy screamed.

"What chu' mean yo man, that ain't the only nigga you gon' spend with?" Benzo stated angrily walking towards them.

"What chu' got Judy?" Grill said anxiously to get it over with so that he could check Benzo. Judy looked at both afraid of what she wanted. Benzo was standing next to her while she was standing in front of Grill and it was like you could hear a pen drop. She whispered, "Samething."

Grill handed Judy the bag, quickly adding up the five hundred with the money in his pocket, totaling up to a grand. As she grabbed the bag, Benzo grabbed her.

"Bitch, I told you, you gon' spend with me," he drew back his hand and slapped her. She withdrew from him, cowering down, bracing for another lick. Grill stepped in between, breaking the grip and pushed Judy behind him.

"Dawg you wanna fight?"

"Ain't no pressure, but you ain't gon' stop nobody from spendin' with me," Grill said.

"Fuck nigga, you don't run nothin' out here. Nigga you fresh off the porch," Benzo said stirring himself up.

During the argument, Judy handed Grill the money and slipped away. As she scurried down the street, the argument continued.

"Fuck nigga? I'ma show you a fuck nigga. Give me one!" Grill snapped as he put the money in his pocket.

"You ain't said nothin," Benzo said.

Grill walked pass everyone who was watching him. He took off his sweater and pulled his gun out of his waistband off his hip. He handed it to Corkey, who was standing by Shika's car. Shika grabbed his things from Corkey and put them in her car.

Grill met Benzo in the middle of the road as the crowd stood and watched. Grill threw his set up, and Benzo charged. Grill timed him perfectly and hit him with an uppercut and a right overhand flush. Benzo was out cold on his feet and fell into Grill. Grill pushed him off, and he fell to the ground. Grill mounted him and hit Benzo two more times. Bango and Lil Gee had to pull him off him.

"Nah, don't touch jit. He wanted to fight, let him fight," Face said.

"Lil bruh don' knocked him out," Dirty said. Grill got up grabbed a bottle of beer off the nearest car and walked back over to Benzo and all the guys who were trying to revive him. He stood over him and poured the beer in his face. When Benzo woke up, he started swinging at the sight of Grill but was punching the air.

"Fuck nigga you gon' respect me! You hear me?"

"What happened?" Asked Benzo in a drunk voice.

Grill walked off and got in the car with Shika while the guys helped Benzo up. Shika's pager continued to go off. She easily made another thousand dollars. She was feeling good. She was more impressed with how Grill controlled the block. She knew he wouldn't advance on Sipes Ave because of all the envy. He needed to get him some new clientele. He was an animal and literally destroyed Benzo and his pride. She also knew he wasn't going anywhere with the boys from the projects. He was so young but so hard. She was in love with him, and she decided then and there she would help him in any way that she can.

"Take me on Dixie," Grill said after not speaking for the last hour.

"Okay," Shika responded submissively.

Pulling up on Dixie Ave. at three in the morning and seeing a few people out was a surprise. Billy and Trab were talking, while Sean and Mark sat in the car smoking a blunt.

"What yall niggas doing out so late?" Grill asked.

"Chillin'," replied Billy.

"Trying to make a lil money," Trab added. Sean and Mark got out of the car and walked towards the others.

"Unc, whats up? Man when you gon' get me some work? The Eastside booming. Shit, I don' ran out. Just got one more piece," Sean said holding out a crummy little piece of crack.

"Shit what you want?"

"I got six hundred," Sean said proudly. Grill looked at Billy and nodded his head. Billy went and got the shoe box. Grill opened the box and placed it on the hood of the car. He pulled out one of the cookies and handed it to Sean.

Sean's eyes got big as if he was using crack.

"How much for that Unc? Man let me get that. I'll bring you the rest of the money." Sean said handing Grill the six hundred.

"Give me five hundred!"

"What? How much?" Sean said excitedly.

"That goes for five hundred all day!"

"Man I ain't never had no cookie, I want it!" Grill took the five hundred and gave Sean back one hundred dollars.

"You want me to cut it up for you?"

"Hell yea, I ain't cut nothin' that big before!"

Grill started cutting the cookie the same way he cut it up for himself. Sean watched carefully without saying a word. Billy, Trab, and Mark just looked on.

"Twelve hundred!" Grill said putting the twenty's in twelve separate piles. Sean grabbed a piece of the crack and squeezed it. He smiled and threw a piece in the air and let it hit the hood of the car.

"Straight drop!" Grill said.

"Yea that's that Iron," Sean said smiling. Then Sean popped one of the twenty's in half.

"Two dimes," Grill said.

"Shit these twenty's," Sean said smiling.

"Man them dimes," Grill said.

"Not how we serving out there," Sean replied telling Grill he had twenty-four hundred.

"Man a lil money been comin' thru here. I'm trying to get me some work." Trab said. Grill grabbed another cookie, cut it in half then handed it to Trab. Trab grabbed it and handed Grill the one fifty he had in his hand.

"You want me to cut it up for you too?" Grill asked.

"Hell yea!" Grill began to cut Trab half of cookie up. Shika got out the car to pass the blunt and asked could she use the phone. When she got on the phone, you could hear her saying that she'd be somewhere in five minutes.

"Man put me on man," Mark said, Grill acted like he didn't hear him and kept smoking the blunt. Grill would give Mark a few pieces from time to time to trick with, but now he was telling him to put him on. Grill had been noticing him hanging around SipesAve. a little more than usual, so he knew that he was dibbing and dabbling. Grill thought to himself, I might as well put him on too. Grill gave him the other half of cookie.

"You on your own."

"Cut it up," Mark said smiling as Grill grabbed the dope out of his hand and cut up the dope for him. Grill took three more cookies out the box and emptied the money on the hood of the car. He did a quick count of fifteen hundred and took two hundred out. He gave two to Billy and told him to take the rest to his father. He didn't really have a count on how much he gave Billy to give to his dad, but he estimated it to be between four and five thousand. The night had been good. Grill hopped in the car with Shika, and they pulled off. Shika did a quick count of Grill's money as she remembered every sale. She knew he had close to five thousand. In her eyes, he was eating, and he was getting it out the mud. She had a motive to help him advance and build up his clientele. Shika had made thirty-eight hundred herself and the night was still young. Her beeper was still ringing, and she was down to one cookie and a half. After riding around serving all her customers, she asked him, "Where to?"

"Sipes." Shika was hoping he didn't say that. Not after he had just got into a fight. She knew he hurt Benzo's pride and she was scared for him.

"You sure?" Grill just nodded his head. They pulled off Highway 46 on Sipes Ave and crossed over King Rd. From the looks of it, Sipes was dead, and everybody went in. The only thing out was the police, and they were parked in Jimmy Hamp parking lot.

Smokey and Andrews were the cops that were out. All they'd do is sit around and wait to find somebody to harass. Grill leaned all the way back as they passed them and Shika instantly went to stuffing shit in the crevasses of her bra.

"They comin." Shika drove with one hand in her pussy the other one on the steering wheel. She was watching the rearview mirror the entire time.

"I told you not to come up here. Ain't nothing out here but the police? You don't gotta be up here all night!" Shika said angrily because she was in this situation.

Shika turned right as she seen the headlights pull out. Ready for whatever, she made another quick right and pulled into a field where at least ten cars were parked.

The House of Pain was jumping. It was a known gambling spot, but the owner also was the bootleg man. He sold blunts, liquor, and weed after hours. To all the OG's, this was the place to be.

Shika quickly parked and got out. You could see the private property signs as they walked up to the house. Shika walked under the carport and Grill followed. All type of men were standing around, watching sports and gambling.

At one corner sat Stack, Red Lewis, T-Red, and DD from Bookertown. The table was covered with money.

"Bet a thousand more broke ass nigga!" Red Lewis said while talking to Stack.

"You ain't said nothin' Chump!" Stack shouted back to him.

"Nah, bet two thousand more since you back-talkin' me. You a has-been. You ain't been nothin' since the first two years you came down here from Lauderdale." Red Lewis shot back.

"I'm gon' be something after tonight. I'ma break you," Stack said.

"Nigga you can't break the bank, I can only give you some more to come back."

"Foreclosure!" Stack said in his raspy voice as he snorted out of a bill. Shika just smiled, hoping that Stack won.

"Poe ass nigga, how much money you got on you? Pull out everything you got and own nigga and I call it!" Red Lewis shot back looking at Shika who was looking at Stack. Stack quickly did his count. He served Corkey for two grand and taxed lil Grill a grand to cook his work. He served Shika four cookies for two grand, and he put four grand back in his pocket and started with a grand. He had a bet with T-Red for two grand. DD for two grand and Red Lewis for two grand. That was six grand he had on the table covered. He saw through the money in his hand, and he had seven grand there. He was up good! Plus the four grand in his pocket. He had seventeen grand right now. He should quit!

But Stack loved and lived to gamble. This could be his chance to come back and take over. He didn't like the way Red Lewis was talking to him.

"Broke ass nigga don't you hear me talkin' to you! I'ma take your money, then I'ma take Twiggy fine ass. Twiggy likes money, and you ain't got none of that no more!"

"Bet nigga, get it all then," Stack said reaching in his back pocket, pulling out four grand. Plus, the seven grand in his hand throwing them in front of Red Lewis.

Red Lewis picked the money up smiling. He knew he had him when he mentioned Twiggy. Every man had a soft spot. Twiggy was Stack's. Stack had broken him plenty nights earlier in his career, coming from a faster city than Sanford. Stack had the flavor, swag, the drugs, and the money but tables turned.

The locals got the money and the drugs now. Eleven grand Red Lewis counted. He only had five grand on him, and he was down ten grand.

He was already aggravated with Stack because since he had been there, they had been snorting cocaine. Stack was being a crab because he knew he had grade A but didn't let Red Lewis bump his bag. Red Lewis had put ounces of clean out numerous of times when they gambled and never complained, but Stack was acting funny.

Red Lewis decided in his mind that he would send Stack home broke to his wife. He had been there before himself and knew the road Stack was headed down. He could easily get six grand from someone to cover the bet. Everybody knew he was rich.

"Somebody let me get six grand so I can send this nigga on his way. Poe ass ain't got no business around the table," Red Lewis said.

Stack was through talking and had called Red Lewis' bluff and awaited the outcome. How a person waits on the results from an AIDS test is how he pulled out his bill, slouching in his chair and waiting on his verdict.

In a few moments, he would be rich or poor. He might as well prepare his self for Twiggy.

"Let 'em fly. Let 'em come out the box," Stack said.

"Hurry and get this shit over with!" Red Lewis let out.

You could hear a pin drop in the house. Big Peewee pulled the cards out the box and turned them over. Everyone was scared to breathe. The only person talking was Red Lewis.

"Break this clown," he repeated.

The ten of diamond came out first. DD's face frowned because that was the card he needed. Stack said nothing or moved. He counted four grand in his head, the two he put up and plus his two. Big Peewee grabbed his money from DD from the bet they had made. More cards were pulled, but the Jack came out of the box. Stack added another four grand to the four he already had. Big Peewee grabbed his money from T-Red smiling.

"Break this nigga!" Red Lewis said chanting to himself as well to others.

"Tighten up nigga, bet them eight grand right there," Stack said snorting the clean cocaine with his hat turned backward.

"Nah nigga bet ten, broke ass nigga. Mines a call away!"

Big Peewee betted everyone in the house a thousand a pop that Stack's card would hit. The others betted on Red Lewis. He betted the whole eight grand he had on him. The house was quiet as they waited on Stack's reply but he didn't say anything.

253

"Bet nigga, get it all then," Stack said.

Shika sensed Stack was broke, but she needed more work. She walked over to him and asked was he still straight. Usually, he would have cursed her or anyone for that matter that broke his concentration, but he remembered what she had spent earlier. He just nodded his head.

"Samething," Shika said handing over the two grand. Stack threw it at Red Lewis and smiled. Red smiled back and told Big Peewee to take off. Big Peewee pulled the cards out the box, and they tumbled out. The crowd couldn't breathe.

Stack's heart was beating out his chest. They were down to the last cards, and everyone was quiet.

"I wish yo poe ass had some more money!" Red Lewis boasted.

"I will after this, make your phone call!" Stack shot back. Big Peewee flipped the card, and it was the queen of heart. Stack looked in Red-Lewis eyes and knew that it was his card.

"Bang Bang!" Stack said. Reaching for his fake pistol at his side and shooting Red Lewis like an old Western flick.

"Original Desperado!" Stack said smiling. Red Lewis flipped his card over and over revealing the queen, and everybody started smiling. Stack had just hit Red for twenty-three thousand for that play. Big Peewee flipped the other card over, and Stack had the King at the bottom of the deck. Big Peewee collected his money from his side bets and came up with sixteen grand. He was a firm believer that the hand is quicker than the eye. He stacked the deck and knew where he had put the king. Stack and Big Peewee were snorting and gambling buddies. They had got one up on Red Lewis. Big

Peewee would play like he didn't know but he was going to tax Stack later. Manuel Hillary, one of the best gamblers and cheaters, was his father and taught him all the tricks and how to cheat. Stack collected his money as Red Lewis called his wife and told her to bring him fifty more grand.

Moments later, a white car pulled up and handed him the money. The two police cars that had followed Grill and Shika earlier was just pulling off. It was close to five in the morning as Red Lewis came back inside the House of Pain and dumped his money on the table.

"I want this mark head up!" He counted ten grand and threw it to Stack, "Poe nigga this forty grand," Red Lewis continued.

"You want me to break you?" Stack asked eyeing the money.

"Now we got about the same amount of money, except I got plenty of this shit!"

"What you saying?"

"I want you head up on the dice. A thousand a roll!"

"I call that!"

Stack walked to the car and got the six cookies out and gave Shika all six. He told her she owed him a grand. She accepted. Shika and Grill watched the two go at it. They started betting a thousand then a thousand more. Then, five thousand.

After an hour or so, Stack overpowered Red Lewis and took all the money he had. Stack took him a good line of coke out the bill and dropped his hat low then walked out of the house. Everyone started to disperse. Stack was a big winner, and so was Big Peewee.

Stack sat at home with a towel in front of him covering the money with his AK across his lap. He was high as a kite. He was not aware that Twiggy was standing over him looking at him in disgust. As she cleared her throat, Stack's eyes opened.

"See you have to get the fuck on. You don't fuck me right, and you are broke all the time. What happened to the old Stack?" She asked with tears in her eyes.

"He back," Stack said smiling.

"Where?"

"Right in front of you. Pack your shit we goin' down south in the morning."

"Boy can't nobody just be taking off work!" Stack hit the light switch behind her head and snatched the towel off the money. Twiggy dropped on her knees in front of Stack and put his dick in her mouth. She sucked it like she was in love all over again. Right when he was about to cum, there was a knock at the door.

Stack shoved Twiggy's head down and pulled his dick out of her throat. That caused him to cum all in her mouth. Twiggy expertly milked it all out and swallowed everything.

"Who is it?" Stack said clutching his AK, adjusting his pants. Stack thought quickly. He knew Big Peewee had set the deck because he had seen him do it when Red- Lewis started the commotion. Everybody's eyes were on Stack. Stack grabbed five grand off the floor and told Twiggy to go in the room with the rest. Stack opened the door with his finger on the trigger.

"Break bread bitch!" Big Peewee said stepping through the door smiling.

"What chu' talking about?" Replied Stack.

"You know I peeled him for you. Why you think I was betting with you?"

"Well if you bet with me, then you came up too," Stack said bucking up, letting Big Peewee in and shutting the door behind him.

"Still break me off, you knew I was coming!" Big Peewee said continuing to smile.

"I'm going down south in the morning. I got to get right. I'm about to blow!"

"Shit I already knew that and nigga you wrong, we about to blow. Bitch, I'm going with you. Fuck you think I'm 'round here for?" Big Peewee said smiling.

"How much you got?" Stack asked.

"Sixteen grand. Plus, what you gon' give me!"

"So you wanna go to Ft. Lauderdale with me, I'm gon' be down there for about a week."

"Wake me up when we get there. How much for the whole brick?" Big Peewee asked. Stack quickly did his math knowing he could get them for nineteen thousand a piece. He was already going to get five bricks himself.

"Twenty thousand."

"I call that. Give me four grand and we even. You gon' have to feed me and take care of me while we are there."

Stack reached in his pocket, snatching the grand off the five thousand stack. He could feel what type of money it was. Shit, he came out a thousand cheaper. He smiled to himself and handed it to Big Peewee.

"Damn, you a beast! It all started from you robbing lil Grill on the sly for his work." Big Peewee said kicking his shoes off while sitting on the couch.

"What chu' talkin' about?"

"Nigga I ain't slow. Jit needed his work cooked up. I made Lil Corkey buy the cookie from me to get in the game. He said he just bought two from you. Nigga I was just with you, and you was broke. Then he showed me the work. It was the same as mines." Big Peewee breezed through the statement because he had figured it out. Stack just smiled, letting Big Peewee know he was right. He could never count him out.

"Go to sleep Big Peewee!" Stack said snorting from the bill and thinking about his next move. He would buy a total of six kilos and step on them while Big Peewee wasn't watching to turn them into eight. Then present the eight kilos.

Big Peewee started to snore, while Stack walked in the room with Twiggy. He wasn't getting any sleep. He had to make a phone call to his brother down south to order the six kilos and let them know that Stack was back in Miami. He smiled.

Grill had Shika to back the car into the rooming house. As she did the door to his buick opened and out came a very small individual with a hoodie on.

"What up?" The person asked, knocking on the driver's window.

"Who the fuck that is?" Shika said looking at Grill.

At first, Grill didn't know who it was, but as the person knocked on the window, he realized it was the young boy, Dunney.

"Roll the window down."

"What up, what yall want?" Dunney asked.

"Damn jit, you just gon' shortstop my money?"

"Oh, whats up?" Dunney asked, looking embarrassed he got caught coming out of Grill's car.

"Man my grandma kicked me out. I don't got nowhere to go." Grill immediately sympathized with the jit because he too was in the same position at one point.

"Get in," Grill said, and Dunney jumped in the back seat.

"That money boomin'," Dunney said smiling.

"Oh yea, what's saling?" Grill said rolling a blunt.

"This," Dunney said showing off the seven pieces of crack he had left from Fonso.

"Man you slanging this bullshit," Grill said while examining it.

"Shit they like it," Dunney said sorting his money.

"How much is that?" Grill asked passing the weed to Dunney.

"Two-fifty!" Dunney said proudly. Shika caught the exchange and started smiling.

"So what you gon' do next?"

"Go buy me some shoes, and when I sale the rest I'ma re-up with Fonso."

Grill liked what he was hearing, and he liked Dunney. He decided to take Dunney in as his little brother.

"Give me them two fifty," Dunney handed over the money without asking questions.

"First you got to get a good quality product." Grill pulled out one of the cookies and showed Dunney.

"How much for this?" Dunney asked eyeing the cookie like it was a kilo.

"Five hundred."

"So, half for two fifty?"

"Yea."

"I want it."

"Check me out. Jit, you my lil nigga. From now on you cop from me. I'ma give you the whole thing. You gon' owe me two hundred and fifty dollars."

"Hell yea, cut it up for me."

Shika listened to the conversation go back and forth and liked the fact that Grill wanted to see the young jit come up.

As Grill cut the cookie up, Dunney was very observant. He watched him closely.

"Before you bring this out, get rid of this bullshit you already got," Grill said.

Light from another car was pulling in off Sipes Ave into the rooming house. It was Judy.

"Baby I been looking for you. I want the same thing from earlier," Judy said with her eyes wide open. You could tell she was high because her mouth and jaws clinched together. Grill gave her seven hundred and fifty dollars' worth of crack for the five hundred. The money continued to come as morning approached. Grill was down to his last two hundred dollars' worth of crack. Shika was sleeping in the driver's seat while Dunney and Grill kicking game. Grill sold the last two hundred dollars' worth, and Shika demanded that he go home as if they stayed together. Judy pulled up again.

"Samething baby." Grill could have easily told her to follow him on Dixie Ave., but instead, he let Dunney serve her. Dunney did exactly what he saw Grill do to her with the cookie he cut down. He gave her seven hundred and fifty dollars' worth for five hundred. She gave Dunney the money, and he counted it quickly. He handed Grill the money he owed him and pocketed the rest. Grill told Shika he was going to go lay down and she asked, "Where?"

"In there, I got a room," he replied. Shika looked at him in disgust but followed Grill inside refusing to let him out of her sight.

"Hold the fort down jit," Grill said to Dunney, and he just smiled.

When they got into the rooming house, Shika was surprised to see all the people up in the crack house. She was even more surprised that his room was clean. Grill fell in the bed, and so did Shika. They both drifted off, exhausted from pulling their first all-night flight together.

Grill sat on the hood of his car with his young gun, Dunney, on Washington St. contemplating on his next move. Mary J had just paid the money she owed him and told him she was moving from Washington St. She asked if he wanted to take over the rent. He agreed. She then threw in at the end that no hoes were allowed over.

Grill rested the whole day Saturday, after pulling an all-night flight with Shika. He hadn't heard from her since. He had to admit he liked her. She was a hustler and gangster as fuck, and that attracted him to her. He would get with her later and ride and smoke a few with her.

Dunney had moved the whole cookie the same night and had five hundred to spend with a clean face. Grill told him to be patient as he got his head together. Sean was looking for him also. He had called Vickie's house and told him he had a grand, and he was on his way from Oviedo or the Eastside as he liked to call it.

Grill just smoked his blunt and watched two dudes help Mary J move her things out of the house. He would have to get furniture for the place, which he didn't have a clue where to start. The house was two stories. He figured he would need a lot of furniture. While deep in thought, a car pulled up with a kid driving, barely seeing over the stirring wheel. It was his little nephew, Renzo.

"Boy, what the hell you doin' driving this car?" Grill asked smiling the whole time.

"Shit, the keys was in this bitch, so I jumped in!" Renzo said, not knowing it was a grand theft charge he was sitting on.

"Man you going to jail, Mary gon' kill you!" Renzo didn't say anything at the mention of his mother's name. Little did his uncle know, Renzo was a runaway. He had got into it with his stepfather, Spanish Joe, and ran away from home. He had already been gone for three days, and he was only twelve years old. He had done made up his mind that he wasn't going back. He needed a place to stay. He couldn't go to his grandmother, so he had plans to stay with Vickie until he bumped into his uncle. He had been joy riding for two days with the kids in his neighborhood.

"Let me hit the weed!" Renzo said to Dunney, sizing him up. Dunney looked to Grill as if to ask for permission. They looked the same age. Grill gave Dunney the nod, and he passed Renzo the blunt.

"Man, follow me!" Grill said quickly looking at the car in front of Vickie's driveway. Dunney got in the car with Grill and Renzo followed him up to Washington St. and made a left on Beardoll Ave.

Grill parked in the abandoned building and Renzo did too. Grill got out his car, and he began to wipe it down from the inside out with an old t-shirt he had in the trunk of his car. Renzo and Dunney just watched. He told them to get in the car.

On the way back, they stopped by the store to buy new locks for the house that Mary J let him take over. When they got there, they noticed nothing was left but the kitchen appliances and a living room set. Mary J had told Grill that he could have it.

Just as they were changing the locks, Sean pulled up. Grill got in the car with him and went to Dixie Ave. He got the shoebox, which contained his last ten cookies and went to his new spot on Washington Ave.

"Man, they love that shit in Oviedo! They call it Iron Mike Tyson," Sean continued, "Mike Tyson, Mike Tyson!" He said in a funny voice. He gave Grill a thousand dollars and told him to save him four of them.

After Sean left, Grill took the five hundred from Dunney and sold him another cookie. Then, he fronted him another. Renzo and Dunney immediately hit it off. Grill made up in his mind that he would sale two more cookies wholesale and grind the rest of it out.

Shika laid in her bed thinking about Grill. She couldn't believe he was so young and getting that type of money on the corner. He was a little rough around the edges but nothing she couldn't fix. She smiled to herself as she masturbated thinking about his tongue between her legs. She was going to turn him out, and it was only a matter of time before she'd make him hers. She climaxed thinking about Grill, then got in the shower and began to start her day.

Meat, Bango, Lil Gee, and Daddy-Low were at the Paint and Body Shop, known as Hanson. Spring Break was this weekend, and they were bringing their cars out. Hanson had met the deadline, and the Midway boys were done. They all played with their Hydraulics why Hanson explained to them what not to do.

CHAPTER 14

ANOTHER LEVEL, WEIGHT MONEY

Grill was riding by the Paint and Body Shop when he saw Daddy-Low standing outside. He pulled up in the shop.

"What's good homie?" Grill asked.

"Just chillin just got this bitch out." Daddy-Low had a Spanish gold on a Delta 88, with triple gold Dayton's on it with flakes all through it. The paint was still wet while Daddy-Low played with the hydraulics.

Meat, Bango, and Lil Gee walked out.

"God damn, Grill 'em up thug!" Lil Gee said smiling. Grill smiled back wondering why Lil Gee was always smiling.

"Damn Grill, why you did Benzo like that the other night?" Bango asked laughing. Before he could respond,

Daddy-Low replied, "Shit he was fuckin' with the man!" Meat just watched as they talked amongst each other.

Grill walked around and inspected all their vehicles and was satisfied with the results.

"Your time next up Grill," Meat said.

"Yea I know. I'm thinking about dropping this bitch off now!" Grill said excitedly, shocked that Meat knew his new nickname.

"Nah, not yet. Wait 'til after spring break. You don' missed the main event," Meat said.

"Well, what's up with the work tip?" That was music to Meat's ears.

"What chu tryin' to do?"

"Shit, it depends. What you got? I want soft, but you gotta cook it for me."

Meat wasn't really into the weight game full time. He just sold it from time to time. He was waiting on the right connect before he grabbed some big shit. Usually, he just grabbed a brick for himself and his young guns.

He would cook up a quarter kilo for Lil Gee and Bango. Who was buying four and a half ounces a piece? He'd cook nine for himself, flip that, then do it again.

"What chu wanna get? Four and a half ounces are going for three grand and a quarter is going for fifty-five hundred," Meat said to Grill.

"I want to get the quarter, and I want you to cook me eighteen cookies. Just like this!" Grill said reaching in his car, pulling out one of the cookies that Stack cooked for him.

Meat immediately recognized the cooking style, and he also knew it wasn't anything but nine or ten grams in the cookie that Stack cooked. He also knew that it was the same dope that Teke had. But what he didn't know was that Grill had enough money to buy two bricks and that he was Teke's co-defendant. He was just amazed at how fast Grill was coming up. He already was buying more than his young guns.

Meat knew he must pull him on board, so to start things off right he would give him a cushion.

"When you ready?"

"I'm ready now."

"Meet me in the circle by Seminole in an hour. Come by yourself!"

"Bet!"

Meat got in the car with Bango and Lil Gee and told them to drop him off at his apartment in the circle. Meat sat in the back seat making fun of Lil Gee and Bango about how lil Grill was passed them.

Meat went into his apartment, pulled the brick from behind the stove and put his beakers on the table. He dropped twelve grams in nine beakers. He whipped up nine straight drop cookies. He kept two grams for himself off every half ounce. He snatched them out the water and repeated the process. The first nine was drying when there was a knock on the door.

"Knock, Knock!" Meat grabbed the .357 off the counter and walked to the door. He peeped through the peephole and opened the door for Grill.

"Go get that cookie you showed me out the car," Meat said. Grill went and got the cookie and walked back towards the apartment. Meat walked him towards the kitchen and showed him the nine cookies that were dry. They all were thicker, and the same size in width as the cookie Stack made for him. Grill instantly saw the difference.

"Damn, you could cook way better than Stack!" Grill said innocently. Meat decided to not put Grill on game about Stack. Instead, he remained quiet. Meat took the other nine out and smoked a blunt with Grill as they dried.

Meat liked the kid and decided then and there he would be his new top gun. He went over a few things with Grill about the game and told him that he was riding shotgun with him to Spring Break in Daytona. Grill gave Meat the fifty-five hundred and dapped him up, then told him that he'd be ready Saturday morning.

Standing on Sipes Ave, Lil Gee asked Bango, "What chu' think he got from Meat?"

"Man ain't no telling. I told you what he was worth when he brought the car and got the gold teeth."

"That lil motherfucker had Sipes on lock the other day!"

"Hell yea, like he had unlimited work."

Shika pulled up on Sipes Ave. and parked her car next to her cousin.

"What's up cousin? Ain't nobody seen Stack?" Shika asked.

"Nah, what you trying to get?" Lil Gee asked.

"I'm tryin' to pay him his money and don't want that bullshit you got."

"Yea right!" Gee said smiling.

"Where my tender at?" Shika asked returning the smile. She fell right into Lil Gee's game. They were cousins, and they acted just alike.

Lil Gee automatically knew who she was talking about, so he decided to play along.

"Spend with me right now, or I will hate on you so bad and run him off. I mean it cuz!" He said, a smile covering his whole face.

"Man you with that bullshit, and if you do, I'll tell Daddy-Low you fuckin' his old lady!" Shika said smiling, enjoying the fact that she had him by the balls. She loved the discomforted look in his face.

Daddy-Low and Lil Gee were really close friends but Daddy-Low's baby mama, Argie, was Lil Gee's ex-girlfriend. Daddy-Low was a beast. They called him the "War Daddy" because he was six-foot-four inches of straight pressure. If you were on his side, you were good but if you wasn't then that was a problem that you would not be able to handle.

Daddy-Low's whole family was considered crazy. He was raised up under his brother, Warlord, who was Teke's, other right-hand man. He stood six-foot-six and three hundred pounds. Being raised up under Warlord, you had no choice but to be an animal.

Warlord kept the other side of town in check ten years ago. He was known to work a single shotgun like it was an automatic. He would reload it faster than you could shoot with your automatic while holding the shells in his mouth, screaming out "Warlord," as he shot, emptied and reloaded. Everybody called Daddy-Low "Lil Warlord"! Lil Gee was terrified of Daddy-Low.

As Shika threatened him, Daddy-Low was coming up the street. Lil Gee looked from Shika to Daddy-Low. Shika watched the exchange and asked, "You wanna play?"

"Man stop playing so much," Lil Gee said terrified.

"Nah, you started it. I wasn't fucking with you," Shika said enjoying Gee's discomfort.

"Man you know that man would kill me if he found out."

"You gon' get the jit for me?" Shika asked quietly as Daddy-Low approached.

"Yea man."

"When?"

"Tonight."

"I swear to God Gee if you don't get him to me tonight. I'm going to tell." Shika said with a huge smile. Daddy-Low was up on them, and the first thing he did was slap Gee across the head.

"Man quit playing all the time," Lil Gee said.

"Freaky Shika, What up?" Daddy-Low asked. Lil Gee slid out of reach and got behind Daddy-Low's back making funny faces.

"That god damn Gee ain't shit!" Gee instantly stopped the funny faces when he heard his name. Daddy-Low snapped his head to see Lil Gee, and he put his head down as if he was looking for something.

Now, Shika was wearing the smile. Daddy-Low turned back around to look at Shika, and she straightened her face. Shika looked over Daddy-Low's shoulder, and Lil Gee made a gesture as if he was humping the air.

"Let me spend fifty with you, to catch my people." Daddy-Low gave Shika a double up.

"Cuz take me to go get me something to eat," Lil Gee said with a smile. They enjoyed the game they were playing on Daddy-Low.

In the car, Lil Gee told Shika that if she told he would also tell that she let him use her house to fuck his baby momma. Shika was scared of Daddy-Low too. Lil Gee sensed it again to make sure it was fear he smelled.

Grill pulled up on Dixie Ave, and Billy was on the side of the house cutting hair along with Pistol Pete. They were the only two not in the drug game, the rest in their age brackets had fell victims to the streets.

Mark and Sean pulled up listening to UGK, Pocket Full of Stones. Mark jumped out of the car doing some crazy dance, and everyone laughed.

"What y'all two up too?" Grill asked.

"Making money, what chu' think?" Mark said, flashing a fat knot of fives and ones. He shook his pill bottle, and Grill just smiled at his nephew.

"How much that is?"

"Three fifty," Mark replied, "One fifty more, I'm going to get me a grill," Mark said doing his funny dance.

"Sean what's up man, how you put up with this nigga?"

"Man that nigga crazy, a straight ass!" Sean said.

Mark looked at his Unc and said, "His name ain't Sean no more, it's Sweet Jones."

"Grill looked from one to the other and seen that Sean had improved.

"Ole Sweet Jones," Billy said still cutting hair.

"Mark you need to flip that money before you get them gold teeth. I'm not giving you nothing else."

"That's what I told him. I'm going to go get me some too. But I ain't goin' broke tryin' to get them," Sweet Jones said.

"Alright, you gon' let me get a cookie for three fifty?" Mark asked, winking his eye at Sweet Jones.

"Bitch you crazy, you can owe me one fifty."

"I call that!" Grill went in the car and grabbed the shoebox out from under the seat and walked back on the side of the house. He sat the box on his Delta 88 and gave Mark a cookie.

"Bruh, let me get a haircut." Grill said to Billy.

"You next." After Billy gave Grill a haircut, he told him he moved into Shannon Dora Apartments near the county jail and Grill slipped him the money Mark gave him.

"Bet that up!" Billy said cleaning his clippers. Grill handed him the shoe box and told him to put it in the trunk.

"You know Renzo don' ran away?"

"I know, he at my house now."

"Doing what?" "Shit, he gon' drive Mary crazy." Before he could reply, Trab pulled up. Everybody called Trab the reverend because he would speak Truth.

"Rev what up?" Grill asked.

"Just the man I'm looking for."

"What's good?"

"You still got some of that?"

"Yea, you got to give me a sermon first." Grill said dead serious.

"Man gon' on with that bullshit," Reverend said laughing.

After grabbing something to eat for herself, she grabbed extra food and confused Lil Gee.

"Who in the hell you tryin' to feed? The homeless?" Lil Gee asked.

"My in-laws," Shika said flashing her trademark smile. She pulled up on Dixie Ave. "Damn, I'm late on the play. You already making progress," Lil Gee said when he noticed where she pulled up at.

Shika got out the car like she owned the place and everybody got quiet as she approached.

"I bet you ain't ate all day," she said, handing Grill the box of chicken with a smile. She must have read his mind because he was about to order pizza.

"Thank you," he said with a smile.

"Billy! What's up brother-in-law?"

Billy just smiled, showing his dimples, knowing Shika was intruding on his brother's space. He would play along.

"Sister-in-law, what's good?" he said snatching some of the Chicken from Grill.

Lil Gee was walking up on the crew.

"Pop belly sixteen," Billy said laughing at Lil Gee. They were old classmates.

"You think everything funny." Everyone back in the day called Lil Gee that.

"Pistol Pete, let me get a haircut," While Pistol Pete cut Lil Gee hair, Shika asked Grill was he going to ride with her tonight. He told her to come get him off Washington St.

Stack and Big Peewee were back in the city. They had gone to Fort. Lauderdale. Stack bought six kilos, five for himself and one for Big Peewee. Big Peewee attempted to watch him close, but Stack knew the hand was quicker than the eye.

Stack had made Big Peewee wait at his mother's house while he went to Miami with his brother to Little Haiti to meet the Haitian connect. He bought the six kilos. He then stopped in Carol City to the flea market off 183rd St. and bought two more bricks of Isotol cut.

Once he examined the kilos during the purchase, he knew he could add two kilos easily. He stopped to his brother's apartment and took out 250 grams out of each brick and put a quarter of the Isotol in each one and shook it up. He did this until it was a good mixture. He had easily turned six kilos into eight, just like that. He rapped them up and pulled up to his mother's house.

Big Peewee was waiting outside with Stack's relatives. Stack talked for a minute and told Twiggy he was ready. He had been down south for a few days. His mission was done. Stack told Big Peewee they fronted him two more for twenty-one thousand, and he would front him one. Big Peewee accepted, not believing he had two kilos.

In the kitchen on Center St. Big Peewee watched Stack closely. It didn't matter to Stack because the damage was already done. He slowly put fourteen grams on the scale for Big Peewee, then put it in the bowl. The cookies came out perfect to Stack. He had hit it just right.

"Knock, Knock, Knock!" That was the sound coming from Stack's back door. He peeped out the blinds and saw that it was Shika. Bingo thought Stack. He was dead broke. He walked outside.

"What's up Freaky Shika?" he said.

"Here go yo money, and I want six of them!" Stack took the money, but he had different plans.

"I'm in the kitchen right now, come back when it get dark. I'ma front you four more."

'Shit you must got a brick in there," she said fishing for information. Stack just smiled as he thought to himself if only you knew. Shika got in her car and pulled off.

Grill was on Washington St. in front of his spot smoking a blunt with Dunney and Renzo when Shika pulled up. He got in the car with her, and she asked for his pager number. She wrote it down at least 20 times, and he was confused.

"Why you did that?"

"So you won't be standing on no damn corner all day. Every time my pager goes off for the hundred, I'm going to let you make twenty dollars, and if it go off for fifty, I'm going to let you make ten."

"That ain't no money."

"I know, but it's so you won't be riding for nothing. Every new person we meet you give them your number. You got to get clientele. A boss don't hang on no damn corner."

Grill liked that she called him a boss. It never dawned on him that he needed his own personal clientele. So he agreed. Before nine o clock, he had made a hundred dollars off Shika and snatched three customers from the Handy Way gas station. They had already spent three hundred with him and kept paging him to come back and serve them. This was another level to the game.

"The trick is transportation and quality work." Shika was certified in the eyes of Grill.

"I see."

"And always get to them on time," she boasted.

Stack was tired. He was taking a short break as he'd like to call it. He had cooked seventy- two cookies for Big Peewee and charged him thirty-five hundred dollars. He also fronted Big Peewee a brick, so he was in the hole.

He also cooked ten cookies for Shika and had nine ounces cooked, waiting on Daddy-Low. At this point, Stack didn't need to do any footwork because that's what Big Peewee was for. He had enough money to sit on and supply his habit. *He liked it this way,* he thought as he smiled to himself.

A knock interrupted his thought. Stack assumed it was Shika when he opened the door, but it was Daddy-Low.

"Low!"

"What's up?"

"Come in." As he let Daddy-Low come in, he saw Shika's car bend the corner. He held the door open for her.

Shika came in and seen Daddy-Low, "Well, well, well. If it isn't ol' Daddy-Low!" Shika said. Daddy-Low just smiled being caught in Stack's house. Stack gave Shika her package, and she said, "I should rob yo' ass."

"Shit, fuck around and get robbed. I know you getting' something big!" Daddy-Low shot back, laughing at how fast she had got in her car.

Once Shika got in her car she immediately went to meet all the people she had lined up waiting for her. She at least had five hundred dollars on hold. Grill easily made him a hundred and had two hundred on hold himself.

They rode through the night, just the two of them, catching customers and meeting new people. Grill's pager started to compete with hers, so Shika decided to toy with him.

"In a minute, you're not making no more money off me." Grill knew it was coming so he just smiled.

"Let's go home. I want to cook you something to eat." She threw a glance at him to see if he caught the *home* thing. He did but didn't acknowledge it.

Shika lived off Sanford Ave, in a nice one-bedroom apartment on a drug-infested strip. The apartment was laid from top to bottom. Everything was new with gold and black interior. It was very nice and cozy, by far the cleanest and nicest place that Grill had been in. Grill heard the bath water running and knew someone was there. He immediately clutched his pistol.

"Nobody but Argie," Shika said to relax him.

"Make yourself at home," Shika said throwing him the remote. She headed to the kitchen to put the cookies up that she had just bought from Stack. Argie came out of the bathroom with a towel wrapped around her head. She was a thick red bone. "So you must be Grill?" She said giggling in her northern accent. Grill just smiled back.

"Pleased to meet you. I've heard so much about you from a lot of different people," Argie said.

"Oh, yea?"

"Yes, indeed," Argie said attempting to play mind games.

"Argie, leave him alone. I did not bring him over here so that he could get grilled by you!" Shika said peeking her head out the kitchen.

"Hoe, shut up! I can talk to my friend."

"Alright bitch, I'ma tell Daddy-Low you still fuckin' with Gee," Shika said smiling.

"Bitch you wouldn't dare!"

"Keep fucking with my man then!" Shika said laying claim on him.

"Nah, it's cool. What's up? Argie is it?" Grill jumped in.

"Yep, the one and only. How old are you?" Argie asked.

"Fifteen, bout to be sixteen though."

"Shika I didn't know you liked them so young!"

"Bitch, I'm only nineteen!"

"But you an old nineteen!" Argie said laughing as Grill joined her laughing at the comment. He could tell that they were close friends.

"I just seen Daddy-Low," Shika said smiling, waiting on Argie to explode.

"Bitch don't nobody care about no Daddy-Low, with his ugly ass!"

"Hoe you do care and tell him that!"

"Bitch, I will and have. He fucked my baby all the way up. Damn baby look just like him!" They all started laughing.

"Where your cousin? You seen my man out there in Midway?" She was asking Shika but looking at Grill to see what type of time he was on.

"Of course, I seen his fat ass that bitch get on my nerve."

"I'm calling him over tonight," Argie said with excitement in her eyes.

"Alright I don' told both of yall! If Daddy-Low find out, he gon' kill both of yall!" Shika said smiling and shaking her head.

"Girl, ain't nobody scared of Daddy-Low! She said, halfway shouting and looking directly at Grill. He just smiled and rolled him a blunt.

Lil Gee was on Sipes Ave, standing next to Daddy-Low and the boys when his pager went off. He looked at the number and didn't recognize it. He dug in his pocket and walked to the pay phone and called the number back.

Grill had just got the phone from Argie to check some of the numbers that had been paging him. The caller ID indicated that someone was on the other line. Grill looked at the number and recognized it immediately. It was the pay phone on Sipes Ave.

"You paged someone?" Grill asked.

"Yea," she said as he handed her the phone.

"What's up?"

Lil Gee realized who it was by her voice and looked at Daddy-Low, then switched the phone to his other ear as if Daddy-Low could hear him.

"Yea," Lil Gee said in his cool voice. His eyes were glued to Daddy-Low.

"You coming through to get this pussy or what?" Grill just looked at her as she boldly said that to Lil Gee. Gee watched Daddy-Low serve someone before he finally responded, "You tryin' to get me killed, you gon' swallow it all?"

Argie could hear him smiling through the phone, "Don't I always?" She responded back to him. Lil Gee's dick instantly got hard.

"Man, get yo cakin' ass off the phone. You got the line all blocked up!" Daddy-Low said, walking towards Lil Gee.

"You still at cuz house?"

"Yea."

"She there?"

"Yea."

"Grill over there?" Argie looked at Grill before she answered, "Yea, how'd you know that?" He hung up.

Lil Gee had plans. He hoped to make Grill his righthand man. He wasn't a flat foot worker. He was an *all the sense* hustler. He wouldn't out hustle you, just out think you.

He knew Meat had recruited Grill, so somebody's position was going to be taken. He doubted that it was his and he wanted to let Grill in on the secret about him and Argie. He smiled to himself thinking about how he would use this to his advantage.

"What the hell you smiling for? Somebody gon' kill you for fuckin' around with their ole lady," Daddy-Low said.

"Yea, right. That's why I got big ass homeboy's like Daddy-Low. You gon' let somebody kill me?"

"Shouldn't be fuckin' people, ole lady," Daddy-Low said smiling while dialing numbers on the pay phone. Lil Gee just walked away, singing Down Low by R Kelly.

Shika brought Grill a plate and sat down beside him. They ate and watched TV. Both of their pagers were going off rapidly.

"See that's how you chill, do what you want and make money," she said.

"I see," Grill replied.

"Everybody that's pagin' you meet them across the street at the Chevron."

"Alright!"

After eating, Shika went into her bedroom, got her some night clothes and preceded to the bathroom. She ran her some bath water and took her a long hot bubble bath. When she got out, she lotioned her body with peach Victoria's Secret and put her Deborah Cox CD in on repeat. The song she wanted to fuck him off of was How Did You Get Here because she swore to herself that she was done with all the love shit, but now she was in love again.

Shika had already made up in her mind that she was going to fuck, suck and lick him from head to toe, without missing a spot. She smiled to herself thinking about how she was about to turn him out.

"Grill come here." Grill walked to the room where Shika was. She was laid across the bed, smoking a blunt. The lights were dimmed low.

"There go a washcloth and towel. Take a shower." Grill grabbed his things and jumped in the shower. After he freshened up, he walked back into the room.

"Lay down on your stomach!" Grill looked for his clothes. She had them folded up on a chair next to the bed with his gun on top of them. Once he turned his focus towards her, he noticed that she was on her knees on the bed. Grill did as he was instructed and laid on the bed naked.

Shika poured lotion on his entire body and started to rub the lotion in, starting with his feet. She then went up to his calves, to his butt and then back.

When she got to his back, she straddled him and rubbed his back until she felt the tension release off his body. He was relaxed.

"Turn over," she said in a seductive voice. She spent around the opposite way, giving him a full view of her plumped ass and began to perform a pedicure on his feet. This was something Grill was not used to, and he enjoyed it. He leaned up against the headboard and fired up a blunt she had in the ashtray.

Shika spent back around and continued to rub lotion all over him while admiring his body. He was slim and cut, and that's how she liked them.

"Stand up," Shika demanded, and Grill did as he was told. She kneeled in front of him, slid his boxers down, and started massaging his dick. The harder it got, the more she smiled, thinking of what she was going to do with him.

She started off by slapping herself in the forehead with his penis, as she played with her pussy. Her pussy was so wet from the anticipation, and she was amazed by the size of his dick. Then she grabbed it with two hands, stroking it with a twisting motion while looking into his eyes.

"Nigga you better not dare take your eyes off me! You hear me?"

She pulled at his dick, stretching it to its full length. Shika coughed up spit and aimed it directly on his shaft as she slowly worked the spit all over. She made sure it was good and wet. She put her hand on the base of his dick and stomach and relaxed her throat muscles and attempted to deep throat.

She tried to stuff the whole thing in her mouth, but she caught herself gagging. Tears were running out the corners of her eyes, but she continued to look up at him. With a full mouth of dick, she knew she had him! Grill held the blunt with his left hand, and she placed his other hand on top of her head, directing him to push her head down on his dick. He quickly caught on and started thrusting his hips into her mouth.

Slob and spit were seeping out of Shika's mouth as she snatched her head away, still holding his dick. She then stroked him in a twisting motion.

"This my dick, you hear me?" She said, slapping the dick over her forehead. Grill dick was so hard it had a mind of its own. She released it, watching it bounce up. The sight of his dick seemed to excite her. She attacked it. With one smooth motion of her hand, she stroked him and cleaned the entire slob and spit off his dick and stroked the head, where her opened mouth waited.

She spat back on his dick and sucked and stroked him fast. When she saw he couldn't take any more, she instructed him to lie down. Grill laid on his back and looked up at her. Shika mounted Grill and put a pillow behind the headboard to stop the noise from what was about to occur. She eased herself on his dick. Once she got it all inside, she placed both of her hands on his chest for leverage. She looked down at him and started to ride him. She started slowly at first and then quickened the pace. Before long she was riding Grill faster than he had ever been riding. It must have been feeling good to her because she was digging her nails into his chest with a death grip. Shika wasn't riding him up and down, she had his dick buried, and she was going back and forth.

Grill grabbed her ass and met her thrust for thrust. The pillow that Shika had placed earlier had fallen from all the commotion, causing the headboard to bang loudly against the wall right above the window.

"This my dick you understand me?" Shika said as her hands moved from his chest to his neck. She was choking him and crying. Her face carted into sheer bliss.

Lil Gee was standing outside the window about to knock on the door, but he couldn't stop himself from smiling. You could hear Shika and Grill from a mile away. He stayed there to listen for a second as the headboard slapped into the wall. He finally knocked on the door.

"Knock, knock, knock!" The door swung open. It was Argie.

"Damn, Grill puttin' it down on cuz!"

"Shit, Shika probably rapin' that boy." They both laughed.

Shika felt a climax coming on. It felt like a big one. Grill dug deeper from the bottom, slamming her into his dick. She dug her nails in him and rode faster. Grill loved the look on her face, so he pulled her into him. He timed the thrust just as she came forward.

"I'm going to cum all over that dick, Daddy! Make me cum all over it," Shika screamed and cried at the same time. It felt like a dam had broken loose. A watery, warm sensation squirted all over Grill. Shika fell forward, exhausted. Never before had she squirted.

"I'm cumming all over you!"

Grill was excited but wasn't finished. He had the stamina and wanted to go longer. As Shika leaned forward, he pushed her head down by the crook of her neck and held it forcefully. He shoved his hips up fast and hard, squeezing her ass with his other hand.

"Yes, Daddy! This your pussy!"

"I can't hear you!" Grill said, feeling himself.

"It's yours," Shika said still cumming. The orgasms felt like forever. Grill had her head pinned in his hand. He released her, grabbed her ass cheeks and pulled her down and came inside her. They both clung to each other for dear life. It was by far the best fuck for both of them. They had that chemistry!

Argie was riding Lil Gee reverse cowgirl. Her eyes were closed for all she was worth. Lil Gee heard the bedroom door open, but he didn't warn Argie. He just kept going.

Grill had to use the restroom after the tiresome fuck he just had with Shika. He opened the door and immediately heard moans coming from the living room.

Lil Gee looked towards the bedroom door as he heard it open and locked eyes with Grill. Grill looked at Argie, whose eyes were closed. Lil Gee gave a thumbs up at Grill and started making funny faces while Argie's eyes were still closed. Grill started laughing.

Argie's eyes popped open at once. She looked at Grill, grabbed the blanket and covered herself in one quick motion and flung her head to look at Lil Gee. He was smiling as usual.

Grill went in the bathroom, and when he came out, Lil Gee was behind Argie fucking her butt ass naked. Grill laughed all the way back to the room.

"What?" Shika asked, already knowing the answer.

"That damn Gee crazy!"

"Tell me about it," Shika rolled a blunt, and halfway through the blunt, they heard a knocking on the door. Shika looked at Grill with fear in her eyes. She didn't know who it could be. Grill sensed it and grabbed his gun.

"Who you think it is?" Grill asked.

"Don't know!" Shika said as the knocking continued.

Shika started to peep out the blinds when her room door swung open.

"Bitch that's Daddy-Low!"

"Girl you better stop playin'," Shika said laughing.

"I swear to God!" He knocked again, "Pussy ass hoe, I know you in there!"

Argie grabbed her mouth, and Shika started putting on clothes.

"Where is Gee?"

"His scary ass is in the kitchen!" Daddy-Low started beating the door, "I'ma kick this bitch down if you don't open up!"

"What the fuck we gon' do? Shika he will kick it down!" Argie was terrified. Grill walked into the living room looking for Lil Gee.

"Bruh, what's up?" Lil Gee said, trying to act as though he wasn't scared.

"What you gon' do boy?" Grill asked enjoying the look on his face.

"Shit, we gon' get in the attic." Grill caught we and seen Lil Gee had made him his codefendant.

"Shit, I ain't going in no attic." Grill said showing Lil Gee his gun.

"Man you can't kill nobody from Midway!"

"I ain't fuckin' his hoe!" Grill explained.

"But you know about it!"

"But I ain't fuckin' her!" Grill repeated himself.

"Don't matter with that fool, you just as guilty."

Daddy-Low banged on the door even louder this time. Shika and Argie ran into the kitchen. They burst out laughing at the look of Lil Gee's ass half way up the latter that led to the attic.

"Man I'm just gon' open the door before he kick my shit down."

"You better not open that fuckin' door. Are you crazy?" Lil Gee said looking horrified.

Grill looked at Lil Gee and couldn't help but laugh. The nigga was scared to death. Shika wasn't going to open the door but kept playing like she was.

"Come down cuz, he gone!" Shika said with the biggest smile on her face.

"Come down my ass! He's slick. He in them bushes, he ain't goin' nowhere!" Lil Gee said looking down at everyone from the attic, smiling.

"Come on bae, that's their problem," Shika said, leading Grill back into her room. Shika told Grill how she never came like that. It was as if she pissed on the bed. Grill told her it was his turn and he took Shika and dominated her all night.

Lying in bed the next morning. Shika woke up feeling good.

"You want breakfast?" Shika asked rubbing on Grill's chest.

"Yea."

"After I get mines!" Shika grabbed his dick and sucked him until he came in her mouth. She swallowed every drop and got up smiling. She was sure of her fuck game and knew she had him to herself.

CHAPTER 15

IN LOVE WITH THE GAME, AND HER

Grill watched Shika back away and realized then and there that he was in love. She completed him in the grown man department. Grill and Shika fucked and made money off their pagers for two days straight. Before he finally made her take him to Midway to re-up.

"I'll hit you up later," Grill said, getting out on Washington St. It was Friday, and Spring Break Daytona was popping tomorrow. Grill decided he would spend some money for Spring Break since he didn't have a car in the game.

"I got the five hundred. Plus, eight hundred more." Dunney said smiling. Grill just looked at the youngster, knowing that Dunney was going to be a problem.

"Man, we need some fire out here like this," Grill's nephew Renzo said referring to Grill's gun.

"Why?"

"People act like they wanted to take Dunney shit!" Grill thought of this, but he didn't want to be responsible if they killed someone for nothing.

"Alright, I'll see what I can do."

"You know they closed the rooming house down. Slap say they pushing it down," Dunney said.

"Oh yea, I haven't heard that!"

"Shit, I been around there and told everybody to come around here," Dunney said devilish. Grill smiled back because he liked what he had heard.

"I'll be right back." Grill jumped in his car, went on Dixie Ave. and grabbed five grand and all his work out of the Delta 88. When he got back, Sweet Jones was pulling up at the same time.

"What up Unc?"

"Chillin."

"Here go another grand."

"Bet!"

"I got my dawgs in the car, and they want to get some too, you got some more?"

"Let me get you out the way first."

They went inside the spot. Sweet Jones had made two grand off one cookie. He was bussing heads in Oviedo.

"Where you been slangin' that shit at?"

"Man, I got them all on a pager." Sweet Jones said.

Grill looked at him and realized Sweet Jones was quicker to the pager game than him. Grill opened the show box and handed him the four he paid for and four additional.

"Ain't no looking back from here!"

"I see you tryin' to take off!"

"I'ma go get me a grill, I'll be through before Friday to bring some of this money I owe you."

"Ain't no pressure."

"You got some for my dawgs?"

"Send them in." Three young guys came in with Sweet Jones. They were all from Oviedo. Each of them had five hundred a piece and was ready to spend. Grill served them all. Dunney sat in the cut, waiting for his turn.

"Let me get that cash." Grill said as Dunney handed him everything. Grill handed him four cookies.

"You owe me a grand," Grill advised Dunney.

"Bet!"

"You want me to cut it up for you?"

"Nah, I got it." Grill just smiled, knowing the kid was taking off. Grill cut up a half of cookie and gave it to Renzo.

"You on your own."

The remaining cookies he took inside Vickie's house and told her to keep an eye on Dunney and Renzo. Grill drove down Sipes Ave and seen his crew, Corkey, Ratty, and Bango.

"What's up with y'all?

"Chillin'," they all replied in unison.

"Y'all gon' get right or what for Spring Break?"

"Let's ride," Corkey said. They piled in the car and drove towards Orlando. They pulled in the Magic Mall. After walking through the mall, Grill stopped at the same jewelry store that Trucker took him to. He looked at the jewelry and decided that he was going to get him a set.

"How much Mommy?" Grill asked pointing at a necklace, where the cross looked broken.

"Too much for you! Six grand," moving it out of his reach.

"You think so?"

"Yea, that's an Avalon, and the diamonds are real US diamonds."

"I got five grand, Mommy!" She quickly did a count, knowing she was winning regardless.

"Where the money?"

"I want the bracelet too," Grill added.

"Three thousand, but I'll give it to you for two thousand total."

Grill dropped the seven thousand on the table, and Mommy snatched it up and counted it quickly.

"I clean for you," she said with a huge smile.

Around the corner at another shop, Corkey had dropped two grand down on him a necklace, and he had already purchased a set of gold Daytons. He just had to get him a car.

They went to the mall and got all types of clothes and went back to Sanford. Grill gave his things to Vickie and decided then and there, he was going to pull an all-night flight.

He cut up two of the cookies and drove to Sipes Ave. and backed into Jimmy Hamp. He wrote down his number twenty times and sat them on the hood of his car. Stack pulled up, then Big Peewee, and then Meat. Little did Grill know, all these people were banging for Boot's spot in the hood. They all were trying to be the next weight man. Stack was in the lead by far, with Meat close on his trail money wise.

Out of all the cut up money that was coming, it was divided five ways between Daddy-Low, Lil Gee, Grill, Corkey, and Bango. The money started coming all night, and so did the crowd of on-lookers. Grill's pager kept going off and he would leave to meet his customers and come back to the block. The ones he had caught that night, he put them on his pager.

Big Peewee served Corkey and all the other people that wanted weight. Meat had Lil Gee and Bango. Grill just worked his pager. He went on Washington St. and cut down two more cookies and came back. The money was booming.

He had easily made twenty-five hundred from his pager and being on Sipes Ave.

His pager kept beeping all night, so he wasn't on Sipes Ave. as much. He was starting to get his clientele up and lots of it! When he came back on Sipes, the police were everywhere. He kept it going to Washington St., to his spot.

Once he got there, he backed in his driveway. As he was listening to Juvenile, Dunney and Renzo came outside.

"What yall lil bad motherfuckers up to?"

"Just tryin' to get this money."

"Get in." Grill smoked blunt after blunt with them and flashed all the cars that came down Washington St. The money was coming from everywhere. Grill's pager kept going off. In the process of serving them, he would meet new people. He swung by the rooming house and directed all the traffic to Washington St.

Before the sun came up, they rode around. They were the only ones up, which made money come harder. At four in the morning, Grill's pager kept going off. Four hundred here, two hundred there. Money was on repeat.

Before long, Washington St. was like a drive-thru. Now, everyone that paged him, he told to come to Washington. Grill didn't receive a page from Shika, so he dozed off on his couch.

Dunney and Renzo were still up. Dunney took charge and caught everything that came. When Grill woke up that next morning, there were knocks at his door. He looked outside, and his car was gone. Before he could react, it was pulling back up, and Dunney was driving as he backed in the yard.

"Man, where the fuck yall been?"

"Had to go serve your people."

The dude at the door had fifty dollars, and Renzo served him.

"All that work you had in that pill bottle gone," Dunney said throwing him his keys and his money.

"And here go your beeper," Grill liked the lil nigga. He was a boss. He didn't have to tell him what to do.

"Damn jit, you about your business!"

"Straight up!" Dunney said smiling.

Right as they were talking, they heard a scraping sound like something was dragging on the pavement. They all looked in the direction. It was a red Cadillac on three wheels coming up the road with one in the air. It was Meat. He stopped in front of Grill's spot and dropped the car.

"What's good?"

"Chillin'," Grill replied.

"I'm 'bout to hit the car wash. I'll be back to get you!"

"I'll be ready!" Meat jacked the front up and pulled off.

Grill grabbed the four cookies out of his shoebox and gave them to Dunney along with his pager and keys. He gave Renzo the.38 pistol that his father gave him and told them to only leave the spot when it was necessary.

Grill threw on his white and yellow Tommy shirt, a blue and white Tommy Hilfiger hat with blue Cargo shorts. He also had the blue and white boat shoes to match. He shined his gold grill and looked in the mirror. He loved what he saw. Oh, I almost forgot, he thought to himself. He pulled out the Avalon necklace and bracelet to match and put it on. Now that's better, he said to himself.

Grill had come up, and it was Spring break of '98. He was doing big things. He had loved the nigga that he was becoming in the streets. He knew he had to learn one more level and that was how to cook. Once he learned that, it was no stopping him.

"Meat out here," Vickie said. Grill grabbed the Glock and jumped in the Cadillac.

"Shit, you got everything?"

"Take me on Dixie Ave for a second." Meat pulled up on Dixie Ave. Billy, Reverend, and Mark were outside. They were all clean. Grill hopped out of the car.

"What's good? Y'all going to the beach?"

"Just about to take off," Billy said.

Grill ran in the house and grabbed eight more grand to put with the three grand he had already had. He handed Billy a grand, and he gladly accepted it.

Grill had to admit, his brother was fresh. He had on all white Polo.

"Damn, you fresh boy!"

"Shit that's what they call me," Billy said smiling, showing his pearly white teeth and dimples. Grill accepted Billy new name as Fresh.

"I see you got that asshole with you." Grill said to Rev talking about his nephew.

"Got to have the Donkey with me," Reverend said referring to Mark and laughed.

"Y'all follow us." Grill got in the car with Meat, and they headed towards Crawford Drive.

First Outlaw pulled out with Lewis behind him followed by Big Lee. They went up Midway Ave towards the block. Sipes was thick!! Whips were out everywhere as Meat bent the corner on three wheels. All the Midway boys lined their cars up, ready to take Daytona by storm.

Meat and Grill were in the Cadillac. Lil Gee and Hard were in the red Buick with Spanish gold Dayton's. Bango and Corkey were in the white pearl bubble back Chevy with gold Dayton's. Outlaw and Big Lee was in the bubble back camillion paint with chrome Dayton's.

Stack and Big Peewee was in the 1973 Caprice convertible on gold Dayton's. Slapp was in the 1969 Impala on triple gold Dayton's. Fonso was in the 1973 Caprice on chrome Daytons. Midway was out and in full effect. The crazy part was that this was not Sanford, this was just Midway! They headed out towards Volusia County. They hit all the back roads because the highways were known to be crowded around this time.

Racing all the way up to International Speedway, they pulled to a Krispy Kreme Donut Shop. With all the excitement from the cars, Grill decided that he had to take his car to Hanson as soon as he got back.

"In Sanford, we bang it out, but out of town we come together." Before Grill could wonder what he was talking about, he looked up and seen a long line of candy painted cars swerving through traffic.

"Damn we deep!" It was all the whips from Sanford. The guy Earl was leading the pack. The one they called Versace. He had a burnt orange '79 Chevy, with the Miami hurricanes bird on the trunk of his car. Cocked up on three wheels Yellow Boy was behind him in a lime green one.

All the bosses got together and laughed and said they would beef when they got back, but now we can take it to the beach. Sanford niggas partied hard on the beach taking over the hotels, cars everywhere, weed smoke constantly was in the air, and drink was out the ass.

They took turns playing their music and working there hydraulics. Grill set in the cut, clutching his pistol, smoking blunt after blunt with the young Midway Boys. Then a Monte Carlo came through followed by a green Cadillac on all gold Dayton's pulling up where the Sanford boys were. The Monte Carlo went into the air.

"There go them boys from Bookertown."

"Thought they wasn't coming."

The window came down on the Monte Carlo.

"Yea I know you niggas thought I wasn't coming. I wouldn't miss it for the world!" DD said showing his grill. He was followed by Lil Dannie, Rikki, and Mole. They parked.

Terry who they now called Dolo walked up on Grill.

"What's up, bruh?"

"Shit you tell me, who that is your brother?" Grill asked.

"Yea, he got that bitch out yesterday!" Dolo was clean from head to toe, and he had a grill as well.

"Who you out here with?" Dolo asked.

"My nigga, Meat," Grill said proudly.

"See you doin big things,"

"Same to you. The two kicked it with the other young bosses from Sanford.

Everyone knew who was next in line to become bosses.

The police pulled a baby blue Cadillac over for hitting switches in the middle of the road. He pulled right in the front of all the Sanford niggas.

Grill recognized the guy that was driving. It was his nephew, Cool. Grill walked up to him, "What's up nigga?" Cool looked up and saw it was his uncle and replied, "Man what the hell you doin down here uncle Grill?"

"Shit the same thing you doin down here." Grill smiled showing him his grill.

"I see you getting it in. Metal Mouth told me you came through." Metal Mouth was Cool's big sister and Grill's niece that he sold the brick too. Grill looked in his eyes to see if he had known anything.

"Them your dawgs? I see y'all deep. You can get me some work? Shit fucked up since sis went to jail," Cool asked.

"Like what?" Grill asked.

"Shit, a half of brick."

"I'll see. When you want it?"

"I'ma come to grandma house Monday."

"Bet."

"Be safe Unc," Cool signed his ticket the officer wrote, turned the music up, and pulled off.

"Who that was?" Meat asked.

"My nephew."

"Where he from? Titusville?"

"Yea, he want a half of a brick." Meat's brain started to calculate numbers.

"You told him to come through?" Meat asked.

"Yea," Grill replied. Meat was glad he hired the young man. He was ready to claim the throne in Midway. He had heard from his Miami connect.

Dolo approached Grill, "Man, you know we got that work out there. My brother straight."

"Oh, yea?"

"Come fuck with us."

"I will."

Sanford partied all weekend in Daytona.

Monday morning around 4:30 am, the FEDs grabbed Meat. They found half of the brick behind his stove.

Cool came on Dixie Ave. He wanted to get the half of brick, but since Meat got caught up, Grill had to go to Stack.

"What's up lil Grill?" Stack said leaning up against a red Audi.

"What's good, I need to holla at you," Grill said. Stack looked at Big Peewee to Grill and got into Grill's car.

"What's up?"

"You got a half of brick?" Stack's eyes never left Grill. Thinking to himself, this young nigga on the rise.

"Yea."

"How much?"

"Give me eleven-thousand lil Grill. I ain't gon' tax you."

"Well, what about the whole brick?" Stack eyes almost popped out of his head.

"Man, you want a whole brick? You don' came up like that?" Stack asked trying to pin his pockets. Grill just smiled.

"I want a half and my nephew want one."

"The one that was on the beach?"

"Yea."

"When you ready?"

"Now, you gon' cook my half?"

"Yea." Stack knew the nigga might have known something in the Cadillac, so he told Grill twenty-thousand for the whole brick.

Grill met his nephew on Dixie Ave. and gave him the half of brick. He examined it.

"How much?"

"Twelve-thousand."

"Damn they taxing," he went into his bag and brought the money out.

"Bet!"

"I got to get on this road, Unc. Fuck with me!" Grill counted the twelve grand. He had three in his pocket and went into the house and got five more.

He pulled up on Stack and gave Stack the money. Big Peewee just looked on in awe. Stack decided not to charge Grill to cook the half of brick, and he wasn't going to cuff any grams this time. He started his cooking process.

He was almost down to one brick left. He would be at two hundred thousand flat once he sold it. He paid off his house. He blessed Twiggy with her share and got his vert out of the shop. He took his kid's shopping, and he did all of this off of lil Grill. He decided to let him see a little profit. Besides he had plans to start serving bricks of soft.

Big Peewee paid him for the brick he owed him and then bought another. Stack fronted him another. He decided to cook the last one then he would be done with crack cocaine. He was going to serve soft from here on out.

Grill stood in the kitchen watching Stack. This was the part of the game he needed. Once he learned how it was done, he didn't need anyone. He would be destined to be on top. He already had a nice percentage of clientele on Sipes

Ave. If the hood found out that he knew how to cook it, that would be more money in his pocket.

Grill's mind was running. He had splurged this week, and it was time to make it back up. He vowed that this week he had to step it up.

He decided that he would go to his father to do a count. Drop his Delta 88 off and push hard. Stack continued to work the metal clothing hanger in the bowl. Then he would take the bowl to the sink and splash cold water on it. He poured the excess water off and brought it back to the counter. Stack slowly drug the substance that turned into jell across the bowl forming a circle. He did this repeatedly until all was done.

Grill noticed that his cookies were thicker and wider than last time.

A knock at the door interrupted Stack as he was about to finish. "Who is it?" Big Peewee had left, and it was only Grill and Stack in the house.

"Shika," the voice replied through the door. Stack opened it, and she walked in, handing Stack his money she owed him. Grill was gathering up the cookies putting them in a shoe box, walking out the door. He walked right pass her smiling.

Grill backed in on Washington St. in front of his spot to smoke a blunt. His two young guns came out of the house. Dunney threw the money on his lap.

"Thirty-five-hundred yours. Fifteen-hundred mines and five-hundred Renzo's." Grill couldn't believe the youngster's had moved all the work. He was proud of Dunney. When he looked up, he noticed what Dunney wanted him to see. He had a grill across the top of his teeth.

"Damn nigga," Grill said smiling.

"Yea man, me, Donkey, and Sweet Jones went and got right. Sweet Jones got twelve." It took Grill a minute to register who Sweet Jones was. Then he remembered that's what Sean called himself. Dunney and Mark who was being called Donkey got six.

"When we gon' be ready for the work? Sweet Jones and those niggas from Oviedo been coming through here."

"Be patient." Grill was waiting on them niggas. That was the main reason he bought half of the brick. He was fixing to start the weight money.

"Y'all get in."

They pulled up on Dixie Ave. He went inside to get his dad and shut the door. "Pop's what's up? How much money I got?"

"Well, you had sixty-thousand. You don' came and got eighteen-thousand dollars in the last week. What the hell you been doing?" It was really sixty-two thousand, but his pops clipped him for two grand for playing the bookie. His pops blew smoke wondering did he catch on. Grill went into his pocket.

"So now you down to Forty-two-thousand," his father said with a grunt, mad that Grill had let some of the money get away. Grill pulled out ten-grand. "Alright, you keep the two-grand but put this ten with it. That will take me to fifty grand." Grill got up after talking with his dad and went to his mother and spoke then walked outside. He decided he would chill tonight and get his head right. He wasn't bringing nothing out tonight.

He hid the work in his Delta '88, dropped Dunney and Renzo off and went on Sipes Ave. He backed in, and Corkey came to his car, and they kicked it. He told Grill he had twenty grand and the gold Dayton's. Grill told him he had fifty grand. Out of all the young hustlers, they were ahead and quickly became partners.

CHAPTER 16

WAR!!!

While talking to Corkey, four cars came through Sipes Ave. back to back. It was the boys from the projects, swerving through Midway, all with rims on their cars. Taz was disrespectful, throwing dirt all over everyone's car. When the crowd looked up, Daddy-Low was on King and Sipes in his car with the road blocked.

He couldn't move. Words were exchanged and the next thing you know bullets started flying.

Shots rang out everywhere. Cars were crashing into each other. Taz was still shooting in reverse. Boom! Boom! Boom!

The police came from out of nowhere. It was pandemonium in Midway. Two people were screaming they were shot. Grill and Corkey ran behind Jimmy Hamp and just like that the war broke out between Midway and the Projects again.

Shika heard about the shootout on Sipes Ave. She heard Taz, and his boys were to blame. She also heard that two people got shot. She paced the floor of her one-bedroom apartment continuing to page Grill.

So far, he had not responded. She was getting angry. Argie called her and told her what happened and told her that Daddy-Low came and got his guns from her mother's house.

Daddy-Low was furious that Taz and his boys came through Midway the way they did. He was slipping, something he didn't usually do, but being that the two local police was on his trail, he didn't ride with his gun.

The police got on the scene as quickly as if they were on the back road waiting for it to happen. A kid name Young Gotti got shot, and a crack head named Bobo got shot in the chest. Bobo didn't look like he was going to make it.

Daddy-Low got dropped off in Geneva to one of the crackers, who came to Midway to get drugs. Him, Looney, and Big Jay were together. They kept a stolen vehicle out here for occasions like this. They had two vans with sliding doors and an S10 Silverado truck.

They drove them back to Midway. Everyone from Sipes was in the duck hole in Midway. It was dead in the danger zone. Daddy-Low pulled up, and niggas came out of the dark from everywhere. All you could hear was guns cocking.

Daddy-Low appointed the best drivers from Midway to drive the three cars, then started picking out who got in what car.

"I'ma tell you now. You don't shoot or get off, I'ma leave you out there with them." Daddy-Low had the look of death in his eyes every time he spoke. Everyone knew he meant business. The last mission they went on there was a dude that they couldn't find. Daddy-Low was the only one calm. He made C-Murder drive to the dude mother's house and calmly got out and walked to the lady's door. He knocked, and when she answered he shot the lady point blank range in the throat and told her to tell him, *a Desperado did it!* Then walked back to the car as if nothing happened.

Grill was the youngest in the duck hole, but Corkey, Ratty, and Little Timmy were out there. Grill had the assault rifle he took from the Haitians and the Glock. It was only one spot left on the back of the truck. Both vans were filled.

Daddy-Low looked at the youngsters carefully. He examined each one. None had been on this type of mission before, even though he knew all of them were ready. He knew Grill was raised by Teke and he knew the nigga bloodline was ruthless.

"Grill, come on. The rest of y'all stay back." All the other young guns seemed disappointed. Grill hurriedly jumped on the back of the truck.

"Man, give me that big ass gun. You can't work that," Daddy-Low said, smiling like the devil. He handed him a .45, so Grill had two pistols.

As they approached the projects, they scoped the scene. Two police cars were in the middle of the projects, facing each other.

The truck was in the front, so they went in the back and turned around. Cake Boy was driving.

"Man, you see them crackas parked over there."

"Man fuck them crackas, they can get it too," Daddy-Low leaned over Snake and said.

"So what's the plan?" Cake Boy asked.

"We gon' go down the middle road and when we come out everybody get it!"

"Just like that," Grill said.

"Lil Grill, let me get in the truck. You get in the van. Cake Boy, fall to the back!" Grill and Daddy-Low switched positions and cars.

Taz and his crew were sitting beside their cars on the middle road, smoking, and drinking.

"Bruh, you aired them, niggas, out," Corey said.

"Good for them fuck niggas," Anton said.

"I was tryin' to kill that fuck nigga, Daddy-Low," Tyger said.

"I tried to knock that lil fuck nigga Grill head off. That bitch was movin'," Freddie Lee said, remembering how Grill shot him.

"Man, y'all niggas out here celebratin'. Y'all better be on point. Them niggas comin'. Y'all got Daddy-Low fucked up," Taz said. He didn't want to shoot Midway up. He was just having fun. Shit got out of hand.

"Let 'em come!" Tyger said in his deep voice.

Before Taz could reply, he saw a van creeping off 1st St, coming their way. The van parked and the sliding door open. Before he could warn someone, shots rang out.

Taz only had enough time to lift his pistol and start bussing. They were under attack. He was bussing his 9mm while backing up in one of the projects.

The shots went on forever. The passenger door of the van flew open and out came Grill.

Boom! Boom! Boom! Grill was working the .45 and the Glock. He was out on feet, followed by several other Midway boys. The guys from the projects were retreating, but Midway kept coming. Daddy-Low was out the truck in his army fatigue jacket, working the assault rifle.

"What the fuck is goin' on? Do you hear that shit?" the black officer said.

"God damn right I hear it. That's an assault rifle. Haven't heard one since Vietnam," the white officer responded. He could see the fear in his partner's eyes.

"I didn't sign up for this. I got children."

"We can't do nothing for them, let's ease on the scene. Hopefully, gunfire will ease up." Neither police officer was ready to die. The gunfire kept going like the fourth of July.

Taz made it to safety. He was in an apartment on the floor. He was out of bullets. Bullets were coming through the walls of the buildings. The little girl on the floor next to him was shot. The shots were still coming.

"Wet all these fuck niggas!" Big Jay said.

The sound of the assault rifle let off, *Braaaat, Braaaaaat, Braaaaat!*

Everyone started to run back like they were going to make it to Midway, but the police had a plan already in motion. They were already setting up roadblocks.

The van Grill was in was in Georgetown.

"Everybody gotta go for what they know. Out on feet! You get caught, shut up and get the gun off you!" Dirty said. He slammed the van in park, and everyone jumped out.

The sounds of the helicopters were so close to the ground, you could hear it as if the blades of the chopper were directly near your ear. Everyone had split up. Grill ran to Ayeshia's house. He jumped the fence and was on the side of her house. Please be home, he thought.

Ayeshia heard the sirens and helicopters and walked on her back porch. Her mother was in the front. Neighbors came outside from everywhere. You could tell by how many police that it was serious.

"One went this way," the young officer said, pointing in the direction of Ayeshia's house.

"Turn the dog loose," another officer said.

The dog immediately started barking. Ayeshia's house sat off the ground, so Grill started crawling under the house. He heard the officer saying let the dog loose and started to panic.

There were spider webs everywhere, and spiders were the only thing that Grill feared.

"The dog just hit. He's in this area," the police said. Grill's heart began to beat faster. He saw the light, so he knew he was almost to the end of the porch. He was afraid to come out in fear that he would be seen.

"Boy I don't know what they did, but them crackas want them," Ayeshia said holding her niece in her arms on her hip. She was literally standing on top of Grill.

The dog barked again, attempting to come through the fence.

"Ma'am, did you see anyone come this way?" The officer asked.

"Nope," Ayeshia quickly replied, "And if I did I wouldn't tell you," she said under her breath.

"Because my dog is indicating that he ran this way. I'm coming around the gate." The officer turned around and started walking toward the front of the house.

"Bae, bae, bae!" Grill said in a voice over a whisper. Ayeshia thought she was hearing things and turned to walk in the back door. Grill knocked on the floorboard, "Ayeshia"!!!!